ENDURANCE

THE HEBRAICA TRILOGY
BOOK THREE

CHRISTINE JORDAN

BLOODHOUND
— BOOKS —

www.bloodhoundbooks.com

Print ISBN: 978-1-917214-56-8

CAST OF CHARACTERS

The Jewish Community
Gloucester

Douce: Widow of Moses

Zev: Silversmith
Arlette: Wife of Zev
Rubin: Son of Zev and Arlette

Baruch: Skermiseur
Brunetta: Wife of Baruch
Tzuri: Son of Brunetta
Ozanne: Daughter of Brunetta

Mirabelle: Widow of Elias

Bonanfaunt the Elder: Son of Mirabelle
Genta: Wife of Bonanfaunt

Belia: Daughter of Mirabelle

Isaac of Lincoln: Husband of Belia
Pucelle: Daughter of Belia and Isaac
Garsia: Husband of Pucelle
Saffronia: Daughter of Pucelle

Abraham of Warwick the Elder: Wealthy Moneylender
Elias of Warwick: Moneylender
Leo of Warwick: Moneylender

Rabbi Isaiah: The Rabbi

Solomon Turbe: Gloucester Moneylender
Comitissa: Wife of Solomon

Abraham Gabbai: Treasurer of Bristol Synagogue

The Christian Community
Civil

King Henry III: King of England (1216–1272)
William Marshal, 1st Earl of Pembroke: Regent to Henry III
(1216–1219)
Ralph Musard: Sheriff of Gloucester (1216–1231)
Simon de Matresdon: Coroner of Gloucester
Geoffrey de Matresdon: Simon's eldest son
Henry de Matresdon: Geoffrey's brother
John Gooseditch: Christian Chirographer of Gloucester
John Rufus: Christian Chirographer of Gloucester

Quinton Brebon: Draper
Vernisse: Daughter of Draper
Lucien: Nephew of Draper

Yvain: Troubadour from Occitan
Guillaume: Poet from Toulouse
Beatriz: Trobairitz
Bertran: Troubadour

Ecclesiastical:

Henry Blunt: Abbot of St Peter's Abbey (1205–1224)
Thomas of Bredon: Abbot of St Peter's Abbey (1224–1228)

Yet there will be a tenth portion in it,
And it will again be subject to burning,
Like a terebinth or an oak
Whose stump remains when it is felled.
The holy seed is its stump.
Isaiah 6:13

CHAPTER

ONE

Feast Day of Simon and Jude the Apostles
Friday 28 October 1216
St Peter's Abbey
Gloucester

Tzuri waited in the cold cavernous cathedral for the arrival of the boy. He breathed in the choking smoke of pungent incense, belching out of the many thuribles, swinging from side to side as the monks of St Peter's Abbey walked along the nave towards the altar. The aromatic smell of frankincense and myrrh mixed with the smell of crushed rosemary strewn across the stone floor was a heady combination. The monk's plainsong chants resounded throughout the crowded abbey, adding to the ethereal setting. There was an air of expectation amongst those dignitaries gathered to see the nine-year-old Henry crowned King of England.

Tzuri stood with his family. His great-grandmother, Douce, was next to him. She was not actually his great-grandmother, but she was known in the family as *safta*, grandmother. Her expression was proud and haughty. A woman of advancing years, she still had an air of vibrancy about her. Her high cheekbones were smooth and wrinkle-free, and her dark eyes darted around the nave, occasionally glancing up to marvel at the vaulted roof. His grandmother, Arlette, stood on his other side. A quiet, angelic being, she had an otherworldly quality. Advancing in years, you could see she had been a woman of great beauty.

Douce turned towards Tzuri and caught him staring at her.

'Tzuri, there are plenty of better-looking women to stare at than me,' she said, her eyes smiling at him.

'There's always me,' said his mother, Brunetta, squeezing his arm.

Douce ignored the comment. She turned away, pursed her lips and stared ahead of her. Tzuri loved Douce but he didn't like it when she was harsh towards his mother. Baruch, his stepfather, told him they would never resolve their differences and were resigned to the end of their days to have a caustic relationship. He gave Tzuri a knowing smile. He had endured their animosity for years.

Baruch stood next to his wife, his battle-scarred face lined with age and in between his parents was Ozanne, Tzuri's younger sister. She had grown into a strikingly beautiful young woman with mahogany-coloured hair that glistened with natural copper highlights, her eyes cinnamon and flecked with bronze. She had many admirers but so far had not found the love of her life. She was gifted musically, spending hours with her aunt, Henne, playing the kinnor, writing poetry and making up songs, singing with the voice of an angel. *Une chanteuse.*

There was a ripple of chatter, then silence, as the young prince entered the nave. The monks of the abbey, joined by several singers of the chapel royal, struck up a shrill chant.

Tzuri's Latin was good enough to recognise the Antiphon, *Firmetur*, 'Let Thy Hand Be Strengthened'. Trumpeters sounded a rousing fanfare, accompanied by a young man banging on a nakerer, a small drum hung around his neck.

The young prince, a diminutive figure, was clothed in what looked like hand-me-downs. A shirt of white silk and a coat of red sarcenet. He made his way towards the altar with slow determination. There was something incongruous in his appearance, thought Tzuri, as he watched transfixed. He looked like a boy dressed in knight's clothing or one of the young monks they dress up at the annual Boy Bishop celebrations. Nevertheless, he had a serious face for someone so young. His jaw was set, and his grey eyes stared fixedly ahead of him.

Standing behind the prince was his mother, Isabella of Angoulême, renowned for her great beauty. Tzuri studied her. A woman in her late twenties, she had cobalt-blue eyes and blonde hair and had already given birth to five children with her recently deceased husband, King John. She was indeed beautiful, thought Tzuri, as she glided past him, her chin tilted slightly upwards. In her hands, she clasped a plain gold circlet. Beside her was William Marshal, Earl of Pembroke and former Sheriff of Gloucester. Tzuri knew him well as his stepfather was a great friend of his. Behind him were the rebel barons who had gone against the prince's father. They included Ranulph, the Earl of Chester; William Ferrers, the Earl of Derby; John Marshal, William's nephew; and Philip de Albanie.

At the head of the procession was the papal legate, Guala Bicchieri, an Italian diplomat and representative of the Pope, accompanied by his deputy Pandulf. In Bicchieri's hand was an intricately worked golden crosier. He was a swarthy man in his late sixties and wore the most colourful religious garb, oozing opulence. Tzuri knew his great-grandmother liked to wear luxurious clothes but today it was the Italians who stood out from those Jews assembled in the abbey to witness the coronation. Also with Guala was Peter des Roches, the warrior Bishop of Winchester and Jocelin, the Bishop of Bath. The Abbot of St Peters, Henry Blunt, who had taken over from Thomas Carbonel upon his death, waited for them at the altar.

A commotion behind Tzuri made him turn around. Vernisse, the draper's daughter, was pushing through the crowd, evincing cross looks and mumbled complaints of 'no manners'. Tzuri's stomach flipped at the sight of her. She wore her hair back beneath a translucent veil, her russet hair flaming in the motes of light. Her jade-coloured eyes widened when she saw Tzuri. She reached him and whispered, 'I thought I'd never find you.'

'I'm glad you did,' he said, looking around him before surreptitiously clasping her hand in his.

Vernisse squeezed his hand then let go, yet she made sure her fingertips remained touching his, lightly inside the folds of her skirt, unseen by those close to them. Tzuri's stomach flipped again, and his pulse quickened. For the rest of the coronation, he worked hard to concentrate on the lengthy proceedings.

When the procession reached the altar, the prince was shown to a faldstool at the side where he sat patiently. William Marshal took his place at the altar. The chanting stopped and Abbot Blunt joined him. He straightened his spine and coughed several times before speaking. Tzuri noticed his hands were shaking as he held the Bible and when he spoke there was a tremulous quality to his voice.

'I welcome all here present on this historic day. It is indeed an honour to be officiating such a noble coronation on this day of the Feast of the Apostles Jude and Simon.'

Abbot Blunt opened his Bible and read the first of the Collect prayers:

'O God, who by the blessed Apostles have brought us to acknowledge your name, graciously grant, through the intercession of Saints Simon and Jude, that the Church may constantly grow by increase of the peoples who believe in you. Through our Lord Jesus Christ, your Son, who lives and reigns with you in the unity of the Holy Spirit, one God, forever and ever.'

'Amen,' replied the Christians.

Vernisse, her voice clear and reverential, joined in. Hearing her voice and watching as she crossed her chest in the Roman Catholic way, reminded him he was in love with a Christian and not a Jew. The Fourth Lateran Council of the Roman Church had implemented harsh and restrictive laws against the Jews. They were supposed to wear a distinctive badge, made of linen sewn onto the breast of their outer garments, to distinguish them from Christians to prevent Jews from having relations with Christians, though this was largely unenforced. Even so, Tzuri had told no one of his trysts with Vernisse.

His great-grandmother would be horrified, his mother indifferent and his stepfather would probably tell him to follow his heart. His heart was aching to be one with Vernisse. The caress of her fingertips on the inside of his hand was tantalising. Excruciatingly pleasurable and unbearable at the same time, heightened by the illicitness of their union.

William Marshal was speaking now. He was a broad-shouldered man with a commanding presence.

'Behold, Right Honourable and well-beloved, although we have persecuted the father of this young prince for his evil demeanour, and yet worthily, this young child whom here you see before you, as he is in years tender, so is he pure and innocent from his father's doings. Wherefore, in so much as every man lies charged only with the burden of his own works and transgressions, neither shall the child – as the Scripture teaches us – bear the iniquity of his father.'

The marshal looked over at the young prince whose face was one of pure bewilderment. He continued.

'We ought, therefore, of duty and conscience to pardon this young and tender prince and take compassion of his age as you see. And now, for so much as he is the king's natural and eldest son, and must be our sovereign king and successor in this kingdom, come and let us appoint him our king and governor; let us remove from us this Louis, the French king's son, and suppress his people, which are a confusion and shame to our nation; and the yoke of their servitude let us cast from off our shoulders.'

There was a great roar, followed by cheering and clapping. William Marshal left the altar. The boy was brought forward and the papal legate, Guala, bid him sit on the thronal chair that had been provided. It was not as grand as the chair that would have been used in Westminster but in the circumstances it would suffice. The boy swore upon the Holy Gospels and the relics of saints that he would observe honour, peace and reverence towards God and the Holy Church and its ordained ministers all the days of his life.

'I will,' the boy answered in his small voice, barely audible inside the nave.

He swore that he would show strict justice to the people entrusted to his care, and would abolish all bad laws and customs, if there were any in the kingdom, and observe those that were good, and cause them to be observed by all.

Tzuri was relieved to hear that he would show strict justice and abolish bad laws. Perhaps the Jewish people would fare better under this king than the last. He listened as the prince paid homage to the Holy Church of Rome, and to Pope Innocent for the kingdoms of England and Ireland and swore that as long as he held those kingdoms, he would faithfully pay the thousand marks which his father had given to the Roman Church.

Then came more prayers. At this point, Tzuri's mind drifted. He was imagining telling Vernisse's father that he wanted to marry his daughter. Tzuri had difficulty seeing Quinton's face. Was it an angry face, red with rage? Or smiling and congratulatory? He couldn't tell. That part of his fantasy was blurry. It would be difficult – marrying someone who was not a Jew. He gripped Vernisse's cold hand. He could not bear the thought that he might lose her. Her cold fingers felt like the delicate bones of a bird. She responded by gently stroking the inside of his wrist with the fingertips of her other hand. It sent a tremor along the length of his arm. If he were not careful, he would embarrass himself. The ceremony droned on. How much longer? He was itching to get away and take Vernisse somewhere they could be alone, where no one would find them.

Then came the anointing. Guala took hold of the boy's tunic and tore it open. In that instant, the nave was filled with the quiet voices of the monks chanting the Antiphon, *Unxerunt Salomonem*, the anointing of Solomon by the priest Zadok. An ampoule of olive oil was opened, and an amount poured onto a small spoon. Guala used this to anoint the boy with the sign of the cross on his head, then hands and breast to signify glory, courage and knowledge.

After this, Guala stepped back allowing Peter des Roches, the Bishop of Winchester to place the circlet that his mother had been holding onto the boy's head. It was a plain band of gold, nothing like the crown his ancestors had been crowned with, but it was all they had. The rumour was that his father, King John, had lost the crown jewels in the Wash whilst fleeing the enemy. At the moment of the crowning, a shout of 'Long

Live the King' rang out in the nave and a third Antiphon was begun. *Confortare*. Be Strong.

Tzuri listened to the singing voices. They were loud and high-pitched at this point, adding to the drama of the moment. Their voices were at times melodic, at times discordant but always masterful. Tzuri felt the hairs on the back of his neck prickle at the opening chords. The sound was nothing like the singing he was used to in the synagogue.

After the Catholic mass had been performed, the bishops and knights in attendance clothed the newly proclaimed king in royal robes. William Marshal stepped forward and in a fatherly gesture placed his hand on the boy's shoulder and led him towards the Chapter House where there was a bounteous feast awaiting the select few who had been invited. As he was led away the monks began to chant *Te Deum* accompanied by resounding peals of the abbey's great bells.

'*Sanctus, Sanctus, Sanctus, Dominus Deus Sabaoth.*'

The panoply of sound filled the nave. Whatever criticisms he had of the Christians they certainly knew how to stage an impressive ceremony of pomp and gravitas. Behind the king, a lengthy line of dignitaries followed. Tzuri noticed Mirabelle, his great-grandmother's arch-enemy, amongst the favoured contingent. Before he had even thought it, Douce whispered to his grandmother, Arlette, a note of disgusted envy in her voice.

'I wonder who she bribed to get that invitation?'

'And how much did it cost her?' replied Arlette, her eyes widening at the thought.

Arlette was a frail woman in her mid-sixties. Frightened of loud noises and strangers, she always seemed like a wounded bird. Tzuri imagined, when she was younger, that she was a stunningly attractive woman. Even now she stood out with her fair hair and lapis eyes. Her vulnerability only seemed to enhance her attractiveness. Her husband, Zev, worshipped her as did her son, Rubin, who had never married and was considered within the family a mother's boy.

'She has the money to waste on such flimsies,' Douce said, her tone now dismissive and judgemental.

A small smile formed on Tzuri's lips. Douce never shunned an opportunity to say something damning about Mirabelle. She had even taken to calling her 'Misabel' because of her miserable face. Tzuri relinquished his hand from Vernisse's fingers and filed out of the abbey, thankful to breathe some fresh air at last. Outside in the precinct, a crowd had gathered. Hundreds were waiting, hoping to get a glimpse of the boy king. Quinton Brebon, Vernisse's father, walked over to them. He greeted the group with a friendly smile.

'Vernisse, I've been looking for you.'

'I was late, Father. I tried to find you inside.'

Quinton was a jovial, amiable man. His reddened cheeks and nose told Tzuri that he liked a drink or two.

'What did you think of the ceremony?' he asked them.

'I thought it was magnificent,' Douce answered, her eyes squinting in the low October sun shining behind Quinton.

Douce had known Quinton for years. She had been buying his superior cloth since he arrived in Gloucester from Paris.

'Why aren't you at the banquet?' he asked in all innocence.

Douce's smiling eyes lost their sparkle. 'We were not invited,' she said, pursing her lips slightly.

'Well, if I was in charge of the guest list, I would have made sure you were invited.'

'Mirabelle was invited,' Vernisse said.

'You mean Misabel,' said Ozanne, giving her grandmother a cheeky smile.

Ozanne often opened her mouth without thinking. Quinton cleared his throat and continued. 'Mirabelle may be one of my best customers – as are you, Douce – but her company is nowhere near as enjoyable as yours.'

Tzuri watched in disbelief. Quinton was flirting with his great-grandmother. Douce was blushing like a new bride and Quinton grinning as if he had just won a prize. He was a widower so Tzuri could see no harm in it.

'You don't have to flatter me,' Douce replied. 'I will still buy your lovely cloth.'

Tzuri wondered if this was Quinton's usual manner with female customers or if he did really like Douce. He was probably half her age but then Douce was still an attractive woman with a slim figure. She had never remarried after the death of her husband, the great Moses le Riche. She deserved some happiness in her old age even if it was just harmless fun.

'I have some new bolts of fustian, fresh off the boat from Egypt just in time for the winter. Also, some mousseline from France, organza and of course, the silk baudelet you like so much. You must come into the shop and see for yourself.'

Quinton pronounced the word Egypt in his native French accent, elongating the 'e'. He was a born salesman and couldn't help selling his wares to his customers even when he wasn't in his shop.

'I will when I have the time,' said Douce, her eyes lighting up when she heard the word baudelet.

Baudelet was a rich embroidered or brocaded silk fabric woven with a warp of gold thread. Supremely opulent and worn on special occasions. Tzuri noticed the brightness in his great-grandmother's eyes glaze over, and a faraway look came upon her as if she were remembering happier times. A sadness seeped into Tzuri's heart. The family had fallen on hard times since the death of Moses and the death of his father, Abraham. The king had demanded Moses's death taxes be paid and when they weren't, the only course of action had been to take their beloved home in Jewry Street.

'Don't leave it too long. You wouldn't want Mirabelle to take the last length.' Quinton winked at Douce. Douce straightened at the sound of Mirabelle's name, almost as if Quinton was betraying her in some way. 'I merely jest,' he said, seeing her reaction. 'I will always save the last for you.'

Douce relaxed her shoulders and gave Quinton a weak smile.

'Come on, Papa, it's time you went home,' said Vernisse, taking his arm.

Tzuri didn't want her to go but he couldn't stop her. It would look wrong. He wondered if Quinton had been drinking earlier in the day and that had made him behave over-friendly. Or maybe it was the Parisian way of selling your wares. He watched with sadness as they walked away towards St John the Baptist's Church. He turned away when the family resumed their conversation about the new king.

'What do you think will happen now?' asked Arlette.

'The king is a mere boy. William Marshal will act as his protector and regent until he becomes old enough to rule the kingdom.'

'How do you know, Baruch?'

'You forget, the marshal and I go back a long way. I fought beside him and King Richard.'

'You never let us forget that,' said Brunetta, raising her eyebrows in mock derision.

'Will he look favourably on us Jews?' asked Tzuri.

'The marshal is a fair and wise man. I have no worries on that score.'

'He can't do much worse than his father,' said Zev.

The conversation hushed. It would do no good to speak ill of the king in public even if he was dead.

'Not so loud,' whispered Arlette.

Ozanne, sensing the tension, changed the subject.

'I love hearing your stories – of your times with the king,' Ozanne said to her father.

Ozanne squeezed Baruch's arm. Baruch placed his hand over hers and beamed. He made no secret of the fact he favoured Ozanne over Tzuri. In the past Tzuri had been hurt by this but since falling in love with Vernisse it hurt less.

They began the walk home. Tzuri lagged behind the others; his mind filled with thoughts of how he could marry Vernisse when Baruch appeared at his side.

'You need to be careful, Tzuri.'

Tzuri stopped and braced himself for a telling-off. 'What do you mean?'

'That girl.'

'Is it that obvious?'

'She's very beautiful and someone will come along and snatch her from you if you don't watch out.'

'Do you really think so?'

'I've been around in my day. I know women.'

'I've seen other men looking at her. But she's not interested in anyone else.'

'Your misplaced confidence will be the undoing of you.'

'You think she's interested in other men?'

'I don't know but if you're serious about her and want to marry her, you better move fast.'

'But she's a Christian. It's forbidden.'

'Then find a way.'

TWO

M irabelle sat at the banqueting table in the Chapter House next to her son, Bonanfaunt. They were surrounded by men of great influence and power. At the head of the long table sat the newly crowned king. He looked small and insignificant. Ill-equipped to reign over the kingdom. The real power was with the man sitting next to him. William Marshal. Mirabelle knew him but not well. That blackguard Baruch knew him better. This thought galled Mirabelle and for a second or two her mouth dried up. She took a sip of Gascony wine. Not kosher but Mirabelle had learned long ago that if you wanted to get on in a Christian country then you had better adopt Christian ways.

The head of a boar with a quince in its mouth stared back at Mirabelle from the other side of the table. At least it was not a pig's head she was staring at although nowadays that also would not concern her unduly. A *sotelte*, a sugar sculpture in the shape of an angel, arrived with the second course. There were many more courses before the banquet would end. She glanced at Bonanfaunt who was tucking into a leg of roasted guinea fowl. He had grown to be a fine and handsome young man.

Married to Genta they now had seven children. Mirabelle had great plans for him but first she must not lose any time in petitioning William Marshal.

Since the death of her husband in Bristol Castle at the behest of King John her finances had suffered. On his death, all of her husband's debts had been taken into the hands of the king and Mirabelle had worked tirelessly to have her finances settled. When the king returned from the burning and sacking of Reginald de Braose's castles at Hay and Radnor in August this year he had stopped off in Gloucester. Mirabelle had taken this opportunity to petition him about the debts owed to her by Henry the Burgess. King John had not exactly been supportive of her efforts. A few days later he sent a writ to Sheriff Musard, commanding him on no account to distrain Henry the Burgess, that is to seize his lands in lieu of payment, for the debt owed to Mirabelle because her husband's chirographs and tallies were in his hands. To add insult to injury, a few days after that, King John granted the house Elias had bought from Walter Kidmore, opposite The Booth Hall in West Gate Street, to that obsequious rat Gilbert de Rue. She was furious to say the least. The only consolation was that on the same day the king also granted to Gilbert de Rue the grand house in East Gate Street belonging to the le Riche family.

Oh, how Moses would be turning in his grave.

A satisfying smile appeared upon her thin lips as she remembered the day the family were evicted. She gazed across at the boy king then at William Marshal the Regent and wondered if her pleas would continue to fall on deaf ears. But the smile did not last long. Mirabelle's thoughts returned to the day when there was a knock at her door and the constable stepped forward to arrest Elias – one of many – who had not paid the king's extortionate tallage. That was the last time she saw him. He died a horrible death, like the rest of his captors, having been tortured and having had his teeth pulled out, one by one. Mirabelle held a deep hatred of John and on hearing the news the king had died she rejoiced. Later, when she heard the rumours that his own monks had murdered him with poisoned cherries, she had laughed out loud. He had been a cruel and sadistic king. Bonanfaunt chastised her and told her she should be more charitable for a woman of senior years. Age does not diminish feelings, she had told him.

'Are you feeling all right, *Ima*?'

Bonanfaunt's voice brought her back to the present.

'I'm well, my son, why do you ask?'

'You were grinding your teeth. You only do that when you're angry at someone.'

'I was just thinking about the injustices meted out to us by that tyrant,' she whispered.

'Who?'

'King John.'

'Today is not the day to dwell on such things. You should be enjoying the feast and the wine.'

Mirabelle patted her son's hand. 'You're right. How did I get such a wise son?'

'I had a good teacher,' Bonanfaunt said, smiling at her.

'I'm going to petition the marshal.'

'Today?'

'Yes, why not?'

'I think the timing is all wrong. I would leave it. He has a lot to deal with today.'

'I want your father's houses back and his loans repaid.'

Mirabelle looked across the Chapter House at Simon de Coco, Richard the Burgess and his son Henry, and lastly Gilbert de Rue. Gilbert caught her eye and gave her a supercilious smile. A morsel of bread stuck in her throat, and she began to cough.

Bonanfaunt patted her back to dislodge the bread. She shrugged him off.

'Don't fuss for goodness' sake. I'm fine.'

She looked back at Gilbert. He was laughing at something with Simon de Coco. A rage burned inside her. Were they laughing at her? The smugness on their faces was almost too much to bear. Not only had they been granted the houses in West Gate Street, but they had the audacity to gloat over her misfortune. Mirabelle imagined them sitting in the houses that she had once owned. Given away by King John. She took a sip of wine to ease the coughing.

If it was the last thing she ever did, she would get those houses back, by means fair or foul.

THREE

The day after the coronation Tzuri asked Douce if she wanted to take up Quinton's suggestion and visit his shop.

'Since when did you take an interest in bolts of cloth?' Douce asked, raising a questioning eyebrow.

'I just thought you might like to have a wander outside. Before the really cold weather sets in. The fresh air will do you good.'

Douce looked at him, unconvinced. 'You know I can't afford his wares anymore.'

'It won't harm to look,' said Tzuri, imploring her.

Douce let out a long sigh. 'Very well. I'll get ready.'

'Where are you going?' asked Brunetta.

'To the drapers.'

'May I join you?'

'Of course, *Ima*.'

Tzuri saw his great-grandmother scowl as she announced: 'Maybe not today, I'm feeling a little tired.'

It was an obvious attempt to avoid being in Brunetta's company. After all these years living under the same roof there was still animosity between them. Douce had recently lost her close friend, Bellassez, who had died of old age leaving Douce alone and without a companion. She had not been the same since Moses had died and losing Bellassez had sent her into a quiet state of mourning.

'Nonsense. You can never be too tired for shopping, *Safta*. Come on. I'd like your company and if you behave yourself, I might treat you to something.'

Douce smiled, warming to his charm.

'Can I come along?' Arlette asked, walking into the hall holding a kitchen cloth in her hand.

Just then Ozanne came bounding into the room, humming a tune. 'Where is everyone going?' she asked.

'To Quinton the drapers.'

'Shopping,' squealed Ozanne. 'Yes, please.'

Douce relented once she knew Arlette and Ozanne were going with them. Tzuri was relieved. He wanted to see Vernisse, and a shopping trip was an ideal cover. They walked towards The Cross. Douce arm in arm with Arlette. Tzuri walking with his mother.

'You like the company of women, don't you, Tzuri?' Brunetta said.

'Is there anything wrong with that?' he asked.

'Not really, I suppose. It's a good way to get to know them better.'

'You are complicated beings, I must admit.'

Brunetta laughed, throwing her head back and flicking her chestnut locks so they flowed down her back. Brunetta was now in her forties but still had a good figure, the natural flow of her voluptuous body swaying as she walked. Tzuri could see why she'd had no trouble remarrying when his father had died.

Quinton's shop was in Grase Lane, a muddle of alleyways that made up the Mercery. They stopped outside a timber-fronted building halfway down a narrow passage with overhanging houses giving it a closed-in feeling and blocking out most of the daylight. It was next door to the *boucherie* or the butchery where Christians slaughtered animals without prayer. Quinton's wares were displayed on a drop-down counter at the front of the house. The women ran their hands over the bolts of cloth, discussing colours, softness. Tzuri held back. Quinton appeared and began talking to the women, coaxing them to buy. When Vernisse didn't appear, Tzuri slipped past Quinton into the back of the shop where the draper stored his merchandise. The back-room walls were lined with bolts of scarlet cloth, silks, linens, wools, *corde du roi*, and moleskins. There was a fresh smell of newly woven cloth. The floor was strewn with threads and cotton dust. Vernisse sat at a long table holding a bone-handled knife that she was using to cut lengths of cotton.

'Hello,' he said.

Vernisse jumped. 'Ouch,' she cried, dropping the knife.

Tzuri looked on in horror as Vernisse peeled her hand from the cloth she was holding to reveal a stain of blood. She sucked on her finger.

Tzuri rushed to her. 'I'm sorry. I didn't mean to alarm you.'

She held out her bleeding finger and said: 'Kiss it better.'

Her boldness made Tzuri's desire for her stronger. He took her hand and kissed the injured finger, licking the blood droplets as he did so.

'My mother swore this always worked on me,' he said.

Vernisse smiled at him with a twinkle in her eye. Then she looked down at the cloth she had been cutting and gasped. There was a tiny drop of dark-red blood on the material.

'Father will be furious with me for ruining one of his samples.'

'Here,' Tzuri said, grabbing the length of cloth and stuffing it under his cloak. 'He'll never know.'

Vernisse laughed. Tzuri bent down and kissed her on the lips. Vernisse pushed him away.

'Be careful, Father might see.'

'Why should that matter? I love you and want to marry you.'

'Marry me?' Vernisse said, her eyes wide with shock.

Tzuri was as surprised as Vernisse at his outburst. He had come along to see Vernisse, not propose to her.

Baruch's words came back to him.

Someone will come along and snatch her from you.

Tzuri now interpreted Vernisse's hesitancy as a sign of another. 'There isn't anyone else is there?'

Vernisse looked past him at the counter where her father was busy flirting with Tzuri's great-grandmother. She grabbed the back of his neck and drew him to her. She kissed him with a passion Tzuri had never experienced. Vernisse was never this forward. Perhaps she was signalling her exclusive love for him. Women were so complicated. Something he could not control was happening between his thighs. He straightened up.

'There is no one else,' she said.

'Then will you marry me?'

Vernisse let out a sigh. 'It's not that straightforward, is it?'

The swelling between his legs subsided, much to his relief. 'Because I'm a Jew and you're a Christian?'

'Yes. The Pope has forbidden us to marry.'

Baruch's words came again into his head.

Find a way.

'Then there's only one thing...'

Vernisse's brow furrowed. 'What thing is that?'

'You'll have to convert to Judaism.'

Vernisse let out a sigh of relief and wiped the curls of her fringe from her forehead. 'I thought you were going to suggest we run away together. I could never leave Father.'

'So you're not averse to becoming a Jew?'

'I don't know. I've never thought about it.'

'But you'll consider it?' A flight of hope beat within Tzuri's chest.

'What does it entail?' Vernisse asked.

'I'm not sure about the practical steps to conversion but knowing my religion it will be a long, drawn-out affair.'

'What about you converting to Christianity?'

Tzuri sucked in air. It had never occurred to him to convert. 'Become a Christian?'

'Why not? Would that be so bad? Anyway, what's the difference? You just asked me to convert to Judaism?'

Tzuri ran his fingers through his ebony hair, his brows knotting together in contemplation. He would still be able to get work as a scribe. His skill with a quill and ink, his neatness, his accuracy when transcribing was well sought after. But there were other considerations.

'I hadn't thought about it that way.'

Vernisse stood up and went over to the bolts of cloth and ran her fingers lightly over them. Tzuri watched her, imagining her touch against his skin.

Finally Vernisse spoke. 'Wouldn't you do that for me?'

'It's different for me.'

'Why is it?'

'I'll be ostracised from my family, from the community...'

Were they having their first argument? Would it be the first of many? Brought about by their different religions.

'It's less complicated for you. You only have your father to think about. Would he disown you?'

'Maybe. I don't know.'

Vernisse had no siblings, her mother had died when she

was a child, and her father had never bothered to remarry. Vernisse looked over towards her father. He was standing outside the shop, talking animatedly with the women, laughing, telling them all how lovely they looked.

'My father is a simple soul. He wants nothing but my happiness.' There was a momentary silence then she said, 'But whether he would think me converting to Judaism and marrying a Jew was his idea of happiness, I really don't know.'

'I love you, Vernisse, and I want to be with you. My stepfather is...' he thought about how to describe Baruch, 'a relaxed Jew, should we say. I don't think he would object.'

'What about Brunetta? I never know how to take her.'

'She's a bit prickly at times but I don't think she would stop me from marrying the woman I loved.'

'Should we find out then?' Vernisse asked, her eyes widening in excitement.

'I think we have to. I can't stand being in limbo. It's killing me.'

Vernisse came towards him. She reached out for his hand. Just as her fingers were about to touch his, Ozanne burst into the room.

'What are you two up to?' she asked, radiating a mischievous smile.

'Nothing,' said Vernisse abruptly, bringing her hand back to her side and returning to the table.

'Come on, Tzuri, you can't fool me. I know what's going on.'

Ozanne could be impetuous at times and Tzuri did not want her stealing his thunder by telling everyone about him and Vernisse.

'Please don't say anything,' he said.

'I won't, you know I won't.'

She turned to leave then swung round. 'If I loved someone enough, I'd run away with them.'

CHAPTER
FOUR

Ozanne considered herself to be a bad Jew. She blamed her stepfather who, in her opinion, was also a bad Jew. For some reason he didn't act like a Jew. For one thing he was a Skirmiseur, a very un-Jewish occupation, earning his money teaching swordsmanship to William Marshal's soldiers. He spent time in Christian taverns with his friend the marshal and other grand knights. He did go to the synagogue now and again, but he wasn't what Ozanne would call an observant Jew. He had a knack of crossing effortlessly between Jewish and Christian ways of life. And no one seemed to question it. Her mother, on the other hand, was unfathomable. At times wilful, at others compliant. It was obvious she and her stepfather shared a deep and passionate love for each other.

Her thoughts turned to her brother and his love for Vernisse. She wondered if they would ever get married or if they would have to run away together and start a new life elsewhere. Surprisingly she was saddened by this thought. She loved her brother and sought his opinion on many things. She would miss him. Maybe he would find a way to marry Vernisse and stay in Gloucester.

Inspired by her reveries, she picked up the kinnor and began plucking at the strings. Simple chords. Then a poem formed in her mind. She went to the small desk in her bedroom and took out a leaf of parchment and her quill and an inkwell. She noticed her fingers were stained with gall-nut ink. She began to scribble down her thoughts.

If love were easy, it would not pain,
If love...
Love.

She had never been in love. A few of the boys in the community had been interested in her, but when they got to know her and realised she was different to most other girls – well, that was what they told her – they lost interest and sought wives that would look after them in the way they expected them to. Ozanne was an outsider. Like her stepfather. He once told her – when he had had a little too much to drink – that he felt like he didn't fit in, that he was considered the black sheep of the family, and it would always be so. At the time Ozanne was a young girl and hadn't questioned him further. Now she wished she had.

How did she know love was painful if she had never been in love or had her heart broken?

Real poetry was surely from the heart. From experience. She needed to go out into the wider world, beyond the confines of Gloucester and her claustrophobic community. Even that thought was unrealistic. How would she ever be able to do that? She was trapped. She dipped her quill in the inkwell and held it above the parchment, letting the dark-brown liquid dribble over the scrawly words she had just written.

Amateur.

A soft knock at her bedroom door made her turn round. She

replaced the quill in the inkwell and dried the inky mess she had made then called out to whoever was at her door. The door opened a crack and Tzuri appeared, looking morose.

'Come in,' she said, smiling at her brother.

Tzuri sat down on her bed, his face bearing the signs of a man in torment. An enormous sigh fell from his lips, and he hung his head.

'What's the matter, Tzuri? You haven't been yourself lately. Is it Vernisse?'

He sighed again. 'It is – and it isn't,' he said cryptically.

'Has she upset you?'

Ozanne was fiercely protective of her brother. Although he was older than her, she had always felt she was the wiser of the two. Or was she just hard-hearted?

'No, nothing like that. I don't know what to do.'

'You love her, don't you?'

Tzuri looked up. 'Is it that obvious?' he said, brushing back thick black locks from his face.

His deep-blue eyes were glassy. Her brother was in pain. She looked down at the spoiled poem and wondered if instinctively she knew more about love than she realised. She stood up and walked over to sit next to him.

'Why so sad?'

'She's a Christian and it's forbidden to marry a Jew.'

'Who says? The Pope? What does he know about love? And who is he to tell people how to live their lives?'

She stood up again, agitated. Why did men – men in particular – feel like they could tell other people – women in particular – how to live their lives. It maddened her.

'What does Vernisse want to do?'

It occurred to Ozanne that if Vernisse thought the Pope had the right to interfere in her life then Tzuri was destined to be thwarted in love.

'We talked about it at her father's the other day.'

'The day when I burst in on you?'

Tzuri managed a weak smile.

'Yes, that day. She said she'd talk to her father about converting to Judaism.'

Ozanne gasped. She hadn't known their relationship had developed that far. 'She's willing to convert?' she asked.

'Maybe. It depends on what her father says. She dotes on him and doesn't want to upset him.'

Another man controlling the life of a woman, thought Ozanne. 'And what about you? Would you convert to Christianity?'

Tzuri became agitated, ruffling his fingers through his hair. 'I don't know. She asked me if I would, but I was non-committal.'

Ozanne's opinion of Vernisse shot up when she heard this. 'So Vernisse doesn't automatically think she should convert.'

'No, and I was surprised by that. I didn't think she'd ask me.'

'What are you going to do?'

'I don't know. What do you think I should do?'

'I think you should follow your heart.'

'I knew you'd say that.'

'Then why did you ask me?' she said, joking.

'I needed to talk to someone.'

A pang of compassion swept over her for her brother. He was hurting and she wasn't helping. 'Have you spoken to *Ima* and *Aba*?'

'Not yet.'

'Perhaps you should. If you know how they feel about you marrying a Christian, that might help you make your decision.'

'But what if they say only if Vernisse converts and then if she doesn't want to or her father won't give his permission...'

'You're torturing yourself. Maybe none of this will ever happen.'

'I keep remembering what you said in Quinton's shop.'

'What did I say?'

Ozanne said all sorts of things and changed her mind frequently.

'You said you'd run away with the person you loved. I was thinking maybe that might be the answer.'

'Don't you dare,' she said. 'I'd miss you.'

'Then why say it?'

'I didn't think you'd take any notice of me. I'm the dreamer in the family. Remember?'

Tzuri's shoulders dropped like a beaten man. Ozanne bent down in front of him and took his hands in hers.

'I'll support you in whatever decision you make. You know I will.'

CHAPTER
FIVE

Mirabelle was alone in her luxurious fortress, a stone's throw from the le Riche household, contemplating her future. Bonanfaunt had travelled to London to do business with Elias le Blund and had taken his family with him, so she had the enormous house to herself. Bonanfaunt had been blessed with children. Six boys, Elias, Isaac, Vives, Jacob and twins Bonamy and Bonavie, and one daughter, Mirabelle, who they had named after her but to avoid confusion the family referred to her as Belina. Mirabelle's favourite was her great-granddaughter, the offspring of Isaac with his wife Rana who they had named Belle. At the tender age of four she displayed frequent bouts of childish spitefulness.

It was only midday, but Mirabelle was already drinking a cup of fine Gascony wine. She preferred it to the kosher wine most of the community's pious Jews drank. She had returned to her bed and was lounging upon a pile of richly decorated tapestry cushions. A fire blazed in the hearth, warming the room. The chestnut bed frame had been imported from France and was elaborately carved with quatrefoils and had extended bedposts reaching halfway to the low ceiling. As usual she was thinking of her financial situation and how she could improve it. It had been impossible to get an audience with William Marshal at the banquet. He was far too busy to see her.

She took a sip of wine and thought about Moses le Riche. The death of Moses had brought good fortune to her and her family. His son Abraham had died suddenly in suspicious circumstances, the details of which Mirabelle had never been able to get to the bottom of. She suspected he had killed himself because he could not cope with the family business, but she had no proof. The le Riche family was full of secrets.

For Mirabelle, Abraham's death was the beginning of the rise in her considerable fortunes. Once Abraham was dead, she pushed her son to the forefront of Gloucester's Jewish life, and he had not disappointed her. They were now the richest family in the community – something she had been striving for all these long years.

Her husband Elias had never been able to achieve such accomplishments in his lifetime. She tried to bring his features to mind but she couldn't and then realised she had not missed him. In fact, when she thought about it, she was better off without him. He had always chided her for her actions with the aim of making her feel guilty. Now she had free rein and could do what she wanted although Bonanfaunt occasionally chastised her.

Life was good for the aging Mirabelle apart from one blot on the horizon. Newcomers to Gloucester. Abraham of Warwick and his family. They had arrived from Warwick under a cloud of suspicion and yet were managing to infiltrate their way into some of the more lucrative business dealings on offer. Their status in the community was on the rise and this caused Mirabelle some anxiety. No doubt they had been the victims of some falling out with the leading Christians of that town. Abraham was ambitious. Mirabelle saw him as an irksome threat to her ascendency. Something would have to be done about him.

A knock at her door disrupted her thoughts.

'Who can that be?' Mirabelle asked herself out loud, disgruntled at being disturbed.

She lay there waiting for her elderly servant, Joan, to answer the door but then she remembered she'd given her the day off to visit her family. Lifting herself from the cushions she then dropped down to the wooden floorboards and peeked out of the window opening. Beneath her stood Abraham Gabbai. Since meeting him at the Northampton *donum* he had become a regular visitor to Gloucester even though he was still treasurer for the Bristol community. She wondered what he wanted. It would be something that her talents would warrant attention no doubt.

Mirabelle trudged down the wooden staircase, her knees clicking with age, and answered the door.

In an undisguised sarcastic tone she said: 'To what do I owe this unscheduled visit?'

Gabbai scowled at her. He was wearing his distinctive pointed felt hat and a dark woollen cloak. His skin was grey with dark spots beneath his sunken eyes. His grey beard, untrimmed and matted, Mirabelle had always thought he looked like a bird of prey.

'I need to speak to you about Solomon Turbe.'

Solomon Turbe was another newcomer to Gloucester. He had arrived some months ago with his wife, Comitissa.

Comitissa.

Mirabelle snarled at the name. How pretentious. It meant Countess in Latin. Who did she think she was with her airs and graces. They were a well-matched couple in Mirabelle's eyes. Solomon was a rough carbuncle lacking in manners whereas Comitissa thought she possessed manners she did not have.

Gloucester was changing and newcomers were frequently arriving and inserting themselves into the community and vying to avail themselves of the spoils. The Warwick family were a prime example. Arrivals from her home country of France such as Isaac of Poitevin and Moses of Paris were less bothersome. In some way it was comforting to hear the mother tongue, in others it was infuriating because they were all after the same thing which meant Mirabelle's family got less of what was on offer. Although she hated to admit it, gone were the glory days of Moses le Riche.

'What about?' Mirabelle asked Gabbai in her brusque manner.

Abraham Gabbai was the treasurer of the Jewish community in Bristol. It was a highly trustworthy position and yet Mirabelle had never trusted him.

'May I come in?' he asked, removing his hat.

Mirabelle huffed but opened the door wider to let him in. He sat down without asking permission. Mirabelle huffed again and sat opposite him.

'We've known each other for twenty years or more. I–'

'Yes, yes. Get on with it.'

'It's about Solomon Turbe.'

'You already said that,' Mirabelle replied, tersely.

'He's been threatening me.'

'Threatening you? In what way?'

'He's threatening to expose me.'

Mirabelle was aware that bad blood existed between the two. This latest accusation was not entirely news.

'What is he going to expose?'

'Some of my financial affairs which as you know aren't always above board. He's threatening to tell Sheriff Musard.'

Sheriff Ralph Musard was a man who strived for an easy life and could be easily bribed. On hearing of his possible involvement she wasn't unduly worried. He could be managed.

'Does Solomon have anything he can use against you?'

Since the Northampton *donum* Mirabelle had been embroiled in a deceit, with the help of Sheriff Musard, of not wholly declaring her financial transactions so that when the extortionate king's tallages came along she would pay less than others in her community. The idea had come from Gabbai. He had told her of the game being played by others across the country, particularly the wealthy London Jews. They would offer bribes to have their tallage assessments adjusted. It was called an 'aid' by the sheriffs for receiving the tallage. A fee if anyone asked. It was unfair on those in the community who paid a lower amount as they would inevitably end up with a greater tax burden, but this did not unduly concern Mirabelle.

If Solomon was referring to this then she was possibly at danger of being exposed herself. She offered Gabbai a dried fig. He took it and placed it between his thin lips and bit into it. Mirabelle stood up and walked over to the table where she kept her fine Gascony wine.

'He says he has but I'm not sure.'

'What does he want?' In Mirabelle's experience people always wanted something. Personally, she never did anything unless it was of benefit to her. 'Money?' she asked.

'He says not. He wants me to use my influence to make him treasurer of Gloucester.'

Mirabelle froze and the wine she was pouring spilled onto the cream linen cloth that was covering the table leaving a dark stain. Her precious son Bonanfaunt was the unofficial treasurer of the community. She had been grooming him since he was a boy to take over from the le Riche family.

'You're not going to, are you?' she said, twirling round to face Gabbai, fixing him with her stone-cold stare.

Gabbai shrunk back in his seat as if he could feel the chill touch of a corpse upon him. 'I told him I'd see what I could do...'

Mirabelle moved towards him, her eyes narrowing to mere slits. 'You said what?'

Her tone was flat and menacing. Despite her advancing years she was a frightening spectacle, like a tigress protecting her young.

'I only said that to get him off my back. I have no intention of helping him in any way. I loathe the man.'

In Mirabelle's eyes Solomon Turbe had gone from a man she disliked to an enemy of her family. There was nothing she wouldn't do to protect her family.

SIX

Tzuri sat in the hall of their new house tapping his foot on the tapestry rug, his fingers thrumming the arm of his chair with the same beat. The family's circumstances had reduced quite dramatically. They had lost the big house in East Gate Street – something to do with his father Abraham's mishandling of the family business. More than that he knew nothing. Whenever he broached the matter, the family seemed reluctant to talk about it and always changed the subject. Their old house, built by the great Moses le Riche was now in the hands of Gilbert de Rue, handed over to him on the orders of King John.

It was more than a sore point for Douce. She had been devastated and at the time thanked *Hashem* that Moses had not lived to see it. Douce's sons Samuel and Justelin had moved to London to make their own way in life and the only one left was Henne, and she now lived with her husband, Vives, and their six children in a small house on the other side of The Cross.

'What's wrong with you, Tzuri? You seem on edge tonight,' Brunetta said.

They had eaten their evening meal and Brunetta was

sipping an apple brandy in front of the fire. Douce was squinting at some embroidery on her lap by the light of a beeswax candle and Ozanne was picking out chords on Old Samuel's kinnor. Zev and Rubin were in their workshop and would be home later. Arlette had retired for the night and Baruch had gone to meet an old friend at his local tavern.

Tzuri crossed his leg over his knee in an attempt to stop the tapping, but it didn't work. Instead it set both legs off. In the end he stood up and began pacing the room. Since his conversation with Vernisse about converting to Christianity his mind had been in turmoil. Did he love her enough to turn his back on his faith? Would his family refuse to have any more to do with him? Would he be banished from the community? It was tearing his insides apart. He hadn't slept well since that day either and he found he was snappier than normal.

'Nothing, *Ima*, I'm just tired.'

'You look like you have the world's burdens on your shoulder,' Brunetta replied, placing an ornate hexagonal needle case on the side table by her chair and replacing its lid.

If only she knew, thought Tzuri.

Just then Baruch walked in. He walked over to Brunetta and gave her a kiss on the cheek. They had been married for almost twenty years, yet they still had a spark for one another. Tzuri often wondered if it had been like that with his mother and his real father, Abraham. That was another touchy subject. His father's death. Abraham had died in some sort of accident and afterwards his mother had married Baruch. What did it matter who was more passionate? Baruch and his mother were happy together and that's what mattered. Would he and Vernisse be like that when they grew old, he wondered.

'Have a word with Tzuri, won't you. He's not himself,' Brunetta said, placing a pin in her mouth and pressing her full lips tight.

'Girl trouble, is it?' Baruch asked his son.

Tzuri could not keep his thoughts to himself for a minute longer.

'Actually, yes,' he said, looking first from his father then to his mother who on hearing her son, removed the pin from her lips, leaving her mouth slightly open in anticipation of his revelation.

'You haven't got a girl into trouble, have you?' said Baruch.

'Tzuri!' cried Brunetta, shocked at such a suggestion. 'Tell me that's not true.'

Tzuri didn't answer.

'Is it that draper's daughter?' asked Baruch.

'Vernisse?' Brunetta added.

'Yes, it is as it happens.'

'Your father should have kept a closer eye on you. I knew there was something going on between the two of you. *Oy lanu*, I don't know what's worse: making a Christian girl pregnant or making a Jewish girl pregnant. Think of the shame.'

'Vernisse is not pregnant, and I have done nothing to make it so. I love her and want to marry her.'

The relief Tzuri felt once he had confessed was instant. The tension in his neck and the knots in his stomach left him. He sat back down and waited for his parents' reaction. For a few moments there was silence apart from the flickering of the candles and the collapsing of red embers from the fire. Douce looked up from her embroidery and Ozanne stopped plucking at the strings of the kinnor.

'But Vernisse is a Christian. How do you expect to marry her?' asked Brunetta.

'I could convert to Christianity...'

Douce, who had been quiet up until now, shot out of her chair and threw her embroidery on the seat. 'If you do that, you'll be dead to me.'

With that she left the room, slamming the wooden door behind her. Ozanne followed her out, leaving Brunetta and Baruch.

Tzuri, open-mouthed, looked at the door his great-grandmother had just exited. He had been half joking when he said he might convert to Christianity, never imagining Douce would react so violently to the suggestion.

Baruch stood up and poured himself a cup of apple brandy and drank it down in one.

'Would she really disown me?'

'Douce is from a different generation. She has suffered a lot by being a Jew and now in her eyes her great-grandson wants to throw all that away.'

'I didn't really mean what I said...'

'Then why did you say it?' Brunetta snapped.

'I suppose I was testing the water.'

'I think you've got your answer,' said Baruch.

'Maybe Vernisse would be willing to convert to Judaism?' Brunetta said.

If Vernisse refused to convert it would mean his children would not be Jewish. They would not be brought up in the Jewish faith, would not be able to attend the synagogue, would not be accepted into his tight-knit community, would not know their grandmother.

'Let's hope for you that she will or *Safta* will never speak to you again.'

SEVEN

Following Douce's outburst that if he converted to Christianity, he would be dead to her, Tzuri knew what he must do. He just hoped Vernisse would go along with his decision. If she didn't, he was unsure how he would feel about it.

He needed to talk to her and soon.

Vernisse went to church on Sunday. She was part of the congregation of Holy Trinity in West Gate Street close by the entrance to Bull Lane. He would wait in Bull Lane and hopefully find a way to steer her away from her father's doting attention. Tzuri loitered almost half an hour waiting for the congregation to leave, dodging passers-by using the lane as a shortcut to the castle, mostly Christians who looked villainous. He could make out the preacher's raised voice through the stained-glass windows, reminding the poor Christians of their sin. There would be a slight pause then a chorus of 'Amen' from the gathered flock. Eventually the church doors opened, and a throng of people spilled out into the street. Tzuri scanned the heads looking for Vernisse's distinctive red hair. He spotted her walking beside a young man he had not seen before. She was laughing and occasionally touching his arm. Her father walked behind them. Was this her Christian suitor? Someone her father approved of. A secret?

Tzuri felt a stabbing pain in his heart. Had he lost Vernisse to a Christian boy? His chances of persuading her to convert were looking slim. Tzuri studied the boy. Tall, square-jawed, muscular, with thin fair hair and blue eyes. In comparison Tzuri was dark-skinned, black-haired and of average build. And he was a Jew.

Tzuri followed the happy threesome until they reached Quinton's shop. Would she kiss him? Quinton unlocked the door whilst Vernisse waited behind him. The young man loitered then followed them inside. Tzuri sank into a pit of despair. He had been prepared to convert to Christianity for this woman. What a fool he'd been. He sloped back home where he sat and ate an entire bowl of his mother's pastries and immediately felt sick.

'What's the matter with you?' Baruch asked. 'Is it what *Safta* said?'

'Not really.' Tzuri put the empty bowl of pastries that he'd been cradling on his lap on the side table.

'Then is it Vernisse?'

Tzuri swung his head up to look at Baruch. 'As a matter of fact, it is.'

'What's happened?' asked Baruch as he sat down on the chair opposite.

'I think I've lost her.'

'What makes you say that?'

'I saw her coming out of church with a young man.'

Baruch laughed. 'Well that's hardly evidence of having lost her.'

'They seemed very friendly.'

'Still not evidence.'

'They looked overly friendly.'

Baruch grinned at Tzuri. 'Why don't you ask her instead of jumping to conclusions. I pursued your mother even though she gave me signs she wasn't interested.'

'That was different. You were old.'

Baruch burst out laughing. 'I still had blood in my veins.'

Tzuri thought for a while. Baruch was probably right. He may have jumped to conclusions. 'Maybe he's a relative,' he said.

'Well, if you want to marry this woman hadn't you better find out?'

The pastries in Tzuri's stomach felt like stones. He looked down at his bloated stomach and thought of the athletically built youth who was charming Vernisse. He wasn't going to win her heart sitting eating until he made himself sick.

'You're right, *Aba*. I'll go and ask her now.'

'That's more like it,' Baruch said, giving him a friendly dig in the stomach. 'Get some fire in that belly of yours instead of those sickly pastries you're so fond of.'

Tzuri stood up, brushed the crumbs from his lap and hurried out the door.

'Let me know how you get on,' Baruch shouted after Tzuri's retreating back.

CHAPTER

EIGHT

Tzuri hurried through the streets of Gloucester with fire in his belly, determined to be firm with Vernisse, but as he got nearer her father's shop the stodgy pastries began to curdle in his stomach. It was one thing talking about this but another acting on it. How would Vernisse react? She could be quite feisty. And what about that young man she was with? At the thought of him, Tzuri sucked in his stomach and straightened his back as he walked down the lane to Quinton's drapery shop.

The streets were quiet as the night had drawn in and Tzuri suddenly realised it was an odd time of day to visit. His resolve began to wane with every step. When he reached the front of the timber-framed building the wooden shutters were up and there was no sign of candlelight. He wondered what Vernisse might be doing. He took a deep breath and knocked on the shop door and waited. It seemed an age before he heard someone coming to the door. He thought of walking away, but some inner resolve made him wait. Then the door opened, and Quinton stood before him. His expression showed he was more than surprised to see him.

'It's late, Tzuri. Is there a problem?'

His tone of voice was querulous with no hint of irritation at the intrusion.

'I'm sorry to bother you at this late hour, Monsieur Brebon, but may I speak with Vernisse?'

Quinton stared back at Tzuri as if he didn't quite understand what he was saying.

'Can it wait until the morning?' he said after what seemed an age.

Tzuri heard someone approaching behind Quinton.

'Who is it, Quinton?' a man's voice said.

Tzuri's stomach dropped. It was the young man from the church. He was in the house at this late hour. He realised the foolishness of his actions.

'So sorry, Quinton. I didn't know you had company,' Tzuri said, beginning to slowly back away down the lane.

Vernisse appeared at the door. 'What is going on, Papa?'

'It's Tzuri, he wants to speak to you.'

'At this hour?' Vernisse said, surprise evident in her voice.

Tzuri saw her push past her father and step out into the lane holding a lit candle. He had taken a few steps back but now stopped in the lane and stared at her. Vernisse turned to her father.

'Give me a moment, Papa. I'll come back inside once I've spoken to Tzuri.'

'But–' began Quinton.

'I'll only be a minute. Please, Father.'

Quinton relented. The young man said nothing. Vernisse walked towards Tzuri.

'What on earth is so important that you want to talk to me at this time of night?' she said, holding up her candle to Tzuri's face.

She must have seen his distress because she moved closer and placed her hand upon his arm.

'What's happened? Is it your grandmother?'

'In a way it is. She says she'll disown me if I convert to Christianity.'

'So you've told them about us?'

'Yes, I couldn't keep it to myself any longer.'

'What did they say?' Vernisse asked.

'*Aba* was quite supportive, *Ima* less so but it was *Safta's* reaction that shocked me the most. I can't lose my family, Vernisse. Have you spoken to your father?'

'Not yet.' Vernisse put the candle holder down on the ground and squeezed his arm. 'But I have given it some thought.'

Tzuri was about to offer to speak to Quinton when he remembered the young man. 'Who is that man in your house?'

Vernisse laughed. 'That's my cousin, Lucien. He's here from Paris.'

'Is he here to marry you?'

Vernisse laughed again. 'Of course not, silly.' Vernisse was close now. She placed her arms around Tzuri's neck and hugged him. Then she kissed him. 'There is no one I'd rather marry than you.'

'Does that mean you'll convert?'

'If I have to,' she said.

'In that case,' said Tzuri, prising her arms from his neck, 'I need to speak to your father and do this thing properly.'

Learning the news that the young man was not a suitor gave Tzuri greater courage. He took hold of Vernisse's hand and pulled her towards the door.

'Wait a minute,' she cried as she bent down to retrieve the candle.

Inside the front of the shop it was dark and full of shadows. Vernisse held up the candle, still holding on to Tzuri's hand, and lit the way to the furthest rear room where a fire burned, and Quinton sat with a cup of red wine in his hand staring into the flames. Lucien sat opposite with a cup in his hand. Tzuri nodded at him. Quinton looked up as they entered, a wistful look upon his face.

'Monsieur, I apologise for the late intrusion but I'm here to ask for your daughter's hand in marriage.'

Tzuri let out a deep sigh. The pastries had lodged in his stomach like bricks. The words had come, and he had said them. Now he must wait for Quinton's reaction.

There was silence in the room.

Tzuri was met with a sea of shocked faces. Eventually Quinton spoke.

'But you're a Jew.'

CHAPTER
NINE

O n hearing Quinton's words Tzuri's heart ceased to beat for a few moments. He needed to gather his thoughts. He was a Jew and there was nothing that could be done about that. He had to win over Quinton. Show him he was serious about his daughter and that he would look after her and make her happy for the rest of her life.

'I am Jewish. There's nothing I can do to change that–'

Lucien, who up to now had not said a word, piped up. 'Then you should not come here with a proposal of marriage.'

Tzuri immediately became suspicious of Lucien's intentions towards Vernisse. Was he sweet on her? Did he want to keep her for himself? He was thinking of an answer when Vernisse cut in.

'Tzuri and I have discussed this at length.'

Tzuri knew that wasn't strictly true, but he listened as she continued.

'Papa, the last thing I want to do is upset you, but we love each other and want to be married. The sensible way forward is if I convert to Judaism.'

Quinton appeared to jolt. He put his cup of wine down on

the nearby table and scratched his chin through his greying beard.

'It sounds to me like you've already made up your mind.'

There was a sadness and an air of defeat in his demeanour. Tzuri had never seen this side of him. Quinton was always so jovial. Amenable.

'I've given it quite some thought. I'm an only child, and you are my only family.' She glanced over at Lucien. 'My only close family. If I convert, I'll still have you, Papa, won't I?'

She waited for him to answer. He was silent, staring into the fire. She crossed over to her father who had been listening to her but not looking at her. She knelt at his feet and took his hands.

'Papa, I love you with all my heart. Say I won't lose you if I convert and marry Tzuri.'

Quinton looked down at Vernisse, his eyes glassy with emotion. 'All I've ever wanted is happiness for you. Since your mother died, I have worried about you. Worried what would happen to you if I died. You'd be all alone in this world. I can't bear to think of that. Of course, I hadn't bargained on you falling in love with a Jew.'

'I hadn't either, Papa, yet that's exactly what has happened.'

Quinton's eyes became filled with tears. He looked at Vernisse. 'Do you really love him?'

'I do. With all my heart.'

He turned his gaze to Tzuri and smiled. It was a sign that he felt no animosity.

'Love is a powerful emotion. I know. I loved your mother.'

Vernisse steered the conversation back to the present. 'If Tzuri converted to Christianity, he would lose more than his family. He'd no longer be part of his close community. He has so much more to lose than me.'

'I can see that. I would have preferred a different future for you – one that is not complicated by differences of faith – but if you love him...'

Lucien stood up. 'Are you just going to give in like that? Allow your daughter to marry a Jew?'

Quinton held out his hands to calm Lucien. 'Tzuri comes from a good family. I believe she will be in good hands.'

Tzuri moved between Lucien and Quinton. Quinton continued: 'Call me a sentimental old fool but I believe that in the end love prevails.'

'Monsieur, you can be sure that I will look after Vernisse and make her happy,' said Tzuri with conviction.

'How can she be happy married to you, a Jew, with all your strange ways?' Lucien said.

Tzuri turned to the angry young man. 'I don't see how it's any of your business.'

'I could make it my business.'

Lucien lunged towards Tzuri.

'Stop it you two,' Vernisse said, pushing Lucien away from Tzuri. 'I won't have any quarrelling over this. If Father has given me permission to marry Tzuri, then that's the last word to be said on the subject.'

Vernisse's tone was firm and determined, Tzuri wondered if she'd be like this in their marriage. What if she were? She might be the only one to stand up to Douce. He smiled inside. Then he remembered his question to Quinton.

'Do I have your permission, Monsieur Brebon?'

Quinton nodded, then as if he had forgotten his manners, he stood up and hugged Vernisse.

'Congratulations, *ma petite*.'

Then he turned to Tzuri and shook his hand. Lucien sat back in his chair like a defeated savage cur. Tzuri's suspicions had been right. Lucien had designs on Vernisse.

TEN

Tzuri had barely slept for thinking about Vernisse and the night's events. When he went downstairs to breakfast his stomach was churning not with hunger but with nerves.

Arlette was standing by the *foudron*, the small stove that Moses had bought in France, toasting chunks of bread on its hot surface. Douce could not bear to leave it behind when they moved so it now stood in the small kitchen of their new home.

She turned when Tzuri came in the room. 'You look tired, Tzuri, is everything all right?'

Tzuri swept his hair from his eyes and nodded. He sat at the table opposite Douce and his mother. Neither Ozanne nor his father were in the room. That bothered Tzuri as so far, they were his only allies in his quest to marry Vernisse. Still, the family had to be told this morning before the news leaked out into the community as these things always did.

He took a sip of weak wine and reached out for some bread to dip into a pot of honey. He needed something inside him before he made his announcement.

'Where did you get to last night?' Brunetta asked him. 'I heard you come in. It was very late.'

'Not like you to be out late,' added Douce.

The women were staring at him waiting for his answer. He stared back. A piece of bread stuck in his throat like a stone, and he began to cough.

'What's the matter with you this morning?' Brunetta said, slapping Tzuri's back to dislodge the bread.

Tzuri took another sip of wine. 'I have something to tell you,' he said.

The women's eyes fixed on Tzuri. Douce's mouth was half open, a piece of bread in her delicate hand.

'I'm going to marry Vernisse.'

'You've said that before. That's nothing new,' said Brunetta.

'It's official now though,' Tzuri replied.

'What do you mean "official"?' Brunetta asked, placing her cup of wine down in front of her.

Tzuri ignored the sick feeling in his stomach and continued. 'Last night, I asked Quinton if I could marry his daughter and he agreed, so it's official. I'm going to marry Vernisse.'

Douce stood up and threw the piece of bread on the table.

'How can you marry a Christian? After all the injustices our family has suffered at the hands of these cruel people?'

'Vernisse and her father are not cruel people. I don't know what happened in the past. That's the past and has nothing to do with me.'

'It has everything to do with you. You are a Jew and don't you forget that.'

Douce spat her words out. Tzuri had never seen her so angry.

Brunetta now stood up. 'Don't speak to my son like that.'

Arlette, still standing by the *foudron*, put the toasted bread she was holding on the platter in the middle of the table. She wiped her hands on her apron. 'Please, everyone. Calm down. Let's sit and hear what Tzuri has to say.'

'He's said enough, hasn't he?' Douce glared at Tzuri, ignoring Arlette's pleas. 'I warned him if he married a Christian, I would disown him. They are demons with their idolatrous cults and heathen practices.'

Arlette let out a gasp. 'You can't do that, Douce.'

'Can't I? Just see.'

A spiteful smirk appeared on Brunetta's full lips. 'Why didn't you disown Baruch then?'

'Brunetta,' Arlette cried out.

Tzuri was taken aback by Arlette's reaction. She had a terrified look on her face. Whatever was playing out between these women it was more than just about him marrying Vernisse. Were his suspicions of long-held secrets in the family about to be exposed? Was Brunetta finally going to stand up to the formidable Douce? He looked from the faces of each of the women, frozen by the scene before him.

'Maybe I should have. Look how he turned out,' growled Douce.

Arlette burst into tears just as Baruch entered the room. His smile disappeared from his face as he took in the atmosphere. It was a cauldron of deep-seated hatred and pent-up emotions.

'How who turned out?' Baruch repeated.

Arlette spoke through her tears: 'Never mind. Your grandmother was speaking out of turn.'

'What's going on?' Baruch said, going over to his mother and placing his arm around her shoulders.

This only made Arlette sob deeper.

'What have you said to upset her, *Safta*?'

Brunetta answered for her. 'She's going to disown Tzuri.'

'He's going to marry a Christian,' said Douce. 'Thank

Hashem my beloved Moses is not here to witness such a wicked thing.'

'There's nothing wicked in wanting to marry Vernisse,' Tzuri shouted.

Baruch raised his hand to quieten what was turning into a hysterical mêlée. 'No one is going to disown anyone. Not today anyway. Let's talk this through like adults.'

Arlette sniffed and blew her nose on a cloth. Brunetta folded her arms and fixed her expression as one of cold defiance. Douce sighed and calmly sat back down.

Baruch turned to Tzuri.

'What have you done?' he asked.

'I intend to marry Vernisse,' said Tzuri defiantly.

'But it's not that simple, is it?'

'Why isn't it?'

'As a Jew, you can't just marry a Christian. Have either of you considered converting?'

At this Douce cried out: 'If Tzuri converts to Christianity, I will never speak to him again.'

'Shush, shush,' said Baruch. 'Let him speak.'

'We have discussed it and Vernisse is willing to convert to Judaism.'

Arlette whispered under her breath: '*Baruch Hashem.*'

At this point, tactless as ever, Ozanne came tumbling into the room.

'*Bonjour,*' she greeted them in a loud cheery voice.

Then she quickly assessed the situation.

'Oh,' she said and sat at the table next to Douce.

Baruch turned to Douce. 'If Vernisse converts to Judaism then will you be satisfied?'

Before Douce could speak Brunetta cut in, 'She better be, or I won't be silent.'

Baruch scowled at Brunetta and Douce glared at her. The

room fell silent again and the atmosphere turned to the kind of tension before a mighty battle is about to begin.

Ozanne, not one to be quiet for long, piped up: 'Surely this is nothing new. Lots of people have successfully converted. Ruth, for example. She was a convert to Judaism – and she was the great-great-grandmother of King David.'

Douce stared at the breakfast items on the table for a few moments. She shrugged her shoulders and suddenly became very small, as if the fight had left her. Baruch seemed to seize upon her temporary state of weakness.

'Well, what do you say? Does Tzuri have your blessing?' Baruch persisted.

Douce looked up at him. Her eyes were misted over with tears, but her face was stony. There was almost a hint of hatred in them.

'He doesn't need my blessing,' she said.

Later that day, when they were alone, Baruch said to Brunetta: 'You shouldn't have said anything. That was a secret I told you in confidence on our wedding night.'

'I know I shouldn't have said what I said, only your bloody high and mighty grandmother has made out she's better than me all these years. I just wanted to expose her as the hypocrite she is.'

'*Safta* is no hypocrite.'

Baruch rubbed at his temples. Brunetta sat down next to him and stroked his forehead.

'I'm sorry. I've made things worse. She just maddens me so and you know she's never liked me from the moment she met me.'

Baruch understood his wife's frustration. Douce could be

challenging. But he was devastated at Douce's outburst. He always thought she loved him despite how he came into the world, despite the conversation he had overheard all those years ago. It was Moses who could not love him, could not accept him. Not Douce. She was his loving grandmother but now it seemed she wasn't. That hurt him more than he wanted to admit. And now because of Brunetta's outburst the house felt like an enemy camp and soon Tzuri and Ozanne would be asking him questions.

'It's time you buried your grievances. What are we going to tell the children?'

'They're not children anymore. Perhaps it's time they knew,' said Brunetta, leaning her head on Baruch's shoulder.

'You might be right but how much do we tell them? Everything? That I'm the product of a violent rape. That I'm half Jewish. That Abraham killed himself. That I am their real father...'

'Maybe not everything,' said Brunetta, placing her hand on his naked chest.

'What then?'

'We could just say... Oh, I don't know,' she said, pulling away from him.

'This is all your fault, Brunetta. If you just kept your mouth shut.'

At Baruch's harsh words Brunetta burst into tears. It was not often she showed such emotion and Baruch felt remorseful. He gave her a cuddle and apologised. Brunetta sniffed and sat up straight.

'Well at least as far as Douce is concerned I won't be the most hated person under this roof. Once Tzuri marries Vernisse she'll likely replace me!'

Baruch squeezed Brunetta and kissed her on the neck. Brunetta responded with a quiet moan. It had been some time since they had been intimate. Arguing like they used to in the old days had woken something inside both of them. She wanted him. He wanted her. He ran his hands up and down her back. She wrapped her arms around his neck and pulled him towards her. Baruch responded by pressing her to the mattress, thrusting his hardness against her yielding body.

They made love just like in the old days. Full of passion and illicitness. Afterwards they fell asleep in each other's arms in the middle of the day.

ELEVEN

By September of the following year the French pretender to the English throne, Prince Louis, had been defeated at the Battle of Lincoln. The marshal had fought and won a decisive battle against him and the French threat to the crown was no more. A peace treaty, signed at Lambeth Palace, made Louis admit that he had never been King of England. He further agreed never to invade England again and for this it was rumoured he had been paid ten thousand marks to relinquish his claims. It heralded a period of peace in the land. King Louis returned to France and the marshal returned to Gloucester.

On hearing he was in the city Mirabelle seized the moment. She dressed in her finest attire of rich silk baudekin cloth, embroidered with a warp of gold thread but before she left the house, she had second thoughts. Would the marshal think she was wealthy in her finest attire and decide not to give her Elias's properties and bonds back? Perhaps she should change so that she appeared more impoverished? Mirabelle let out a loud huff. She was not to be judged by anyone. Slamming the door behind her she walked to the castle.

At the barbican she demanded to see the marshal.

'The marshal is not here,' said the porter. 'You'll find him at The Booth Hall.'

Mirabelle huffed at this news. She would have to go down West Gate Street where the house that used to belong to her husband was. It pained her to walk past it knowing it was still in Gilbert de Rue's hands.

When she arrived at The Booth Hall, she was in no mood to be told to wait but she had no option. The marshal was in a meeting and couldn't be disturbed. Eventually, the guard led her into the great hall where the marshal stood by a long oak table. He turned to look at her. Even though he was almost seventy, he was still an imposing character. He stroked his moustache which was now peppered with grey. Mirabelle walked towards him. It was only then she spotted the sheriff, Ralph Musard. He had already proved himself to be corruptible. Mirabelle had offered him bribes for aiding her with her tallage assessments. The marshal, on the other hand, was a known supporter of the Jews and understood their usefulness in a Christian world. Now an old man, battle-scarred, he still had a twinkle in his eye. She imagined his young wife, Isabel de Clare, kept him youthful.

'What can I do for Mistress Mirabelle this fine day?' said the marshal.

He was in jovial spirits. Mirabelle smiled back at him and nodded at the sheriff. 'Sir, I petitioned King John for the return of my husband's property. Sadly, the king died before the transaction could be finalised.'

'I believe the king gave by way of a gift two of your houses. One to his cook, Simon de Coco, and the other to Gilbert de Rue. Is that not so?' Sheriff Musard said by way of clarification.

At the mention of de Rue's name Mirabelle squirmed. 'That he did, and I made fine of fifteen marks for their return.'

The marshal's eyes widened. 'You paid King John fifteen marks?'

'I did, sir, and I think it only right that those properties be returned to me.'

'If that is the case I will need to investigate further.'

'My husband, Elias, has been dead these past years at the hands of men under the orders of King John. I think the least thing our new king can do, by way of reparation, is honour his father's promise.'

'He said he would make enquiries,' said the sheriff.

His comment was designed to shut her up, but she was not going to pass up her opportunity to petition the marshal in person.

'And what about my husband's bonds that the king committed to your custody?'

'Rest assured, Mistress Mirabelle, I will make enquiries and if what you say is true, I will make the necessary reparations.'

Mirabelle detected a curtness in his reply. She was in danger of pressing her cause too forcefully, something her son often accused her of. His admonitions made little difference. If anything, as she got older, she was more insistent having seen the injustices towards her kind.

'I appreciate your efforts, marshal. I'll let you get on with the rest of your day and trust I shall hear from you in due course.'

He bowed to her. The sheriff did not. She nodded to both men and left. She had gone as far as she could. Her fate was in the hands of the marshal.

TWELVE

The process of conversion was lengthy. Vernisse would have to face the intense questioning from members of the *bet din* – the rabbinical court that rules upon a conversion. Tzuri was in the back room of her father's shop coaching her on how best to answer their questions.

'It says in the Talmud that you must be asked why you wish to become a Jew.'

Tzuri quoted a passage: 'Why should you wish to become a proselyte; do you not know that the people of Israel at the present time are persecuted and oppressed, despised, harassed, and overcome by afflictions?'

'Are they?' Vernisse asked.

'You know they are.'

'I don't. I've never witnessed anything like that in this city.'

'I can see that you not only require religious education but a lesson in history. But that will have to wait for another time. You need to concentrate on your conversion studies. Otherwise we can't get married.'

'I didn't realise it would be so arduous.'

'So when they ask you why you want to become a Jew–'

'So I can marry a Jew?'

Tzuri, frustrated at her flippancy, sighed. 'No, that's not the answer, you have to say something like: "I have an unquenchable desire to live the rest of my life as a practising Jew observing the six hundred and thirteen mitzvot".'

'How many?'

'Six hundred and thirteen. You should know this from your studies.'

'I do. I was just teasing you.'

'You have got to take this seriously, Vernisse. At least until you have your certification as a Jew.'

'Then can I do and say what I want?' she asked, grinning.

Tzuri pretended to pull out his hair. 'Ugh, you make me so mad,' he said.

'I have an unquenchable desire for you,' she said, sidling up to him and planting a kiss on his cheek.

'Stop that,' he said. 'You know we have to wait until our wedding night.'

'I know, but it's fun to play around.'

Tzuri laughed. He could not resist her. She had the knack of making him relax and see the lighter side of life.

'I love you,' he said, kissing her on the lips.

'And I love you. Now remind me again... how many mitzvot? Six hundred and thirteen. If I learnt one a day, it would still take me almost two years.'

'You don't have to know each one in exact detail–'

'I wonder if it would be simpler for you to convert to Christianity,' she said.

Tzuri slammed his fist on the table making Vernisse jump. 'Don't you take anything seriously? You're worse than my sister.'

'Calm down, Tzuri. I hope you're not going to be this serious once we are married.'

Tzuri thought for a moment. He *was* being far too serious. He was startled by his angry outburst which was out of character for him.

'I'm sorry, Vernisse. It's just that I so want to marry you. It makes me mad when I think I might not be able to.'

'You worry too much. Nothing is going to come in the way of us getting married. I'm sorry too. I'll try to be more serious in future.'

Tzuri wrapped his arms around her tiny waist.

'That's why I love you so much. You know just what to say to make me feel better.'

CHAPTER

THIRTEEN

For months Douce had hardly spoken to anyone, except maybe to ask Arlette to pass the honey pot at the breakfast table. Tzuri could not bear to see his great-grandmother in such a sullen mood and to know that he had caused it pained him. He was torn between his love for Vernisse and his love for his family. He had to make amends. He saw his chance early one morning when he found Douce sitting outside in the small courtyard at the back of the property. The sun was blinding for such an early hour and cast a warm glow against the stone wall of the house. Tzuri approached her and in his most cheerful voice said: 'You're up early, *Safta*. Enjoying the morning sun?'

Douce remained tight-lipped. Tzuri sat next to her on the bench. She shuffled slightly away from him. He realised he was not going to win her over by buttering her up. He had to tackle the problem head-on. Vernisse's case for conversion was to be heard at the *bet din* where they would need to be convinced that she was sincere, was converting for the right reasons and that she was converting of her own free will. Where she might fail was whether she had a thorough knowledge of the Jewish faith and practices and whether she would live an observant Jewish life. Tzuri had spent the last few weeks tutoring her in preparation for her visits to Rabbi Isaiah.

'I know you don't approve of my marriage to Vernisse.'

Douce huffed as if he had made an understatement.

'But once she has converted, she will be Jewish and all her – and my – children will be Jewish and brought up in the Jewish faith. Surely that is enough.'

Douce let out a deep sigh.

'I never wanted to hurt you, *Safta*. That was the last thing on my mind. But you must see how much I love Vernisse and how much she loves me.'

Tzuri heard faint sniffles and saw a tear trickling down the taut cheekbone of his great-grandmother. He put his arm round her shoulders and drew her to him.

'Please don't cry, *Safta*. Everything will turn out all right.'

Douce lay her head on his chest then pulled back and wiped the tears from her face. 'I've tried my best since Moses passed. I've tried to keep this family together. To keep it strong–'

'But it is strong, *Safta*.'

'You have no idea what I've gone through to keep this family going.'

Tzuri thought about his mother's words to Douce.

I won't be silent.

The family's secrets.

'What did *Ima* mean when she said she wouldn't be silent? Is there some reason why you are so against me marrying Vernisse?'

Douce placed her hand on his. 'I'm old-fashioned. Of a different generation. I've strived so hard to keep this family's reputation and standing in the community. To be better than that conniving Misabel.'

'Is that what's troubling you? Worrying about what

Mirabelle thinks of us? You shouldn't let that come between you and your family.'

'I know, I know, but I'm a stubborn old woman.'

Tzuri was beginning to understand why Douce was so set against the marriage. Her reputation.

'Vernisse will be an asset to this family. Quinton will be my father-in-law. Just think, you might even get a bigger discount than Mirabelle.'

Douce sniffed and smiled at the same time. Introducing a bit of levity was working. Was she finally coming round?

'After the *bet din* Vernisse must visit the *mikveh*. Mother and Arlette are going to be present. I'd really like it if you were there too. She will need someone of your stature and wisdom at the *tevillah* to guide her.'

Douce wiped her nose with the hem of her shift. 'I'm a foolish woman, Tzuri. I sometimes wish Moses was here to guide me.'

'What would Moses do?' Tzuri asked.

He had never known his grandfather but his reputation in the family and the wider community was legendary.

'He would tell me to stop this nonsense, bury my grievances and go to the *tevillah* for the sake of the family. So I will go, Tzuri.'

She stood up and walked back into the house. Tzuri sat a while longer wondering if there was something Douce wasn't telling him. That thought didn't hold his attention for long as he was meeting Vernisse later and they were going to see the rabbi together.

FOURTEEN

On the day of the *tevillah* – the full immersion in the pure waters of the *mikveh* – Vernisse was taken there by Brunetta, Ozanne, Arlette, and Douce. Arlette had supported the marriage from the beginning and was fond of Vernisse. Ever the peacemaker, she was relieved to hear that Douce had finally come around to the idea.

Once inside the *mikveh* the women helped to prepare Vernisse for the immersion. Vernisse had been horrified to find out that three male members of the *bet din* would be present to ensure the full immersion took place, but they would leave once she was immersed. Brunetta had assured her that her modesty would be protected at all times. After undressing, she was wrapped in a large clean cloth, and this was only removed when she reached the top of the stone steps. Vernisse shivered as she took each of the stone steps that led into the dark, icy water. She would have to immerse herself fully in this cold water and not just today but every month. She stopped to get used to the cold. Brunetta coaxed her to go further in. She stepped deeper into the *mikveh*. Rabbi Isaiah, Abraham of Warwick, and Bonanfaunt stood with their backs to the stone bath. Once

Vernisse was immersed to the neck they were asked to turn around. Rabbi Isaiah recited the blessing said before immersion:

'Blessed are you, Lord our God, King of the Universe, who has sanctified us with His commandments, and commanded us concerning the immersion.'

'You must put your head under the water fully then come to the surface,' directed Brunetta.

Vernisse nodded, her teeth chattering.

Something Brunetta said triggered in Arlette a flashback of the night she tried to take her own life in the *mikveh*, followed by another flashback, both coming unbidden, of the night of the rape. She saw Brito's cruel face bearing down on her as if he were there in the flesh. Her vision blurred and her body felt clammy. She reached out to take hold of Douce's arm for fear she was about to faint.

'Arlette, are you unwell?' said Douce.

Arlette shook her head. She didn't want to spoil Vernisse's experience of the *mikveh* and turn everyone's attention on her. She took a deep breath in and thought of the irony of her life. If it wasn't for the rape, Baruch would not have been born. He would not have had Tzuri for she was certain that Tzuri was his and not Abraham's. How things had come full circle. Baruch was half Jewish and now Tzuri had fallen in love with a Christian. There was one crucial difference. Vernisse would be fully Jewish in a few moments' time and her relationship with Tzuri was consensual.

Vernisse's head disappeared beneath the cold water. A few seconds later she emerged, breathless, gasping and with a smile upon her face. She was officially a *giyoret*, a convert. The *bet din*, having witnessed the proceedings, would issue Vernisse with a certificate of conversion, a *Shtar Giur*, certifying that she was a Jew.

The *tevillah* had symbolically cleansed her of her past misdeeds and her future and destiny would now be very different from that of a Christian had she remained one. It was now Vernisse's turn to recite a blessing for as a converted Jew she was entitled to do so.

Still breathless from the cold water Vernisse recited the well-rehearsed blessing:

'Blessed are you, Lord our God, King of the Universe, who has sanctified us with His commandments, and commanded us concerning the immersion.'

The women clapped in celebration and satisfied that the convert had completed the immersion, the officials left, leaving the women to help Vernisse out of the water and wrap her in dry cloths for modesty. They all hugged her and Douce cried.

Vernisse was now a member of the family and of the Jewish faith. Her children would be born Jewish and more importantly, Tzuri's children would be born Jewish. The mood in the *mikveh* had changed from solemn ritual to celebration at welcoming a new person into the fold.

Whilst the women fussed around Vernisse, drying her and helping her into dry clothes, Arlette saw that Douce had left the group and appeared to be upset. She went to speak to her.

'Are you all right, Douce?'

Douce wiped her tears with her hem and took hold of Arlette's hand. 'Abraham once told me that I had to be part of the modern world and that I should change, move with the times. I haven't exactly moved with the times, but strange times have been foisted upon me.'

'Vernisse is a lovely girl, and she loves Tzuri and she's been doing so well at embracing the faith.'

'You know I can't remember the last time I was truly happy. I used to be content when Moses was around. We had our troubles back then, but we faced them together.'

Arlette looked at the smooth skin of Douce's cheeks. She was about to turn seventy-five years of age but to Arlette she still looked in her fifties.

'I know it's not the same, but I will always be here for you, Douce. Please come to me anytime, whenever you need me.'

Douce stared into Arlette's lapis-blue eyes. 'You have been a blessing to this household since you arrived in such dreadful circumstances, and you've had your own troubles to deal with, yet you've carried on. Never complaining. I am so proud of you, and so proud to call you my daughter.'

The two women hugged each other and let the tears fall. Then it was time to leave and join Tzuri and the others.

Arlette helped Douce to her feet. 'Come on, Douce. Tzuri will be so excited to see Vernisse. We will have another wedding in time, and you will have more great-grandchildren. It's time to rejoice.'

Douce was led out into the sunshine. She squinted and managed a weak smile. She gripped Arlette's arm.

'I hope you are blessed, as I have been, with great-grandchildren. They are truly a blessing from *Hashem*.'

'We both will be, Douce. Tzuri loves Vernisse and she has sacrificed so much for him. I'm happy to welcome her into our family and can't wait for my first great-grandchild.'

CHAPTER
FIFTEEN

Bonanfaunt and Belia were out collecting money together. They had just visited Abbot Blunt to collect the weekly interest on a loan the abbey needed to extend its precinct wall. The city was bustling as it was market day, when hundreds of people made their way into the centre to either trade or buy goods.

When they reached The Cross, they stopped. Sheriff Musard was standing on the stone steps of the preaching cross holding a length of parchment and attracting quite a crowd. His voice carried across the hubbub.

'By order of the Earl of Pembroke, William Marshal, I proclaim that throughout my bailiwick, whether on foot or on horseback, and within the city of Gloucester or without, Jews shall wear the badge made of linen or parchment of the two tablets of stone on the breast of their outer garment, that in this way they may be distinguished from Christians.'

A raucous cheer went up. Bonanfaunt turned to Belia. Her face was white and her mouth slightly open.

'What is he saying?' Belia asked in a low voice.

'Sounds like he's implementing the Fourth Lateran Council of 1215.'

'Why do you always talk in riddles, Bonanfaunt?'

'If you kept up with what's going on in the world it wouldn't sound like a riddle. The Catholic Church are clamping down again on our rights and freedoms.'

'So what's new?' Belia said.

'What's new is the edict is finally being enforced.'

They stood amongst the mainly Christian population of the city who were becoming more hostile towards them. There were shouts of 'Jew bastards' and 'unclean Jews'. Someone recognised Bonanfaunt as Mirabelle's son.

'Oi, where's yer badge, Jew Boy?'

The man slammed both hands on Bonanfaunt's chest causing him to stagger backwards. Others joined in.

'Dirty Jewess,' said another and spat at Belia.

Belia let out a shriek. Bonanfaunt put his arm around her and glared at the man. The man backed off when he saw that Bonanfaunt was a lot taller than him.

Sheriff Musard continued, 'I further proclaim that today I have been instructed by the Earl of Pembroke, William Marshal, to instruct our bailiffs and the castellan to oversee the election of twenty-four burgesses to guarantee the safety of both persons and property of all Jews living in this city and to be reminded that the king has granted his firm peace to ensure Jews in this city suffer no injury or molestation as his father, our late King John, wished it to be so.'

'Looks like we'll need it,' Bonanfaunt said. 'We better get home and tell *Ima*.'

They pushed their way through the crowd, Bonanfaunt keeping a protective arm around Belia whilst holding on tightly to his money chest.

Mirabelle was sat at her desk counting gold and silver coins and making entries onto a length of parchment when Bonanfaunt stormed in and slammed his wooden money chest onto the table opposite. She stopped what she was doing and stared at her son in shock. Normally a mild-mannered man with a calm demeanour she could not believe the rage he was displaying.

Mirabelle put down her quill. 'What's happened?'

'The sheriff is fomenting hatred out there against us Jews.'

'I was spat at,' said Belia, becoming tearful.

Mirabelle clasped her hands together and said: '*Oy lanu*. Not again. I thought we'd seen the last of that type of behaviour.'

'Yes, again,' said Bonanfaunt.

'Years ago, when you were both little children, we had some trouble with the Christians, but we've had relative harmony since then.'

'What happened?' asked Bonanfaunt.

Mirabelle shook her head. As much as she loathed the le Riches, the horror of that night, when poor Arlette was attacked, and her own house was desecrated, had not been spoken about in years. It was better forgotten.

'What started it?' she asked.

'We were standing on The Cross listening to the sheriff making one of his proclamations–'

'He said we had to wear a badge on our outer garments to mark us out as Jews,' Belia interrupted.

'It's outrageous, *Ima*,' Bonanfaunt said. 'It's marking us out like cattle.'

'At the end of the day that's all we are to them,' Mirabelle said, standing up and walking over to the small table where she kept her Gascony wine. She poured a generous measure into a walnut wood cup. 'I'm not going to wear one,' she said defiantly.

'I don't want to wear one but what can we do? The sheriff says we must. How embarrassing,' said Belia.

'You should be proud to be Jewish,' Bonanfaunt said.

'I am but I don't need to wear a stupid badge to show I am. Perhaps the Christians should be made to wear a... oh, I don't know... a dead animal around their neck to show they are Christians.'

Belia was pacing around the room, her face red with fury. Bonanfaunt, on the other hand, had regained his composure.

'I thought our lives might improve with the new king after his promises in the abbey.'

'They weren't his promises were they. They came from the marshal and his cronies in the Council of Regency,' said Mirabelle with the bitterness of past experience.

'So the king doesn't make his own decisions in his own country?' Belia said, her complexion turning from puce to pink.

'He's still only eleven,' Bonanfaunt pointed out. 'What I don't understand is why now when this canon was passed in 1215?'

'Something is afoot, knowing these Christians as I do,' said Mirabelle, 'they'll be seeking more tallages to bleed us dry.'

'You may be right, *Ima*. If you remember the Fourth Lateran Council of 1215 not only spoke about a dress code for Jews but they sought to restrict Jewish usury. If they prevent us from lending money with interest the family business will be over. We will be destroyed, unable to work,' said Bonanfaunt, becoming agitated at that thought.

'It's only jealousy on the part of the Christians. If their religion hadn't forbidden them from lending money at interest, they would be doing it,' said Belia.

'And reaping the rewards,' Mirabelle added.

'If this is the start of a change towards us, we had better be more vigilant,' Bonanfaunt said.

'Is there nothing you can do, *Ima*?' asked Belia.

Mirabelle drained her cup. 'I'll speak to the sheriff.'

'I'll call for a *bet din*. We need to discuss the community's response to this.'

'I may have more success with the sheriff,' she said, rubbing her fingers together to demonstrate she intended to bribe him.

Belia sniffed and wiped her nose with the back of her hand: 'That usually works,' she said, grinning at her mother in a conspiratorial way. 'They're so greedy these so-called righteous Christians they'll take money for no effort.'

'More like corrupt,' said Mirabelle.

CHAPTER

SIXTEEN

Zev and Rubin had decided to work late in their workshop as they had a large order to fulfil for the abbey in Worcester. The workshop was towards the end of Longsmith Street where the city's blacksmiths had similar sites. The business was doing well, and they had more than enough work. Zev was hoping to join one of the goldsmiths' guilds that were beginning to pop up in London and other big cities across the country. They were called goldsmiths, yet they were open to silversmiths. He was getting on in years and he had to be realistic, and it would make it easier for Rubin to later be admitted. In the meantime, Zev had devised a hallmark on the underside of the salvers he made. A simple Z for his name followed by a G to denote it had been made in Gloucester.

Zev had built a bloomery from stone in the courtyard at the back of the workshop. This is where he turned the raw material of iron ore, through a process of cupellation, into silver. The dome-shaped furnace was a source of warmth in the colder winter evenings when they worked late. Zev had just finished fashioning a silver chalice for the abbey when he felt the need for a rest. He left the workshop and sat on a wooden stool, feeling the warmth coming from the bloomery. A heavy set of bellows lay nearby and in the corner was a store of seasoned wood for the fire. A hefty mallet he used to pound off the slag after the smelting process stood upright not feet away. He could hear Rubin in the workshop humming a tune. He often would hum one of Ozanne's songs. Zev took in a deep breath and leant against the wooden wall of the workshop and relaxed. He thought of Arlette and wondered what she would be doing. Waiting for his return, for even though it had been years since his attack when he was almost beaten to death, she still spent her evenings fretting until he came home safe.

He still could not believe his luck in having such a wonderful and beautiful wife. The years and struggles she had endured had taken their toll on her mental health, but Zev loved her with great tenderness as one would love a wounded bird. His strong desire to protect her from the evils of the world were still present. It formed a bond between them that would never be broken. He prayed that she would die before him because it was his true belief she would not survive long in this cruel world without him.

Rubin was working on a large silver cross the abbey used in their lavish religious ceremonies, engraving the letters IHS, the Catholic Church's holy name for Jesus based on the Greek spelling ΙΗΣΟΥΣ. Zev did not agree with the Roman Catholic religion, he viewed it as harsh and cruel in its teachings, but the artistic licence that was emerging was, for him as a creator, very appealing. It was keeping him in work. The sound of gentle tapping and scraping as Rubin skilfully used his burin, a sharp metal tool with a v-shaped end, was soporific. Zev closed his eyes and before he knew it, he had nodded off. But not for long.

His head jolted heavily, and his chin lifted from his chest, waking him from his slumber.

It hadn't taken long following the sheriff's proclamation for a murderous mob to begin roaming the city centre. The market taverns had been open since morning and news that the Jews had to wear the badge had travelled amongst the revellers. There were cries in the street of the retribution that would be upon any Jew who disobeyed the order. By that evening, most Jews were locked inside the safety of their own homes apart from Rubin and Zev.

Zev raised his weary old bones from the stool. The beating he had received from Brito had left him with arthritic pain and constant headaches, but he never complained. A sharp pain like an arrowhead pierced his brow in between his eyes. He rubbed at it.

Then he heard a terrific bang.

'*Aba*,' cried Rubin.

Zev, acting on instinct, ran back into the workshop. The secure doors that formed the entrance had been battered down with one blow by a mob of men who had stormed into the building. Rubin held the burin in his hand, staring open-mouthed at the mob. He had always been a boy of tender persuasions. Feminine in his ways. The way he walked, his quiet voice, his sensibilities and his closeness to his mother. He had never married, and Zev had always thought he knew the reason but had never broached it with either Rubin or Arlette.

He was shaking and backing away from the men. Zev ran back into the courtyard to retrieve the mallet, shouting at Rubin to pick up a hammer and follow him.

He was not as nimble as he used to be or as strong. The beating had seen to that. He grabbed the mallet and swung round only to face an advancing mob who rushed at him, forcing the mallet from his hand and wrestling him to the floor. Once on the floor they set about attacking him with wooden staves and metal shovels. His only concern was Rubin.

'Run, Rubin, run. Get help.'

He had no idea if Rubin had managed to escape for a hefty kick in the head rendered him unconscious.

Arlette's smiling face was the last image he saw.

Baruch had been out hunting all day with John of Monmouth. The marshal was in his seventies and spent much of his time at his family estate in Caversham in the south of the country. In his absence Baruch had taken to hunting with his fellow knight and they had become friends through their common interests. When Baruch arrived home, he found Arlette sitting on the floor, her arms wrapped around her knees shivering in the corner of the room. He ran over to her and knelt by her side.

'Are you all right, *Ima*?' Baruch said. 'The colour has drained from your face.'

Arlette stared back at him as if she didn't recognise him and said nothing.

Baruch shook her. 'What's happened?'

'It's Zev,' said Douce. 'He's dead.'

Baruch stood up and wiped his brow with his forearm. 'How?'

Believing it to be an accident or just old age, Baruch was horrified to learn he had been killed by a mob. 'When did this happen?'

'Not long before you arrived,' Douce replied.

'Where? Did they come to the house?'

'At the workshop.'

'Where's Rubin?' he said, scanning the room for his brother.

Wherever Zev was Rubin trailed behind.

'He's in the kitchen getting his burns bandaged by Brunetta and Ozanne.'

'Does anyone know why?'

'The sheriff made a proclamation on The Cross demanding all Jews wear a badge to mark them out as Jews. It seems some people took the law into their own hands when they realised not every Jew was wearing the badge and went on the rampage.'

'Why Zev?'

'He has many valuable items in his workshop. The mob knew there would be spoils to be had. They just use any excuse to go thieving,' Douce said.

'This is much more than thieving. It's murderous,' Baruch said, his face red with anger.

Arlette wiped a silent tear from her cheek.

'Where is Zev now?'

'We left his body at the workshop. It's very badly burned. The mob set light to the place. Stole the silver and left Zev and Rubin for dead.'

'How did Rubin get out?'

'Zev was already dead when the mob left. Rubin was knocked out. He woke to find the fire raging around him but managed to escape. He has serious burns on his hands and face.'

Baruch had spent a pleasant day hunting in the royal Forest of Dean and had arrived home to tragedy. He buried his head in his hands. The news of Zev's death was such a shock he could hardly comprehend it. Zev was one of the kindest men on this earth. To die because he was a Jew. That's when the rage set in. He turned to Arlette who had not said a word.

'I'll find who did this and I'll get revenge for this family.'

'There's no point,' said Arlette. 'They will only kill you.'

Baruch knew his mother's words rang true. In his heart he knew this was going to be another case where a Jew was murdered, and no one would be brought to justice for it. It was a fact living in a Christian country.

Jews' lives didn't matter enough.

SEVENTEEN

Arlette sat down beside the empty seat where Zev should have been sitting. Rubin, his hands and arms covered in clean bandages, sat next to her, his face smudged with soot. Douce sat stone-faced showing little emotion.

The only man to have loved her was gone.

Why had *Hashem* seen fit to take from her so much she treasured in this life?

Her parents.

Her innocence.

Her happiness.

Little Elias.

Moses.

Abraham.

Now Zev.

It was decided to leave Zev's body where it was until first light when they would bury him. Baruch, Rubin and Tzuri had gone, acting as *shomerim*. Arlette had been asked if she wanted to attend but she could not bear to see Zev's burned body.

Brunetta came into the kitchen with a pot of steaming broth. She set it down on the table, ladled some out and put it in front of Arlette. Arlette just stared at it then pushed the bowl away.

'You must eat something, Arlette. Keep your strength up.'

'For what?' said Arlette, staring ahead of her, her eyes dead-looking, like the fish at market.

'For Rubin, Baruch and Tzuri. They need you now more than ever.'

You could always rely on Brunetta to come out with such platitudes, thought Arlette. She meant well but this was the last thing Arlette wanted to hear. That she had to be strong for others. She had never been strong. She had endured.

Endured the vagaries of life.

Endured being raped.

Endured being rejected by a man who saw her as sullied.

Endured an existence of shame. Of pity.

'Poor Arlette.'

'Shame about Arlette.'

She'd had enough.

For almost seventy years she had endured.

Enough was enough.

She didn't have the strength to survive without Zev. He kept her sane. Kept her safe.

Without him she was nothing.

Nothing.

The black shroud, as she called it, settled upon her soul, choking the light out of her. Her heart was beating fast and the darkest of moods had descended. Memories and shadows of feelings, pain, revulsion, resurfacing after all these years. Events that had haunted her all her life. The memories returned with such force she felt like she might be sick. The sour taste of bile filled her mouth.

The suddenness of its coming shocked her. She had kept it

at bay. Locked it away in a dark dank cave where no light could be shed.

It hadn't crept out but jumped out like a lion on its prey.

I am its prey, she said in her head.

Then she looked about her.

Were they looking at her?

Could they hear her thoughts?

She stood up, unsteady on her feet.

'Where are you going?' Brunetta asked, standing up.

'Nowhere,' Arlette said.

She stumbled as she walked. Brunetta rushed to her side to steady her.

'Why don't you lie down until the morning. Baruch will arrange everything. You must rest.'

'Yes, I must rest,' Arlette heard herself say.

Her voice seemed far away.

She felt bone weary and could hardly make it up the stairs, her heart thudding.

Brunetta helped her with her clothes and put her to bed.

Arlette sunk into the mattress and closed her eyes.

EIGHTEEN

When morning came Baruch woke early to an eerily quiet house. Brunetta lay asleep next to him, her warm body comforting him in his grief. He had left Tzuri and Rubin at the workshop. They were both fit and had age on their side and could endure a long night of vigil.

Usually Douce was downstairs making breakfast, accompanied by the sound of clanking pots and pans and the roar of the cooking fire. This morning felt different. A sense of foreboding overcame him. He thought of his mother. Arlette. Brunetta had mentioned in her sleepy state last night that Arlette had been acting strangely and that she had put her to bed early. He leapt out of bed, his limbs stiff from the hunt the day before, and rushed to her bedroom. When he opened her door, he could see her still shape underneath the coverlet. He instantly knew she was dead.

He approached the bedside on tiptoe so as not to awaken Brunetta who was asleep below. He touched Arlette's cheek. It was as cold as alabaster. He sunk down on the bed beside her, put his head in his hands and wept.

His mother was dead. Zev was dead. All in a short space of

time, yet the grief he felt for Zev was nothing compared to the sorrow that overwhelmed him at the sight of his mother's lifeless body.

She'd had a hard life. It had been a struggle. He hadn't helped in the early days, but he hoped she had forgiven him. Since his return to Gloucester he had tried to make up for his past mistakes. He pulled back the coverlet. She lay with her arms across her chest just as she had been put to bed. He took her cold hand.

'Forgive me, *Ima*. I never meant to hurt you. I didn't understand how much you'd sacrificed for me.'

A fierce wind rattled the shutter outside. It made him jump. Was it a sign from his mother that she understood? That she forgave him? The tears came unbidden.

His mother had died peacefully in her sleep. Her struggles finally over. She had slipped away, her heart broken over the death of her beloved Zev. The man who had saved her and without whom she would never have survived this cruel world.

She had finally let go of the fragile thread that held her to life. She was at peace now.

Baruch stayed with her until Brunetta came in search of him and found him acting as *shomerim*. Brunetta fell to her knees when she saw him. Baruch fell into her embrace and sobbed loudly. Brunetta stroked his hair and held him tight.

Later that morning the family laid Arlette and Zev to rest, side by side, in the family plot in the cemetery their grandfather Moses had built, and where those who had gone before now lay.

A testament to the endurance of the le Riche family.

NINETEEN

When news of the deaths of Zev and Arlette reached Mirabelle, she was not unduly upset. The le Riche family had been a source of vexation to her for years. 'But *Safta*, their deaths are a tragedy to this community. What if it had been one of us?' Pucelle questioned her.

Pucelle had never got on with Mirabelle. She had always been the favourite of her grandfather but when he died in Bristol Castle, she was shocked at the callous way her grandmother had taken the news. Not a tear shed, and yet she had cried buckets.

Mirabelle flicked away the question with a gesture of her hand.

'That family is cursed. It always has been. That woman, Douce, wears her sacred amulet around her neck all the time and what good has it done for her. Nothing. She's a superstitious old nobody.'

'That's such a harsh thing to say, *Safta*. The enemy is not the le Riche family but the Christians who set upon us and want to take our money from us. There's enough ill will and nastiness in this world without you adding to it,' Pucelle said.

'Without the Christians we would have no money. The relationship is beneficial to both parties, and you would do well to remember that,' Mirabelle said, raising her voice.

Belia and her husband, Isaac, came into the hall just then with their son-in-law, Garsia.

'Why are you screaming at each other?' Belia asked.

'Pucelle thinks she knows it all as usual. She thinks I should be sad because of the deaths of those two hapless le Riches.'

'It would show some humility,' said Garsia.

He was usually quiet around family arguments but when it involved his wife, he always took her side.

'There's no point in reasoning with her, Pucelle,' Belia said. 'She absolutely can't see reason when it comes to that family. They've been feuding since they arrived in Gloucester, and I don't think *Ima* is going to change at her age.'

Pucelle huffed and folded her arms. 'I think it's terrible that one of us has been murdered and poor Arlette has died of a broken heart.'

'Her heart was broken years ago,' Mirabelle said.

'What do you mean?' Pucelle asked her, unfolding her arms.

'She only married Zev to protect her honour. Zev the butcher boy would never have been Douce's choice. She had her sights set high did that one and look how it turned out.'

Pucelle stepped towards her grandmother. 'What happened to her?'

'*Ima!*' shouted Belia. 'Stop now. You should know better.'

Mirabelle's lips pinched together. She knew she had gone too far when her daughter shouted at her. The attack on Arlette and the calling off of her betrothal to Deudonne, who was Isaac's brother, was something the family had an unspoken agreement not to discuss. Isaac had so far not joined the argument. He had helped himself to a cup of wine.

'I don't mind that you talk about Deudonne. He's happily married now to someone else. It's in the past,' said Isaac.

'Happier than he would have been if he'd married into that cursed family,' said Mirabelle.

'They're not cursed.'

'I don't know what else you'd call it,' said Mirabelle.

'Unlucky,' said Isaac, draining his cup of wine and seemingly unmoved by the conversation.

'Oh, *Aba*, does nothing rile you?' said Pucelle, walking over to her father and giving him a hug.

Isaac smiled. 'I've learned not to take anything too seriously in this life. I leave that to your grandmother. She worries enough for all of us.'

Pucelle and Belia laughed.

Garsia gestured with his hand for calm and said, 'Just let it go.'

'Yes, let's not argue amongst ourselves,' said Belia, turning to address her mother.

'Have you spoken to the sheriff about the badge? That's the cause of this latest violence against us.'

Mirabelle raised her stiff bones from the chair. 'I plan to speak to him today.'

'The sooner the better,' Belia said. 'Given the current mood in the city.'

'Do you want me to come with you?' offered Isaac.

'I may be old and creaky, but my mind is still sharp. I can still do business without anyone's help.'

The hall went silent, a heavy atmosphere settling amongst its occupants. Mirabelle walked from the hall, her role as matriarch intact.

~

She found the sheriff outside The Booth Hall talking to Richard the Burgess and his son, Henry. Simon de Coco, Gilbert de Rue and Nicholas de Santa Brigida were with them. Mirabelle shuddered at the sight of them. The men who had been favoured by King John and had benefited from her husband's death. They were talking about the election of the burgesses to sit on the new body to oversee the protection of the city's Jews.

'*Hashem* help us,' she muttered as she approached them.

When she reached them, Gilbert de Rue turned his back on her. He was aggrieved because as a result of her petition to the marshal she had been successful in having the house in West Gate Street returned to her. She hadn't been so successful with Simon de Coco who was still living in one of her houses. She did not give him the satisfaction of acknowledging his presence. She pointedly ignored the others and gave her full focus to the sheriff.

'Sheriff Musard, good day to you. I was hoping to have a word with you in private as a matter of urgency,' she said.

'What about?' he asked her, stepping to one side.

'Can we go somewhere?' she said, glancing at the burgesses who were eavesdropping.

The sheriff bid them farewell and walked away. It was obvious to Mirabelle that he had guessed what it was she was so eager to talk to him about. They had an understanding. A relationship based on mutual benefit. Mirabelle asked for favours, and he granted them in return for a fee. She preferred to call it that rather than what it really was which was a *douceur* or bribe.

'Why are you enforcing the wearing of the badge on us?' she asked, using her polite business voice so as not to put him on the defensive.

'I have no option. It's an order from the Regency Council.'

'I see,' she said. 'This has put you in a difficult situation.'

Sheriff Musard said: 'I'm so glad you understand, Mistress Mirabelle. My hands are tied.'

'What I don't understand is why the Council is enforcing this edict three years after its passing.'

'I cannot say as I'm not privy to the discussions of the Council.'

'I must say it's quite concerning. The community isn't happy about it.'

'I dare say they're not,' he replied. 'I take it you've heard about Zev?'

'I have but I'm not here about that.'

'I thought you might not be.'

'You know my views about that family.'

'I do indeed,' the sheriff said.

'There must be a way of not enforcing this order?'

'There is actually,' he said.

Mirabelle was taken aback. Perhaps a bribe would not be necessary.

'There is talk of introducing a licence.'

'How would that work?'

'You pay a fee for a licence that exempts you from having to wear the tablet.'

'Who is the licence paid to?' Mirabelle asked.

'To the Regency Council of course.'

Mirabelle smirked. The council was enforcing the badge as a covert way of introducing another tax on the Jewish community.

'How much would this licence cost?' she said, eyeing him with suspicion.

'In the case of Gloucester, it could be as little as twenty shillings for the year.'

Mirabelle did a quick mathematical calculation in her head. She was expecting the sheriff to say an extortionate amount and it turned out to be reasonable. She calculated her entire family would be paying mere pennies for the licence.

'That is very gratifying to hear, sheriff. Good day to you.'

The wearing of the linen tablet was over before it had begun. They would simply pay for the licence. Bonanfaunt shouldn't be so dramatic and think always of the worst outcomes, she thought, as she made her way back down West Gate Street, stopping off to buy some figs from the market.

CHAPTER

TWENTY

For more than a year life for the le Riche family was uneventful until Baruch received some sad news. His friend and mentor these long years, William Marshal, was dead. It was not a huge surprise as he was aware the marshal had resigned his role as regent to the king even though King Henry was still a boy. Baruch knew he would never have done that if he were still capable of continuing. Since then he had spent time at his home, Caversham Hall, near Reading, with his wife, Isabel, and their children.

'This is surely the end of an epoch,' he told Brunetta.

Brunetta, disinterested in politics, shrugged her shoulders.

'He has done well to live this long. He must be in his seventieth year if not more. Not many knights of his rank live that long and not many can say they have served four kings during their lifetime,' said Baruch.

Brunetta continued to embroider a fine piece of silk and did not look up.

'I'd like to pay my respects,' he said.

Hearing that made Brunetta look up. 'You want to travel all the way to London?'

Baruch smiled to himself. Brunetta probably still hadn't forgiven him for going off without a word. Whenever he suggested travelling somewhere she always worried.

'You've no need to worry. My wandering days are over. I'd like to pay my respects to a great man and a friend. That's all.'

As he finished his sentence Ozanne came bounding in. Baruch noted how she could never walk anywhere.

'What's "all"?' she said, catching the end of the conversation.

'Your father wants to travel to London.'

'Ooh, can I come with you, *Aba*? I'd love to go to London. I hear it's a very exciting place to visit.'

'Of course,' Baruch replied without hesitation, and turning to Brunetta he said: 'There, will that stop you worrying?'

Baruch walked over to Brunetta and kissed her forehead. She reached out her hand to him and squeezed it. Baruch took it as a sign that he had her permission.

'That's settled then. You better get packing, Ozanne. We're off to the big city.'

Ozanne screeched with excitement causing her mother to jump, pricking her finger as she did. In her irritation Brunetta said: 'When are you going to start behaving like a respectable young woman and more importantly, when are you going to get married?'

Ozanne's screeching stopped, followed by a long-suffering groan. 'I've told you so many times, *Ima*. I'm not interested in marrying.'

'No woman says that. Every young woman looks forward to getting married.'

'Well, I'm not every young woman, am I?'

'You can say that again,' Baruch said under his breath.

'Baruch, can't you talk any sense into her?'

'You know how wilful your daughter is. She's a mind of her own.'

Baruch reached out to Ozanne. She ran to him and gave him a hug. Baruch hugged her and stroked her long thick hair that fell halfway down her back.

'Thick as thieves,' said Brunetta, returning to her embroidery.

Baruch learned that the marshal had died at his family estate in Caversham, that his body lay in Reading Abbey and that he was to be taken to Westminster Abbey for a funeral service and then buried in Temple Church in London. Baruch and Ozanne had time to pack and say their farewells before embarking on what would be a long and arduous journey. He was used to such journeys, but he wasn't sure how Ozanne would cope. She had never been further than Hereford.

'Hurry up, Ozanne. The horse and cart are here,' Baruch shouted up to his daughter.

Ozanne came bustling down the stairs holding a large bundle of clothes in one hand and her old kinnor in the other.

'What do you want with that? Can't you leave it here?'

Ozanne put on her shocked face. '*Aba*, you know I can't live without my music. It has to come.'

Baruch rolled his eyes and shrugged. 'Come on,' he said, taking the heavy bundle from her. 'What have you got in there?'

'Just some writing materials.'

'You're going to write music on the way there?'

'If the inspiration comes which I am sure it will, then yes,' she said, flouncing past him and climbing into the front seat of the cart.

Baruch had indulged her in her passion all her life. He could not deny her now. He smiled at her as she sat clutching her kinnor on her lap. She was dressed in a plain shift with a thick woollen shawl over her shoulders. The weather was improving but the nights were still chilly. Ozanne was a puzzle to him. One moment her head in the clouds, the next a woman of practicalities.

TWENTY-ONE

When they finally reached London, they headed towards the River Thames to find lodgings.

Ozanne had been full of wonder almost the entire journey. Now she disembarked the cart with a weary slump.

'I never realised it would take us so long to get here,' she said to Baruch. 'I feel like I've travelled to the ends of the earth.'

Baruch laughed as he led the horse to the farriers to be looked after overnight.

'More like the centre of the world. This is London where everything happens. Wars are started, corruption is rife. Skulduggery lurks in every corner.'

'I must say, it's quite a smelly place. I thought it would be cleaner.' Ozanne stepped over a fresh dollop of horse excrement. 'I'm not sure this will inspire my music.'

Baruch laughed again. She had a lot to learn.

They found a humble tavern with rooms for the night a few streets back from the river. By the time they had settled in their room it was early evening and Ozanne's stomach was rumbling.

'Can we go downstairs to eat? I'm famished.'

Baruch nodded. Then as she was about to leave, he grabbed her arm.

'Just be careful down there. We are in London now. There'll be lots of strangers and strange people. Stay close to me,' Baruch said, instinctively patting his hand on the sword he always wore.

Ozanne bounded down the staircase and into the tavern bar room. She was met with a sea of faces. All heads turned to look at her.

'See what I mean,' Baruch whispered.

Ozanne took her father's hand and pulled him close.

They sat at a table by the window. She looked out into the street while waiting for the food and drink to arrive. Despite being a side street, it was bustling with a string of people. Traders, fish sellers, women selling oysters. Oysters were one of her favourite foods. She dug Baruch in the side.

'Do they have oysters, *Aba*? I'd love some, would you?'

The waiting wench arrived at their table with a leather tankard of beer and a jug of red wine.

Baruch said: 'A dozen oysters, please.'

The wench smiled at Baruch in a flirtatious way. Ozanne had not seen her stepfather as a man who women would be attracted to. He was just her stepfather, but she looked at him now and could see, despite the scarring on his face and the deep furrows in his forehead, that he had a certain something. Baruch picked up the tankard and drank most of its contents in one.

'You must be thirsty from the journey, *Aba*.'

'Do you want to try some?'

Ozanne took the tankard and held it between both hands. She took a sip and then another.

'I think I may also be thirsty.'

Baruch laughed and took the tankard from her.

The wench brought them twelve oysters, winked at Baruch then returned to serve them their main meal of soused herring and bread. Baruch poured them both a cup of wine.

'How did you meet Mother?' Ozanne asked.

A knowing smile crept upon the scarred face of Baruch, as if he knew a secret but he wasn't about to tell his daughter. She was intrigued and emboldened by the wine she was now drinking so asked him another question. 'Did you know her before my father did?'

His smile widened. She could tell there was more to know.

'You could say that.'

'Tell me,' she pleaded.

His smile disappeared. 'There's nothing to tell. I married your mother after your father died.'

'You must have known her when they were married?'

'I was away at war for long periods of time. I didn't know anyone in Gloucester that well.'

Ozanne shrugged. It was obvious whatever had taken place in the past her stepfather was not going to enlighten her, so she let it go.

The tavern was noisy with drunken chatter. They sat for a while in silence drinking their wine. Then Ozanne heard a stringed instrument being plucked. She turned around on the bench to see a jongleur tuning his citole, a wedge-shaped instrument. From her knowledge of music and musical instruments she knew it had probably been carved from a single block of boxwood and had six strings. The jongleur held it by the thumbhole near the neck of the instrument and he tucked the trefoiled end into the crook of his left elbow. In his hand he held a plectrum which he used to expertly pluck the strings. It was a very different instrument to the kinnor in look and tone. In contrast the kinnor was a flat lyre-shaped stringed instrument.

Ozanne had a woozy head from the strong wine her father had allowed her to drink. She sat mesmerised at the strange groups of people who had gathered to enjoy the evening's entertainment. Then a voice floated over the chatter as loud and clear as if the person were sat next to her. She looked up to see a young troubadour sitting on a three-legged stool alongside the jongleur. His voice was deep, sonorous and he was singing in a language she at first could not understand. It sounded like French, but it wasn't. She turned to her father and asked him: 'What language is that, *Aba*?'

'It's Occitan, the language of the troubadour.'

Ozanne swung back and gazed at the man. She studied his features. His eyes were a shade of verdigris, his nose broad at the bridge, his lips full and sensuous. His hair was his most striking feature. Black as a starless night, hanging in thick, glossy ringlets past his shoulders. Ozanne listened intently and was able to make out one or two words. He was a troubadour, a singer, a poet. Like her. They performed a few pieces then the jongleur put down his citole and picked up three bone-handled knives, ceremonial and carved. He threw them up in the air and miraculously managed to juggle them successfully without dropping them or cutting his hands. Ozanne was so enthralled by the jongleur's antics she did not see the handsome troubadour approach her.

He sat beside her on the bench. Ozanne was startled by his forwardness. She wasn't used to this kind of behaviour. Yet at the same time she liked it. She felt special, as though he had singled her out above all others. She looked behind her to see what her father's reaction was, but he had started an animated conversation with a man on the next table and hadn't noticed.

'*Bonsoir*,' the troubadour said.

'*Bonsoir*,' Ozanne replied.

He must have detected that French was not her mother

tongue. He answered her in English. 'Do you mind if I sit here for a while?'

'Not at all.'

'What's your name?'

Again Ozanne was startled by his forwardness, yet she answered him. 'Ozanne.'

'A beautiful name for a beautiful young woman.'

Ozanne blushed and took a sip of her wine.

'And where are you from?'

'Gloucester. It's a small city in the west of the country.'

'Is it as pretty as you?'

Ozanne blushed again. 'Where are you from?' she asked, emboldened by the wine.

'I come from Occitania, a region in France united by a common culture and language.'

'Yes, your accent is strange. I speak a little French – my great-grandfather came from France. Well, he's my great-uncle really.'

'It's Occitan. Your English king spoke Occitan...'

'Which one – not Henry?'

'No. Richard. The one they called the *Cœur de Lion*.'

'Oh,' Ozanne said.

She should have known. Her father knew him well, fought beside him. She didn't know why but she suddenly felt perturbed by her lack of knowledge. Why didn't she know the names of the kings of England or what languages they spoke. It reminded her that she was an insignificant, parochial girl, imprisoned in her small city of Gloucester. In contrast he was so knowledgeable, urbane and so, so handsome. Ozanne had never seen or met anyone quite like him. He caught her looking at him and in her embarrassment she turned away from him but not before she saw his eyes light up in a smile. A hot flush rose all the way from her décolletage to her cheeks. She glanced at Baruch. He was talking to a man, his hands moving expressively. She wondered if he was recounting tales of his battles with the king.

'*Je suis le Chevalier au Lion. Mon nom est Yvain.*'

'Your name is Yvain and you're named after the king?'

Yvain tossed his head back and laughed. Ozanne was overwhelmed by the rapidity of his words and his accent was hard to understand.

'Not after the king, after the knight of the lion, a character in Chrétien de Troyes's story. My father named me after him. We are a family of troubadours. *Mon père*, bless his soul, was also a troubadour.'

He was now speaking a mixture of French, Occitan and broken English. His voice was seductive. She could listen to him all evening even if she never understood a word of what he said. In her effort to impress this captivating young man she brought the subject back to the king.

'My father knew King Richard,' she said, hoping this would make him see her differently, more interesting.

'Did he?'

'He fought beside him and was there when he was kidnapped.'

Yvain looked across the table at Baruch.

'He looks like a man who can handle himself.'

'I'm sure he could in his day, but he's given all that up now since he married my mother.'

'A romantic at heart.'

Ozanne laughed. She had never thought of her stepfather as romantic. 'He probably was,' she said, smiling.

Yvain stood up. 'I have to sing some more songs to earn my living. I hope I see you later.'

He bowed before her then walked over to his companion. Ozanne watched as he picked up a gittern, a teardrop-shaped gut-stringed instrument with a rounded back. Plucking the strings with a quill plectrum, he began to sing. Ozanne was lost in him when abruptly she heard her father call her name, his voice raised as if he had been trying to get her attention.

'We ought to be going,' Baruch said. 'It's late.'

Ozanne drank the last few mouthfuls of her wine and stood up to leave. The sound of the gittern reached her. Yvain's voice soared above the clamour. Foolishly, she fancied he was singing to her and her alone. She tried to catch his eye so she could wave goodbye, but his eyes were closed, lost in the haunting melody. Baruch took her arm and led her out.

Ozanne had never felt so miserable in all her life.

TWENTY-TWO

Ozanne and her father rose early. She dressed in a sumptuous outfit that Quinton had made for her of samite trimmed with off-white miniver whilst Baruch was dressed as a skirmisher with his trusty sword at his side. They drank some weak ale and ate bread in the tavern before making their way to Westminster Abbey. Only a few early risers joined them. Ozanne was hoping to see Yvain one last time, but he was not there.

'You looking for someone?' her father asked.

He was being sarcastic. He knew only too well who she was looking for.

'No one in particular,' Ozanne replied, hoping to sound as nonchalant as possible.

'I may be wrong, but you seemed quite taken with that young troubadour last night. He certainly was interested in you.'

'*Aba!*' she protested.

'You know you can't hide anything from me, Ozanne. I know you too well. We're cut from the same cloth you and I.'

'What do you mean?'

She thought she knew what her father was alluding to, but she wanted to hear it from him.

'We're different. I was always the black sheep of the family. The odd one out. I never fitted in. There were reasons for that, I found out later.'

Ozanne thought her stepfather must still be under the influence of drink from the night before. She had never known him to talk so candidly. She wanted to argue with him, say he was wrong because she did fit in, but she knew he was right. She'd always been the outsider. The dreamer. The only female in the family who didn't see their sole aim in life to be a wife. Her father did know her. She reached out and placed her hand on his and gave it a squeeze. He looked haggard. Older.

'I do feel like that sometimes, *Aba*. I know there are things you don't want to tell me. I know there are secrets in the family.'

Baruch nodded whilst looking into the distance. He sighed then stood up. 'We ought to make a move. This will be a long day.'

They walked to Westminster Hall and as they got nearer, the streets became busier until they joined a throng of people walking along the narrow paths. Ozanne found the atmosphere exciting. There was a sense that something was about to happen. She had to almost run beside her father to keep up with his long strides.

'Is London always like this?' she asked.

'Only when a royal dies or is crowned.'

Baruch took hold of her hand and led her through the crowds. He was a commanding figure and people parted way. Eventually they reached the entrance to the hall. The funeral cortège had just arrived.

Isabel de Clare, his young wife who was still only in her forties, wore a white robe with a translucent veil over her head and face. Her flaming hair, inherited from her mother, the Irish princess Aoife, flowed in curls down her back. She was surrounded by mourners.

'Who are all those people?' Ozanne asked her father.

'That's Isabel, his wife, and those are his ten children.'

'Ten?'

'They were very much in love,' said Baruch, smiling.

Baruch knew all the children, especially the older ones. Ozanne wanted to know all about them.

'That's the eldest child,' said Baruch, pointing to a man in his late twenties, dressed in knightly garb. 'William, after his father.'

'Who's his wife?'

'Sadly he's a widower. His wife died in childbirth with their first child. He has never remarried.'

Ozanne winced. Baruch scanned the members of the family.

'Richard, the second son, doesn't appear to be here. Not sure why. After Richard they had a daughter, Maud. She seems to be the only one lucky enough to have had lots of children. That's her there with her husband, Hugh Bigod, and their four children.'

Ozanne saw a brood of children standing by Maud. The eldest, who looked about ten, had a baby in his arms.

'It must be a family curse,' said Ozanne, 'affecting only the males in the family.'

Baruch didn't respond.

'Who's the monk?' she continued, seeming surprised that the son of one of the greatest knights should have a son in the clergy.

'That's Gilbert. He took minor orders. Then they had Walter. He isn't married either. Then they had another daughter. There she is. Isabel, named after her mother. Looks like she's had a baby.'

Ozanne looked at the woman holding an infant. It looked to be the same age as Maud's baby.

'Is that her husband?' she asked, a slight disdain creeping into her voice.

'That's Gilbert de Clare, twenty years her senior.'

It must be a family tradition, thought Ozanne, *marrying older men*.

'The marshal, the old goat,' he said, affectionately, 'arrested him a couple of years ago.'

'What for?'

'Oh some squabble.'

She could tell her father knew more but wasn't about to tell her.

'Oh and there's Sibyl. She's had a baby too. I hadn't realised she'd got married. I'm out of touch,' Baruch said, a hint of regret in his voice.

'Who are the others?'

'Now that's Eva. She's named after her Irish grandmother, Aoife. And the two youngest are Anselm and Joan.'

'My goodness, his wife looks remarkable given she's had all those children. Can I meet them?'

'You will but maybe later. They're starting to file into the abbey.'

Baruch and Ozanne followed the mourners, keeping towards the back. William de Humez, Abbot of Westminster, assisted by William de Sainte-Mère-Église, the bishop of London, were to officiate. Fellow monks walked in front of the coffin, swinging thuribles and filling the air with swirls of pungent incense as they made their way to the altar.

Baruch and Ozanne took seats towards the back of the abbey.

Ozanne had little recollection of the lengthy service; her mind clogged with thoughts of Yvain. His voice played over and over in her head in that seductive accent. Occasionally she heard the Christian words of 'purgatory' and 'hell' and 'redemption', but they flew in like a light cloud and out again, not settling on her consciousness.

She was still thinking about him when they reached the Templar Church where the great marshal was to be buried.

'You seem far away, Ozanne. Is something troubling you?'

'Oh no, *Aba*. Nothing could be further from the truth. I'm having a great time. I'm...'

She stopped herself, realising that wasn't the sort of thing she should say at a funeral. Yet it was true. She had seen so many interesting things. And met the most romantic man she ever hoped to dream of meeting.

The marshal's cortège was led to Temple Church by retired Templar Knights, seen as rebels by many. Ozanne found them a frightening force to behold. The two Williams, the abbot, and the bishop walked at the front. The walk along the Thames took longer than usual as the cart carrying the bier trundled along, the horses labouring under the weight of the stone coffin.

Finally they arrived at the church. The marshal had arranged to be buried in front of the rood screen, in the round nave. His stone coffin was draped in fine silks that fluttered in the gentle breeze as the bier was carried into the abbey. Baruch later learned they had been brought back by Geoffrey, the marshal's almoner from the Holy Land, thirty years before.

Entering through a square porch the church opened into a round nave. Ozanne was immediately struck by how different it was to most other churches. Other Christian churches were cruciform. This was circular.

'This is such a strange shape for a Christian church,' she whispered to her father. 'Is it not Christian?'

Baruch smiled at her and stroked her hair. 'This is a very special church, Ozanne. Christian through and through.'

'Why is it called a temple?'

'It's based on the Holy Sepulchre in Jerusalem. The Knights Templar built it.'

'Who are the Knights Templar?'

'A band of brothers who organise the Holy Crusades.'

'Are you a Templar?'

'Goodness no. It's made up of crusading monks. They're not allowed to swear, no gambling, no drunkenness, and definitely no sex.'

'Goodness.' Ozanne laughed. 'That wouldn't suit you.'

'Quite. They'd never let someone like me in.'

'Even though you were the marshal's friend?'

'Even that.'

'Didn't you go on crusade with the king?'

Baruch had told Ozanne many tales from his youth. She had not taken much interest until now.

'I was at the battle of Acre with the marshal and King Richard.'

'Where's that?'

'In the Levant.'

Ozanne shrugged her shoulders. She was no wiser.

'It's near Jerusalem.'

'Did you go there?'

'No. I was under orders, and we never got to go there even though it was close by.'

Ozanne wanted to question her father more, but the service started, and the church fell silent. To Ozanne's relief it was much shorter than the Westminster service. Hubert de Burgh talked about how the marshal had been the greatest knight in all the world. How he had trained, took part in jousts and tournaments, of how he had served under four English kings: Henry II, Richard the Lionheart, King John, and lastly the boy king, Henry III. He talked about his recent victory at the Battle of Lincoln in his advancing years. His final achievement was to be formally made a member of the Knights Templar which was why he was being buried in this hallowed church.

Ozanne began to understand how her father had been in a privileged position to serve with him as a fellow knight.

Abbot William then gave an impassioned sermon. Since the start of his illness the marshal had confessed his sins every eight days to Abbot Simon of Reading. He paid tribute to his wife, Isabel, who gave one hundred sous to the abbey while his body lay in the chapel. The chapel that he had made glorious and beautiful apparently. When he came to the part about his illness, she saw her father's hand go to his bowed face. She was sure he was wiping away a tear.

The abbot continued: 'Look, sirs, how it is with this life: when each of us comes to his end his senses are all gone, and he is nothing more than so much earth. You see before you the greatest knight in the world that ever lived in our time, and what is there to say now, by God? This is what we all must come to. We have before us our mirror; it is mine as much as yours. And now let us say the Our Father, praying that God may receive this Christian in his heavenly kingdom, in glory with his elect, believing as we do, that he was truly good.'

After the service Baruch made his way over to Isabel. He took Isabel's hand in his and bowed his head.

'I'm so very sorry for your loss.'

'He is a great loss to many, Baruch. I thank you for coming today.'

'I wanted to pay my respects to him. He was a very good friend of mine.'

'I know, he spoke of you often.'

'Did he?'

'Yes, he called you his personal Jew. Not in an offensive way. You know he wasn't like that.'

'I know. He got my family out of many scrapes in the past.'

'He was like that.' Isabel smiled for the first time. It seemed to help talking about him.

'When he became Regent of the King, he confided in me and a few others.'

'Was something troubling him? I knew little about his royal affairs. He was quite circumspect in that regard,' Isabel said.

'He told us he felt as if he had ventured into a wild sea where sailors found no shore or anchorage. He said, "If all the world had abandoned the king except me, I would put him on my shoulders and carry him without fail from island to island, land to land". I remember it so well. I was full of admiration for him.' Chuckling, Baruch added, 'He even said he would beg for bread if he had to, to protect and save his king.'

She dabbed at the corner of her eye. Baruch could tell it was one of the many tears she had shed that day. He changed the subject. 'I was expecting to see Brother Aymeric. Is he ill?'

Isabel gestured towards a newly sunken grave on the floor that Baruch had not noticed. 'He lies there.'

'I had no idea.'

'He was at my husband's bedside in the weeks before he died but sadly only a few days before my husband passed, he also passed. He said he so greatly loved William's company on earth that he wanted to be buried beside him to be his companion in heaven.'

'He was a truly loyal knight and a worthy Master of the Temple.'

Isabel nodded. She was a great beauty and Baruch could see why his friend and mentor had fallen so deeply in love with her.

'It's a great comfort to you that you have your children with you. I noticed Richard is not here.'

'He's in France at the court of King Philip. We sent word but I think perhaps he has not received the news in time.'

'I'm sure he'll be home soon. A shame he missed his father's funeral.'

'I'll bring him here to pay his respects.'

William, the marshal's eldest son, approached. He had inherited his father's title as first Earl of Pembroke. 'I was with Father when he died. He went peacefully.'

'That's good to know,' said Baruch. Baruch felt a pull on his sleeve. It was Ozanne. No doubt feeling a little lost amongst people she didn't know. He had neglected her. 'This is my daughter, Ozanne.'

'She's very beautiful, Baruch. You must be proud,' said Isabel.

'I am. Very,' he said, squeezing Ozanne across the shoulders.

'I must go and thank the abbot and the bishop before they leave.'

'Of course.' Baruch took hold of Isabel's hand once more, kissed it and bid her goodbye.

CHAPTER

TWENTY-THREE

Once back in Gloucester Ozanne could not settle. She pined for Yvain but told herself she was being ridiculous as she barely knew him.

One good thing had come from her misery. Her poetry composition and songwriting had matured. She understood how the troubadours were able to write with such passion, such worldliness. It was their lived experience. Whilst only brief, her trip to London had left her wanting more. More excitement, more adventure. A restlessness had crept into her bones. Her sleep was fitful, and she could not sit for long without wanting to jump up and move around. Her mother had noticed.

'What's the matter with you, Ozanne?' asked Brunetta. 'You can't sit still for a moment. Anyone would think you had something biting you.'

Ozanne was scribbling the word *Amour* on a length of parchment. She had created a pattern of differently shaped letters and flourishes. A mix of *Love*, *Yvain* and her own name all intertwined. Her mother's question irritated her, and she lost concentration.

'You don't see me scratching, do you?'

'No, I haven't but you know what I meant. You haven't been the same since you went to London. Did something happen to you there?'

'No. What has *Aba* been saying?'

'Nothing. He just said there was a boy there who took a liking to you.'

'He wasn't a boy, *Ima*. He was a man.'

'That's probably worse. I know what men are like.'

Ozanne knew that Baruch was Brunetta's second husband and that her first husband, Ozanne's real father, Abraham, had died suddenly. Most women only got to know one man in their lives unless they were of a certain kind.

'You don't talk much about *Aba*.'

Brunetta ignored her.

'What was he like? My father.'

Brunetta set down the lace trim she was sewing on her lap. Ozanne could tell she was searching for something to say. Since Douce's outburst Ozanne had suspected there were things she didn't fully understand about her stepfather or her real father.

'He was quiet.'

'Not like Baruch then.'

They both laughed. It was rare to be alone together. There was always someone else in the house and they had never been close. Ozanne was her father's favourite and he doted on her. She seized the moment to question her mother.

'Did you love him?'

Brunetta hesitated then swallowed hard. 'I loved him. He was a good husband.'

Ozanne said, 'I don't remember him.'

'You were only little when he... when he died.'

Brunetta's cheeks were reddening. She scratched at her neck then sniffed and dabbed at the corner of her eye.

'I'm sorry, *Ima*. I didn't mean to upset you. I was just curious to know how you knew you loved *Aba*.'

Brunetta sniffed again, smiled then answered. 'When you meet the one, you'll know. Your whole body will tell you.'

An image of Yvain came into Ozanne's mind. His rugged jawline, the flecks of copper in his verdigris eyes. His voice. For a moment she was unaware her mother was staring at her.

'You look like you may have already met him,' Brunetta said. She put down her sewing, sat beside Ozanne and took her hands in hers. 'No wonder you're so restless. You must miss him terribly.'

From a place within her she never knew existed surfaced a powerful emotion. She broke down and hugged her mother.

'His name is Yvain and he's French.'

CHAPTER

TWENTY-FOUR

The atmosphere in the le Riche household since Zev's and Arlette's deaths was unbearable and arrangements for Tzuri's long-awaited wedding did not lift the mood. What should have been a happy occasion to look forward to was being marred and not just because he was marrying a former Christian. Douce had been affected the most. Some days she could be quiet, tetchy on others. It was on those days that everyone tried to avoid her, especially Tzuri and Brunetta.

Brunetta was avoiding everyone, hiding away in her bedroom cleaning and tidying. Since the passionate lovemaking with Baruch she had been in a reflective mood. Her conversation with Ozanne had been revealing. Her daughter was in love. It was a love doomed to fail but she could not tell Ozanne that.

How would she ever see him again? It was a blessing. Troubadours were famously nomadic and promiscuous. A wicked smile formed upon her lips. She ran her tongue over her bottom lip as she thought of her conduct as a young woman at an age not far from Ozanne's. How reckless she had been, how wanton.

What would her mother have thought, said or done had she known? Her mother, Abigail, was long dead and her truculent brother, Josce, had moved away to London. She didn't miss him. The only member of her family she did miss was her younger sister, Glorietta. She couldn't wait to be married and had met a boy from Hereford and moved there years ago. She visited Gloucester occasionally and she had travelled to Hereford once or twice, but their lives were very different, and they had lost touch.

The door opened and Baruch stood there. He had been teaching swordsmanship at the castle. The skin on his neck was glistening with sweat, his straggly hair dripping at the ends. Whether it was her thoughts or something more primal, she felt that same passion for him on the day of her wedding to Abraham. He must have seen the desire in her face for he threw down his sword, walked towards her and without speaking, picked her up and threw her on the bed. Baruch could still make her heart melt and her thighs throb. They were not as agile as they had been in the past, but their lust was as keen as ever.

Afterwards they lay in each other's arms, breathing heavily from exhaustion.

'I didn't think we'd still be doing this at our age,' Brunetta said, giggling like a bride on her wedding night.

'Me neither but I'm so glad we still can.'

She imagined Baruch missed his mother more than he could say. In contrast she had not mourned her own mother anywhere near as much. The upsurge in their lovemaking was probably a way of him coping with the loss. Baruch rolled over on top of her and began to kiss her neck. She could feel him hard against her thigh. It was like being young again. Brunetta wrapped her thighs around Baruch and gave into him again. As she lay next to him, she drifted off. When she woke Baruch was snoring. She dug him in the ribs, and he woke with a jolt. It must have been the soldier in him as he instinctively went to his side thinking he was wearing his sword. It made Brunetta laugh. Spending time like this with Baruch made all the heartache and strife melt away. Her thoughts turned to Ozanne.

'Our girl is in love.'

'Is she?' He seemed surprised.

'You should know. You were there when she met him.'

'Who?'

'You can be such a clod at times, Baruch. The troubadour.'

'Oh, him. She did seem distracted by him, but I thought that was all in the past and she'd forgotten about him.'

'Far from it. She's in love and pining for him. Haven't you noticed how she's behaving since she returned from London?'

'Not really. Her moods are always changing. I can never keep up.'

'I think it's time she found a husband, don't you?'

'The troubadour?' Baruch questioned, somewhat surprised.

'No, you idiot. A nice Jewish boy.'

Baruch grinned at her. 'Like me you mean?'

'Not quite like you. A little more stable.'

'More like a Jew you mean?'

'Yes, if you want to put it that way.'

'That's a bit hypocritical, isn't it? Don't let Tzuri hear you say that, or Vernisse for that matter.'

'That's different.'

'How is it?'

'It just is.'

'I don't see that it's different.'

Brunetta struggled to answer. 'Tzuri is different. He's more stable than Ozanne.'

Baruch thought for a moment. 'It's true. Ozanne is more like you. She has a wild side, wild and sensual.'

'Be serious for once, Baruch.'

'*D'accord*,' he said. 'You're right as always. She needs a husband because,' he said, squeezing her bare bottom, 'look what she's missing out on.'

He wrapped his arms around her and squeezed her hard.

'Not again,' Brunetta said, putting up little defence.

CHAPTER

TWENTY-FIVE

One evening Abraham Gabbai was making his way along West Gate Street towards The Booth Hall. As he walked, he thought he heard footsteps behind him. He stopped and turned around. The street was empty. A stray dog emerged from the alley and loped towards the darkness of Holy Trinity Church's porch. Gabbai carried on, quickening his pace. He had not gone too far when he was aware of someone gaining on him. Before he could fully turn, he felt a blow to his head. Then another. He fell to the ground, dazed. It was then the blows began to rain down upon him until he fell into unconsciousness.

When he woke sometime later a man was standing over him. Instinctively Gabbai flinched, expecting more blows.

'Steady on there,' the man said in a reassuring voice. 'How do you feel? You've had a nasty fall by the look of you.'

'I was attacked. Did you see who it was?' Gabbai asked, trying to sit up.

'When I came along you were out cold. I didn't see anyone. Here, let me help you up.'

Gabbai got to his feet, felt for his money pouch which was intact then felt dizzy. He fell against his Good Samaritan.

'Where do you live? I'll help you get home.'

'I'm staying with Leo of Warwick. His house is opposite The Booth Hall.'

Gabbai carried on to Leo's house with the aid of the stranger and was glad to finally arrive at his door. He thanked the man and went inside. When Leo saw him, he let out a gasp.

'What on earth has happened to you?' he said, coming towards him to help him to a chair by the fire. 'That's a nasty gash you have on your forehead.'

Gabbai put his hand to his forehead, and it was wet. He looked at his fingertips and saw fresh blood.

'I was attacked.'

'Who by?'

'I didn't see who it was, but I have my suspicions.'

'Who would do such a thing? Were you robbed?'

'No, my money is still here,' he said, patting his bulging money pouch.

'Then who do you suspect?'

'Solomon Turbe. He's been threatening to do something to me for years.'

'Then you must go to the sheriff in the morning and report this.'

'I'll fetch my daughter Jivette. She'll clean you up and show you to your bed. Hopefully, you'll sleep well and feel better in the morning.'

Gabbai held on to his friend's arm. 'Thank you.'

The next morning Gabbai woke with a searing pain in his head. His wounds had been cleaned by Jivette and the gash on his forehead was no longer bleeding but he felt like he had been rolled down a rocky cliff. Every bone in his body ached and when he tried to raise his head he slumped back on the bed. Eventually he fell asleep and woke later that day.

His first thought was that he must find Sheriff Musard and tell him that he had been attacked. Still unsteady on his feet and with blurred vision he sought out the sheriff in Gloucester Castle. The castle was an impressive stone structure. At the barbican he was stopped by the guards.

'What business do you have?' the guard asked, barring Gabbai's way with his pike.

'I've come to see the sheriff to report a crime.'

'Wait here.'

The guard left, returning minutes later to let him pass and show him into the sheriff's private quarters. Sheriff Musard was sitting in a throne-like chair by a lit fire. The sheriff motioned to Gabbai to take a seat opposite him.

'What is it you want to see me about today?' Sheriff Musard said.

Sheriff Musard was a man in his early fifties with an air of authority about him. His long legs stretched out in front of him by the hearth and his pale-blue eyes stared at him for an answer.

'I was attacked last night on my way home.'

'I can see you have some injuries. Who did this?'

'It was the Jew, Solomon Turbe, who maliciously wounded me in the king's peace.'

'You're certain of this?' Sheriff Musard pressed him, his eyes narrowing with a questioning look.

Musard was no fool. Gabbai knew if he confessed to not actually seeing his attacker then the sheriff would take a dim view of his accusation.

'Yes, I'm certain it was him.'

'Did you see him attack you?'

'Yes.'

'What with?'

Gabbai had not expected this question. He paused for a moment. He hadn't seen the weapon.

'A club of some sort.'

'Why would Solomon Turbe want to do you harm?'

'He's jealous of me, of my position.'

'I'm sure many people are jealous of you, Gabbai, it doesn't mean they would want to harm you.'

'I think he meant to murder me. I was lucky to survive.'

'Do you have any witnesses?'

Gabbai had not expected to be cross-examined. He thought his accusation would be believed given his obvious injuries.

'It was dark but yes it was him.'

Sheriff Musard scratched at his beard. 'Without a witness it will be difficult to arrest him.'

'Do you think I gave myself these injuries?' Gabbai said, becoming indignant and pointing to the gash on his forehead.

Gabbai's face was swollen on one side and a purplish bruise was appearing below his right eye. He looked a sorry sight.

'No, I suppose not.' Sheriff Musard stood up. His tall figure towered over the seated Gabbai. Gabbai got the impression his time with the sheriff was over. 'I'll arrest him today and have him questioned. Where will I find him?'

Gabbai stood to leave, a smirk forming upon his thin lips.

'He'll be at his house in East Gate Street. The one next to the le Riche family.'

'Very well,' said the sheriff, concluding his business.

'Thank you, sheriff. Appreciate that.'

~

Solomon Turbe was sitting in the dining hall with his wife eating supper when a knock came at the door. At first, he ignored it but then the knocking became more insistent.

'Who can that be?' asked Comitissa, popping a pickled cucumber into her mouth. 'Are you expecting someone, Solomon?'

'Not at this time of night.'

'You'd better go and see who it is. It might be business.'

Solomon sighed, took a bite from the chicken leg he'd been feasting on and raised himself from his chair. As he made his way to the door the banging became louder. It did not sound like business to Solomon. More like trouble. He opened the door a crack and asked who was there. The door was pushed towards him, and he staggered backwards with the force.

'Solomon Turbe,' said Sheriff Musard. 'You're under arrest for the malicious wounding of Abraham Gabbai against the king's peace.'

'What?' Solomon said, almost choking on the chicken he had been chewing.

A scream came from the dining hall and Comitissa's corpulent figure came waddling to the door.

'This must be a mistake. My husband couldn't possibly do something like that. Who has accused him?' Comitissa asked, red-faced.

'Abraham Gabbai has made the accusation, and I must arrest you, Solomon, until I can find out more and gather any witnesses.'

Solomon, still stunned by the accusation, stood with his mouth half open.

'When is this wounding supposed to have been carried out?' Comitissa enquired, sensing her husband had been rendered speechless.

'Last night in West Gate Street when Abaraham Gabbai was making his way home.'

'It's a lie, my husband was here with me last night. He did not go out.'

'That may be so but until I can get to the bottom of this accusation, I must arrest your husband.'

Sheriff Musard grabbed hold of Solomon's arm and pulled him into the street.

Comitissa screamed again. 'You can't take him,' she said, coming outside to follow them.

The sheriff had two armed guards with him.

'Restrain her.'

The men took hold of Comitissa, one on each arm.

'You can visit your husband tomorrow. For now you had better go back inside.'

'I'll be all right, my dear. It's a mistake. Don't worry about me.'

As Solomon was led away, he could hear Comitissa howling and wailing. He could do no more but await his fate in the morning.

CHAPTER

TWENTY-SIX

Ozanne was excited to hear that King Henry was visiting Gloucester with his entourage of animals. Since his coronation in St Peter's Abbey, King Henry had visited Gloucester several times, usually with the marshal by his side. On those occasions her father would seize the opportunity to visit his old friend and partake of a few flagons of ale, but those days were long gone.

The city was a hive of activity as she walked with Baruch towards The Cross to pay a visit to Quinton. Ozanne had her eye on a bolt of samite for a robe she wanted to have made for Tzuri's wedding. As they made their way through the bustling crowd, they heard the familiar sound of jongleurs dazzling the crowd with their magic tricks and their amazing juggling skills. She tugged at her father's sleeve.

'*Aba*, let's take a look.'

Ozanne dragged him over to the front of St Michael the Archangel's Church on The Cross where a band of itinerant jongleurs were putting on a show. As she gazed in wonderment at the performers, she felt her father's hand upon her forearm.

'Come, Ozanne,' he shouted, making his voice heard above the appreciative crowd. 'Let's go.'

Although it was only midday, the crowd had already taken advantage of the ales and wines being offered by the street traders and had become rowdy.

'*Aba*, let's stay awhile. It looks such fun and...' Ozanne stopped in mid-sentence; her expression frozen in shock. She put her hand to her heart. She heard her father's voice.

'Ozanne, I really think–'

'*Aba*, is that Yvain?'

Baruch cleared his throat and looked in the direction she was pointing. 'I can't be certain–'

Ozanne shrieked with delight, freed herself from his grip and ran towards Yvain. Baruch followed her, but he wasn't as fast-footed as Ozanne, and she had already reached him by the time he caught up. Yvain was leaning against the stone wall of a house opposite the church clutching his gittern to his chest. He also seemed to be in shock.

'Yvain, what are you doing here?' Ozanne asked, not concealing her excitement at seeing him again.

'We're accompanying the king's tour.'

'When did you get here?'

'Yesterday.'

'Where are you staying?'

Baruch interrupted. 'Ozanne, stop asking so many questions. Can't you see the man needs to get on with his entertaining.'

'That's all right, I'm taking a break.' Yvain smiled at Baruch and held his hand out to him. Baruch shook it. 'Hello, it's good to see you both,' Yvain said, not able to take his eyes from Ozanne.

'You remember us?' Baruch said.

'*Bien sûr.* You were in London for the marshal's funeral.'

'That's right. What a good memory.'

'I have never forgotten it,' said Yvain, somewhat dreamily.

'*Jamais*?' Ozanne asked.

'Never,' Yvain said with conviction.

Baruch shuffled on his feet and cleared his throat. Ozanne sensed he was a little embarrassed by Yvain's outburst. Ozanne couldn't be more thrilled. She studied Yvain's features. He looked even more attractive than she had remembered. His skin was bronzed from the sun.

'Have you been travelling?'

'Yes. We just got back from Italy. How did you know?'

'Your skin. It has the colour of a strong sun.'

Yvain smoothed his hand across his cheek. 'How observant of you.'

'We must go, Ozanne,' Baruch said, tugging at her sleeve.

'Please, *Aba*. I'd like to stay a little while longer to hear Yvain sing again.'

'That won't be until this evening at the celebration in The Booth Hall,' Yvain said.

'Ooh, can we go, *Aba*?'

'I'm not sure.'

Ozanne pulled a face. Her father had never been able to say no to her.

'You'll have to ask your mother,' Baruch said, taking her arm.

Baruch had never deferred to her mother for permission in his life as far as she could remember. Why now?

She was about to argue with her stepfather when Sheriff Musard appeared at Baruch's side. They exchanged greetings and Ozanne, seeing that Baruch was distracted by the interruption, whispered to Yvain, 'Will I see you later?'

Yvain flashed a look at Baruch to check he wasn't listening then nodded confirmation at Ozanne.

'At The Booth Hall?' he whispered.

She nodded back. Ozanne's heart fluttered in her chest. There was no point lingering with Baruch present. She turned to him. He was discussing the arrest of Solomon Turbe for assaulting Abraham Gabbai. She had never liked the man and thought that he probably deserved the beating. Poor Solomon was still locked up in the castle gaol awaiting trial. Ozanne could not stop looking at Yvain. Her whole body trembled in his presence. As she waited for her father Abraham Gabbai approached.

'When are you going to hold the trial for that scoundrel?' Gabbai demanded.

'Soon enough,' said the sheriff. 'Isn't it enough that he's incarcerated in the castle awaiting trial?'

'But when is soon enough?'

The sheriff stiffened. Gabbai was annoying him.

'In due course. I am a very busy man. The halimot court takes up much of my time and I am not long back from London. You must learn some patience, my friend.'

Gabbai grunted as Sheriff Musard turned away from him and continued his conversation with Baruch.

'*Aba*, let's go now,' she said.

Baruch said his farewells to Yvain and to the sheriff and walked away arm in arm with Ozanne. Ozanne was a quiver of emotions. She had never forgotten Yvain and it seemed he had not forgotten her. When they reached Quinton's shop her thoughts were on Yvain and not the bolt of cloth. Thankfully her father hadn't noticed.

Ozanne spent the rest of the day planning how she could sneak away and successfully bring about her secret tryst with Yvain.

TWENTY-SEVEN

Ozanne slept in the small room at the back of the house. After supper that evening, she made a point of yawning loudly, told everyone she was exceptionally tired and that she needed an early night.

Now she lay on her bed, fully clothed, barely able to contain her excitement. She listened out for her stepfather who was usually the last to retire. As soon as she heard his bedroom door click shut, she leapt out of bed and tiptoed to her own door. It creaked as she opened it. Damn. Not daring to move, she listened some more and hearing Baruch snore, she picked up her outdoor shoes and tiptoed down the stairs, barefoot.

Outside, the street was quiet. A man was walking unsteadily on the other side. She waited for him to pass and be out of sight then put on her shoes and ran towards The Booth Hall. She had no idea where she would find Yvain. Would he be inside playing, or would he be outside waiting for her? She hoped the latter.

The closer she got to the hall the busier West Gate Street became. It was full of largely drunken men with women of a questionable nature. Her secret tryst seemed ill-advised. She thought of turning back but her desire to see Yvain was so strong she put her fears to the back of her mind and carried on. She reached the hall unmolested and stood by the entrance. She hadn't been there long when a man, looking worse for wear, approached her.

'Looking for some fun, missy?' he asked, his eyes hungry with lust.

Ozanne stiffened at his approach. He reached out to grab her arm. She sidestepped him and he fell against the wall.

'Bitch,' he cried out.

Ozanne had no option but to run inside the hall out of his lecherous reach.

The hall was packed with revellers. She had been inside many times for markets or the odd court case and had felt safe but not tonight. The atmosphere was lawless, irreverent, and intoxicated. She better understood what her father meant when he told her tales of what he got up to in his youth. Looking around her, she realised he had probably left a lot out to protect her. Still, she was determined to stay until she found Yvain. There was music coming from the other end of the room so keeping her gaze firmly to the ground, she pushed her way through. Something inside was propelling her forward. An inner force. An inner hunger.

When she got to the front of the crowd, she saw him. He was strumming his gittern, accompanying an older man who was speaking with a French accent. A poet. His poem was not about love as she had expected but about the Crusades. Ozanne knew little about politics, but she knew enough to know his words in certain Christian circles would be deemed heretical. The poet's impassioned words struck her.

Dawn broke,
A thousand fluttering flags,
Soon to be stained,
With blood.

What on earth could he be speaking of? A massacre of some sort? Her gaze was still fixed upon Yvain, willing him to look at her. As if he felt her stare upon him, his head flicked up from his strumming and he stared straight at her then smiled. Ozanne's stomach flipped. The performance ended and Yvain made his way to her. She was unsure what to expect or what to say. Yvain took her hand and led her to the back of the hall where there was a small door that led to a rear courtyard.

Once alone, Yvain put his arm around the small of her back and drew her to him, then kissed her. A tender kiss. Her first proper kiss. Ozanne was no longer aware of her surroundings, no longer aware of her feet touching the ground. The world seemed to spin and she in it, alone with Yvain. When the kiss ended Ozanne could barely catch her breath. Her surroundings returned and she was once again on terra firma although her stomach felt queasy.

'I've wanted to do that for so long,' Yvain said, his eyes fixed upon her, his voice rich and deep.

Ozanne blushed. Yvain stroked her cheek.

'You are mesmerising,' he said. 'When I knew we were coming to Gloucester I prayed I would see you.'

'You remembered where I was from.'

'Ozanne, I remember your every word.'

He took her hands and clasped them in front of him then leant over and kissed her again. This time she responded to his soft lips and let herself fall against his warm body as he cupped her face. The kiss went on forever and Ozanne was hoping it would never stop, nor the burst of emotions his presence was causing within her.

'I thought I'd find you here, *garçon amoureux*,' a voice said.

Shocked, Ozanne pulled away from Yvain.

'Guillaume, what are you doing out here?'

'Looking for you.' Guillaume, the poet from earlier, bowed in front of Ozanne. '*Enchantée.*'

Ozanne knew a little French from Douce and her grandmother, so she understood him but was too embarrassed at being caught out to reply.

'This is Ozanne, Guillaume. The young woman I told you about who I met in London.'

Guillaume's eyebrows raised in a look of knowing towards Yvain, then he turned to Ozanne and smiled. 'Yvain has spoken about you. In fact, he does nothing else.'

'That's not totally true. I have other conversation topics.'

Everyone laughed including Ozanne. Yvain's friend had a warmth about him. He made her feel safe and welcome in their company, which surprised her as she didn't know them, they were Christians, and she was unchaperoned. She should be feeling like an outsider, yet she did not. Quite the opposite.

'I was listening to your poem earlier. What was it about?' she asked Guillaume.

'The massacre at Béziers. You know of it?'

Ozanne shook her head.

'This cannot be. I think I need to educate you,' he said in a light-hearted fashion.

'Be gentle with her,' Yvain said. 'I've only just found her again. I don't want to lose her so quickly.'

'You think I'm going to frighten her away?'

'No, maybe just bore her to death,' Yvain said, slapping his friend on the back in a brotherly fashion.

'Come, let's sit down and talk. I'll tell you all about it.'

Ozanne turned to Yvain for confirmation. Yvain put his arm on Guillaume's shoulder.

'This man is my best friend. We have worked together and travelled to many places. I trust him with my life.'

Guillaume winked and said, 'And you trust me with your woman?'

Yvain didn't answer him but took hold of Ozanne's hand and led her back into The Booth Hall. The music had stopped, and the hall had emptied out a little. They walked over to a bench where they were serving weak ale, cider and wine. Guillaume bought them each a cup of wine and they sat down at a small table nearby. Ozanne felt very grown up. Yvain sat close to her with Guillaume opposite them.

'You mentioned Béziers and something about a massacre,' Ozanne said.

Guillaume leant forward. 'Our illustrious Pope sent an army of Crusaders into the city of Béziers to kill the Cathars. Twenty thousand were slaughtered.'

Ozanne winced. She had never heard of the Cathars.

'Why did he do that?'

Guillaume's lip curled. 'Because he was a corrupt, evil man.'

'Was?'

'He died.'

'So is there a new Pope?'

'The equally illustrious Pope Honorius III.'

'Is he also evil and corrupt?'

Yvain and Guillaume laughed together.

'They all are,' said Guillaume.

Ozanne had never heard a Christian talking in such a disparaging way about the Pope, one of the most powerful men in the entire world. She had always thought he was revered by all Christians but then she didn't know any Christians that well. Not even Vernisse.

'Are you a Cathar?' she asked Guillaume.

Guillaume laughed. 'I am a non-believer; someone the Pope would call a heretic.'

'You are not Catholic?'

'I was born a Catholic. My parents are Catholics, but I soon realised that religion was the root of all evil in this world.'

Ozanne turned to Yvain. 'What about you? Are you a non-believer?'

'We think the same,' Yvain replied.

'You would probably get on with my father. He pretends to be a Jew to keep the family happy, but I don't think he really believes.'

'And what about you?' Guillaume asked her.

Ozanne had never been asked that question. It threw her for a moment.

'I've never really thought that deeply about religion. I go to the synagogue with my family. I enjoy *Shabbat* and the food every Friday and the Jewish holidays are fun–'

'Sounds like you're just going along with things for an easy life,' Guillaume said.

'Go easy on her, Guillaume. Not everyone thinks like you.'

'My apologies, Ozanne. I get carried away. Yvain is very good at keeping me in check.'

'I don't mind. I find it interesting. Is all your poetry about death and massacres?'

'Would you rather I wrote about love?'

Ozanne thought about her own pathetic efforts at writing lyrics. They were all about love. So predictable. Not about important matters such as hatred and evil.

'I suppose I wasn't expecting words of hatred–'

'Not hatred. Justice. There is a huge difference.'

'*Pardon*. I have a lot to learn.'

'*Pas de problème*, Ozanne. Many people live under the shackles of ignorance.'

'Guillaume, I said go easy,' Yvain pressed.

Ozanne placed her hand on top of Yvain's. 'It's all right. I'm not offended. I'm intrigued. I'd like to know more about your poetry.'

Yvain bought more cups of wine and the conversation continued late into the night. Ozanne was so engaged with everything Guillaume and Yvain had to say that she forgot the lateness of the hour. Realising the hall was almost empty and the performers were long gone she stood up.

'I better go home. My family will miss me. Then I'll be in trouble.'

'Let me walk you home,' Yvain said, leaping to his feet.

Ozanne held out her hand to Guillaume to shake. He took it, turned it over and kissed the back of her hand.

'*Bonsoir, mademoiselle*,' he said, also standing. '*A bientôt.*'

'I do hope I'll see you again. I've really enjoyed our conversation this evening.'

Ozanne left with Yvain. Dusk had turned to dawn. The streets were empty. Ozanne felt a rising panic at having stayed out so long. Then she scolded herself for being so conventional. If Tzuri stayed out all night nothing would be said to him. Why should it be different for her?

'You seem locked in thought,' Yvain said.

'I was just thinking what my parents would say if they knew I had been out all night in the company of two men unchaperoned.'

'I should have taken you home sooner,' he said, stopping in the street. 'I didn't want you to go.'

'I didn't want to go either. I don't want to leave you now,' she said, emboldened by the wine.

Yvain took hold of her hand and led her into Foxes Lane. It

was narrow, damp, dark, and smelt of urine. Not an ideal place to conduct a romance, she thought.

He pulled her towards him and kissed her. His kiss was more impassioned than earlier. He pressed his groin against her. She felt something becoming harder. Unused to male attention of that kind and being alone in an alleyway she pushed him away.

'Sorry, Ozanne. I forgot myself for a moment. It's because you are so exquisite, and I have missed you so much.'

'I don't have any experience of men... in that way.'

'Let me take you home,' he said, putting his arm around her shoulders.

'I'm sorry too.'

'You have nothing to be sorry about. It's me who needs to apologise.'

They walked as far as the corner near her house.

'I don't think it wise for you to come any closer. I wouldn't want anyone to see us together.'

'*D'accord*. When will I see you again?'

'Tomorrow? Midday. On The Cross. Where we met today.'

Yvain kissed her on the cheek. '*Bonsoir, ma chérie. Jusqu'à demain.*'

'I love it when you speak French.'

'I prefer to speak Occitan! *Fins demà.*'

A cockerel crowed in the distance, piercing the quiet of dawn. Ozanne giggled and left him standing in the street.

TWENTY-EIGHT

S heriff Musard had a busy day ahead of him at the halimot court. He had not long returned from London where he had attended the lavish second crowning of the king, who was now a boy of twelve years. It was thought by the powers that be that there had been some irregularities with his original crowning at Gloucester. With his mentor and protector the marshal gone, he was being guided by the new regent, Hubert de Burgh. The Westminster crowning was a far cry from the rushed event in St Peter's Abbey. This time the young king wore full regalia of a gold crown studded with diverse stones, not the circlet his mother lent him, a gold sceptre and silver gilt staff and a tunic with a dalmatic of red samite. It had been a tiring journey there and back and he wished he could have postponed today's court.

The halimot court had plenty of business to attend to, such as quitclaims, grants of fee farms and messuages. The Matresdon family were to attend in order to sort out some land business and the Abbot of St Peter's, Henry Blunt, would also be there to grant in *frank almoin* some acres of meadow in Pulmede as well as various other orders of business. He would be glad when it was all over so he could invite the brothers to the castle for a few glasses of wine and some lunch.

The Booth Hall was of impressive proportions. Timber framed, it had three floors with an open gallery on the first floor. He entered the packed hall and took his seat at the back facing a crowd of dignitaries all vying for his attention and rulings.

Walter the Scribe sat next to him recording the business of the day. The first up was Abbot Blunt.

'Good morning, abbot. How are you this bright morning?' the sheriff asked.

Henry Blunt stood in front of the sheriff, a heavy woollen alb tied at his waist. Beads of sweat glistened on his high forehead.

'Unseasonably warm,' said the abbot, wiping his brow with a cloth he produced from underneath his alb.

Sheriff Musard unfurled a length of parchment on the table in front of him and read aloud: 'Grant in *frank almoin*, in consideration of six marks of three acres of meadow in Pulmede in the parish of Westburi lying between the meadow of the king and the land held by Henry the deacon which is called Newelende. The annual rent is one penny payable at the Feast of St Michael. If the grantor fails to make warranty of the said land to the grantees when called upon, he shall make recompense to the grantees with land of equal value out of his tenement, in Gerna or in his meadow or in his arable land. Agreed.'

Sheriff Musard looked back at the abbot. The abbot nodded.

'Witnessed here today by Walter the Scribe, Simon de Matresdon, Geoffrey de Matresdon and Henry de Matresdon.'

Walter the Scribe took his quill, dipped it into the inkwell and scratched an entry onto the parchment on which he was listing the day's business.

The rest of the morning passed without incident and when the last of the business was concluded, Sheriff Musard approached the Matresdon family and invited them to the castle. It had become something of a habit. A congenial lunch amongst friends. Geoffrey and Henry were brothers about the same age as the sheriff, and Simon their father was the coroner in Gloucester.

As they left The Booth Hall and walked across Barelands, the sheriff was making small talk asking after Alice, Simon's wife, and his grandson, Phillip, when on reaching the inner walls of the castle some minutes later he heard a cry. He looked up at the battlements of the keep and saw an object falling through the sky. Then a dull thud. At first the sheriff thought the object a bundle of clothes, some rubbish the guards had jettisoned from the roof. He sent the porter ahead of them to see what it was. It wasn't until he got closer that he saw it was Solomon Turbe. Solomon had been incarcerated awaiting trial, accused of the assault of Abraham Gabbai. He rushed over to him and knelt beside him. Solomon was still breathing.

The sheriff looked up towards the battlements to see if he could see anyone but there was no one. Had Solomon been pushed over or had he jumped off, meaning to kill himself? How had he escaped from his cell? All of these thoughts ran through the sheriff's mind as he knelt by the injured man.

'Solomon, who did this to you?'

Solomon was seriously injured and could hardly speak. His words came out in rambling gasps. Sheriff Musard thought he heard the word 'Gabbai'. Had Gabbai wreaked his revenge on his fellow Jew? Was it Gabbai all along who had hoodwinked him and led him to believe that Solomon had injured him? Perhaps he had caused those injuries to himself. It was a conundrum.

He turned to Simon. 'I fear this man is gravely injured and his time on earth will not be long.'

Simon shook his head at the broken body of Solomon lying on the ground.

'It's a bad business, sheriff.'

'Yes, but perhaps fortuitous that you should be here.'

'I deal with the dead,' Simon said. 'This man is still alive. Send for me if that changes.'

Sheriff Musard nodded his head and bid Simon farewell. Simon left with his sons, no doubt he was going to call into a local tavern for lunch and a few ales. The sheriff's plans for a congenial lunch had been ruined. He was furious at the disruption, but he would have to stay and see if he could get any more information from Solomon.

'Take this man to the infirmary and see to his wounds,' he shouted at the guards.

Solomon was raised from the ground and carried towards the small infirmary, all the while crying out in pain and rambling. Sheriff Musard followed them. Once inside, he shouted to one of the guards to fetch a physician.

The sheriff's men laid Solomon upon the bed. His injuries were significant. He was no physician, but it was obvious if a man fell from such a height, he would be lucky if he survived. How he had survived thus far was a miracle. He grabbed a low three-legged stool from the corner and drew up next to Solomon. He was delirious and rambling.

'Solomon, you must tell me what has happened to you?'

The sheriff bent down, close to Solomon's mouth so he could hear him better.

'*Melec Sha'ul. Melec Sha'ul.*'

Solomon was not making sense. The sheriff knew some Hebrew words but not these, if indeed he was speaking Hebrew.

'Bring Rabbi Isaiah here at once,' he commanded one of his guards.

Rabbi Isaiah was well respected in his community. The sheriff had very little to do with him, but he would be an impartial person to call upon in such circumstances where trust was in little supply. He would also be needed if Solomon were to die.

The sheriff returned to his private quarters until the guard returned with the rabbi. Rabbi Isaiah was a tall man with kind grey eyes and a long straggly beard. The sheriff lost no time in taking him to Solomon.

Lying on a bloodied hospital mattress the sheriff was relieved to see that he was still alive.

The rabbi knelt by Solomon's side. 'Who has done this to you, Solomon?'

Again Solomon repeated the phrase, '*Melec Sha'ul. Melec Sha'ul.*'

'What's he saying?' the sheriff asked impatiently.

'He's repeating the name of Saul. King Saul. From the book of Samuel.'

'What does it mean?' asked the sheriff.

Rabbi Isaiah scratched his head. 'It is said that when the Philistines fought against the Israelites, they sought out King Saul – *Melec Sha'ul*, and their archers critically wounded him. Saul then said to his armour bearer, "Draw your sword and run me through, or these uncircumcised fellows will come and run me through and abuse me". But his armour bearer could not do it; so Saul took his own sword and fell on it.'

'So Saul killed himself rather than be slain by someone who is not circumcised?'

Rabbi Isaiah nodded.

'The uncircumcised being a Christian.'

'That would be a sensible conclusion.'

'Rabbi, do you think Solomon is saying that he was attacked by Christians but rather than die at their hands he chose to throw himself from the tower?'

'I can't say for sure but that might be the interpretation.'

'Can you ask him, Rabbi, who did this to him?'

Rabbi Isaiah bent down once more to ask Solomon in his own language. 'Who do you accuse of pushing you, Solomon?'

Solomon grabbed hold of Rabbi Isaiah's arm and in a moment of clarity he looked upwards towards the rafters and cried: '*Lo!*'

The sheriff understood that word. It meant 'No'.

This made no sense, thought the sheriff. Either Solomon had done this to himself, or someone had pushed him. To confound matters, just as the sheriff was puzzling on this, Solomon's wife, Comitissa, appeared. She gave out a piercing shriek so loud Rabbi Isaiah jolted and held his hands to his ears. On seeing her husband she fell to his side and took his hand. Through her tears she spoke to him.

'Solomon, who has done this to you? Speak out now. Was it Gabbai?'

There it was again, the name, Gabbai. The sheriff was beginning to think he was at the centre of a conspiracy to murder but who was the guilty party? Solomon's eyes rolled around in their sockets and then he opened them wide and stared at Comitissa, shrinking back onto the mattress as if he'd seen an enemy.

'Flee hence for 'tis by thy plot that I am slain!' he croaked.

Comitissa let go of her husband's hand with a gasp. 'How can you say that, my love? You are not thinking straight.'

Then she stole a glance at the sheriff. The sheriff stared back at her. Was she in on this plot to kill Solomon? Was she and Gabbai in it together? Were they lovers? The sheriff's mind was frantic with questions and possible motives. It was all very puzzling. He was used to dealing with drunken street brawls or petty squabbling over land in the halimot court but not this. Solomon's moans grew louder, and his delirium grew worse in the presence of his wife.

'Get her out of here,' the sheriff shouted to his men. 'And lock her up.'

The men pounced on Comitissa, grabbed her by the shoulders and hoisted her up. Comitissa let out another piercing scream. The sheriff winced at the noise.

'And shut her up,' he shouted.

One of the men gave Comitissa a swipe across the cheek. For a moment she was silent then she began to wail as she was led away.

The sheriff went back to questioning Solomon, but it was no use. The man was demented and was making no sense. The sheriff thanked the rabbi and left, leaving Solomon's injuries in the care of the physician and his soul in the care of the rabbi.

CHAPTER

TWENTY-NINE

Mirabelle sat with her son, Bonanfaunt, and her daughter, Belia, and their growing offspring. The house was full of the noise of children playing. Although the occasional screech hurt her ears Mirabelle was comforted in the knowledge that her lineage was secured, unlike that of Moses le Riche whose empire was crumbling if not completely gone. She had successfully secured her son Bonanfaunt's place as the head of the Gloucester community. No one had risen to the competence of Moses. His son, Abraham, had died in mysterious circumstances, Douce was no moneylender and her sons had left home. All that remained of the once great empire was Douce. Baruch, the black sheep of the family and his stepson who, to Mirabelle, looked remarkably like him, his stepdaughter Ozanne and his wife Brunetta. None of them players in the business of high-wealth moneylending. How times had changed.

It was a change that Mirabelle welcomed. At last her dreams of being influential and wielding power had finally become a reality. She looked across at her handsome son. He was a shrewd moneylender, a good husband and father. His only drawback was he lacked the duplicity that Mirabelle felt was an essential quality in ascending the power ladder. If she wasn't careful her family might sink to the bottom. For that reason she still wielded influence behind the scenes.

'Did you hear they put all the Jews of London in the Tower on the day of the king's coronation?' said Belia.

'Yes, but that was for their own protection,' Bonanfaunt said.

'That was a drastic measure, wasn't it?' said Pucelle.

Pucelle was too young to remember the terrible events of King Richard's coronation. Mirabelle raised her eyebrows at her. She suspected Pucelle had been a little frightened of her as a child. Now a woman in her thirties and mother to three children, Pucelle was no longer afraid of her grandmother.

'Don't you know about the terrible riots when Londoners attacked the Jews?'

'When was that?'

'You were only a baby,' Belia interjected.

Pucelle glared at her grandmother and put her hands on her hips. 'So how was I supposed to know?'

'We should never forget. It's our shared history. It's what keeps us together. Our faith and our history,' Mirabelle said, glaring back at her granddaughter.

Pucelle huffed and returned to counting and stacking the coins in front of her. Mirabelle smirked, knowing she had won yet another argument with Pucelle. There was a welcome silence until the door to the great hall opened and in rushed her son-in-law Garsia.

'Solomon Turbe has fallen from the castle tower,' he said, out of breath.

'Is he dead?' asked Mirabelle.

'Not yet, but he's in a bad way.'

Mirabelle shot a menacing look at her son-in-law, Isaac, son of the late, great Aaron of Lincoln, once the richest man in the country and richer than the king. Sadly, his father's business acumen had not rubbed off on Isaac, but with careful grooming over the years Mirabelle had taught him the seedier side of the business of money and power. He had become her lackey. Her son, Bonanfaunt, to her shame, had too many scruples and was morally incorruptible.

'How did he fall?' asked Bonanfaunt.

'They think he was pushed,' said Garsia.

'By whom?' asked Bonanfaunt.

'He said it was his wife. She's been arrested.'

'Comitissa? Surely not. She has many faults, but I don't think she'd do something like this. Not to Solomon. They're devoted to each other,' said Bonanfaunt.

As head of the community, Bonanfaunt would likely be called upon to discuss the matter at a *bet din*, literally meaning *house of judgement* but it was more like a court where they would hear complaints relating to civil, or religious and sometimes criminal matters. Along with Rabbi Isaiah they had been appointed judges but as this was a case of attempted murder and Solomon had already been arrested and was awaiting trial for assaulting Abraham Gabbai, Bonanfaunt didn't think they would be able to intervene. The king's charter, which gave his community immunity from English courts and certain protections, did not cover matters such as murder.

A conspiratorial smile had formed upon Mirabelle's lips. She put her hand to her mouth to conceal it and coughed. 'Serves her right,' Mirabelle grunted.

Pucelle had been listening to the conversation and studying her grandmother's reaction. '*Safta*, how can you be so heartless?'

Pucelle's husband, Garsia, coughed pointedly. It was a sign to his wife to be quiet, for whenever Pucelle challenged

Mirabelle it always turned into a heated argument and his wife was not always on the winning side.

'I won't be quiet,' she said, acknowledging her husband's gesture. 'This is a case of attempted murder, not some seedy backhand dealing *Safta* usually dirties her hands with.'

Mirabelle's stare hardened and her cheeks began to flush. Pucelle needed to be taken down a peg or two. That husband of hers needed to control her a little more.

'Garsia,' she said in a controlled voice.

Garsia was small in stature and was a little afraid of Mirabelle. Mirabelle was fully aware of the effect she had on people and used it to her advantage. At the mention of his name, he sat upright in the chair to catch his breath. His youngest child, Saffronia, ran over to him and sat on his knee as if she sensed her father was in trouble. The child turned to Mirabelle and scowled. Garsia didn't know where to look. He didn't have the courage of his wife to stand up to Mirabelle, yet Mirabelle would always try to pit one against the other when an argument loomed. He didn't answer. Instead, he wrapped his arms around his daughter's thin frame and cuddled into her.

'Garsia, you need to teach that child some manners. As to your wife...'

Still Garsia remained silent. There was no point in engaging with Mirabelle. She was ruthless and never backed down in an argument.

'That's enough. Leave them alone, *Ima*,' demanded Bonanfaunt.

Mirabelle pursed her lips. She knew she had gone too far once Bonanfaunt intervened. That was her cue to keep silent.

CHAPTER
THIRTY

That same morning Ozanne woke late. She was in a deep sleep when her mother knocked on the door and opened it without waiting to be called in.

'Are you ill?'

'No, why?'

'Breakfast has been ready for ages. I've been calling upstairs for you. I thought I ought to check you were well.'

'I'm just tired, that's all.'

Brunetta sat down on the bed beside her and touched her forehead. 'You said you felt tired last night. Perhaps you're coming down with something. I'll make you some chicken broth.'

Brunetta stood up and left.

Ozanne stretched out underneath the bedclothes. Memories of her tryst came rushing in. She lay there, an image of Yvain's face in her mind's eye. Then she thought about his manhood pressing against her. It was a sign that he desired her. Why had she been so prudish? Jewish laws around relations between men and women taught that it was not sinful and was to be enjoyed by both. That, of course, was once you were married. And married to a person of the same faith. Yvain was neither Jewish nor of any faith. He was impossibly adorable and intriguing, and Ozanne could not keep her thoughts away from the events of last night. If her mother knew where she'd been and what she'd been up to...

'*Sheol*,' she said, repeating what had been her grandfather Zev's favourite phrase.

Tzuri was marrying a converted Christian. Her brother had set a precedent. Look how the mere announcement of a marriage to a Christian had affected the family. Douce was an embittered old woman who barely spoke to anyone. Realising she had slept late, she shot out of bed to get ready for another assignation with Yvain.

Ozanne spent some time choosing what to wear and settling on a robe that would emphasise her figure, she dressed and went downstairs into the kitchen. Brunetta and Douce were around the kitchen table preparing the meal for *Shabbat*. The smell of *challah* yeast and roasted chicken made her stomach rumble.

'Where are you going?' Brunetta asked her.

'Just out,' Ozanne replied, nonchalantly.

'You're all dressed up for just out,' said Douce, kneading a blob of rich dough.

'Am I?' Ozanne said.

Ozanne had dressed in one of her finest robes. A tunic of taffeta with a sarcenet lining. On reflection, she should have dressed more plainly for she was now drawing unwanted attention.

'Where exactly are you going?' Brunetta asked her.

Ozanne had to think quickly. She needed to tell them she was going somewhere that would not spark suspicion.

'To the drapers,' she offered.

'You were only there the other day with your father. Why do you have to go back so soon?'

'I'm going to see Vernisse.'

Douce let out a groan. She picked up the lump of elastic dough and threw it back down on the table with a slam. A puff of flour dust flew into the air.

'You're going to have to get on with her now she's converted. She'll be living under the same roof as you once they are married.'

Douce grunted again. 'Whenever that may be,' she said, huffing and pressing with force into the dough.

Douce was referring to their wedding date which had been postponed twice since Vernisse's conversion.

'You know Vernisse is worried about leaving her father alone and Tzuri wants to make sure Vernisse is happy with the arrangements,' Brunetta replied petulantly.

'As long as Vernisse is happy,' Douce said in mocking tones.

'*Oy lanu,*' Brunetta began.

Suspecting another argument was about to commence, Ozanne snatched a bread roll left over from breakfast and stuffed it in her mouth. It seemed her mother had forgotten to interrogate her further on where she was going and for once she was grateful for Douce's outburst.

Once outside in the brightness and warmth of the late May sun, she had the feeling of having a chain released from around her neck. Her whole body relaxed as she made her way to The Cross but when she saw Yvain waiting for her some other sensation took over her body. An intense hunger.

Yvain came rushing towards her. In the middle of The Cross, he embraced her. Afraid they may be seen she pushed him away.

'Let's go somewhere less crowded,' she said to him. 'I know somewhere.'

They walked together towards the river.

'Did you get home without your parents noticing you'd gone?'

'Yes, I crept up the stairs like a thief. My stepfather was snoring loudly.'

Yvain laughed. 'I'm glad you didn't get into trouble on my account.'

When no one was in sight she grasped Yvain's hand and held it tight. Once they reached the riverbank and found a clump of bushes, they sat down out of view of anyone passing by.

Yvain knelt beside her and took her in his arms. As they kissed, he gently pushed her to the ground so that she lay on her back. He then moved his body so that he was on top of her. It all happened so fast. His warm hand went beneath her tunic, and he traced her inner thigh with his fingertips. Ozanne began to moan. Like a hunger that wouldn't be satiated she held him tight and opened her thighs to let him in. There was no stopping it. She was hungry for it, for him. She wanted to consume him, for him to be part of her.

When it was over, rather than feel sullied, she felt liberated and alive.

After a while Yvain spoke. 'I didn't mean that to happen.'

'Neither did I,' said Ozanne, with a slight snicker.

'You're not mad at me?'

'Not at all. I was a willing party if you hadn't noticed.'

Yvain let out a sigh of relief. 'I love you, Ozanne.'

Ozanne's heart stopped beating for a second. She couldn't breathe. Had she heard him correctly?

'I said I love you, Ozanne. Say something.'

Ozanne threw her arms around him. 'Oh, Yvain. I love you too. I never want to leave you.'

Yvain prised her arms from around his neck. 'That's the problem. I'm leaving tomorrow.'

Ozanne's chest constricted with shock. 'Leaving tomorrow?' She could hardly believe what he was saying. 'But you can't. We've only just–'

'We're going to the Holy Land. Guillaume and I.'

The Holy Land was on the other side of the world. Yvain's words cut into her like a carving knife. She put her hand to her stomach.

'Come with me,' he said.

Come with me.

Come with me.

Stupefied by his suggestion she could not sort her thoughts or words into any cohesive form.

'What?'

'Come with me to the Holy Land,' he repeated.

The Holy Land had always seemed to her a land of adventure, of warm winds and cold nights. Of deserts and dark men. Baruch had told her tales. She had dreamed of going there but never thought it possible. It was only a dream. A fantasy.

Until now.

'All right,' she said.

'You mean it?'

'I've never been so certain in my life.'

After the *Shabbat* meal Ozanne went up to her room and packed a small bundle of clothes. Her writing materials and ink she placed in a small wooden chest and to her old kinnor she attached some rope so she could sling it over her shoulder. Then she waited.

On the tenth chime of St Peter's Abbey's bells, she heard

Baruch climb the stairs and go into his bedroom. It wasn't long before he began to snore. Ozanne collected her possessions and left the house. She took one last look at her home before striding along East Gate Street to The Cross where Yvain was waiting for her.

'You're certain this is what you want?' he said.

'With all of my heart,' she replied.

CHAPTER

THIRTY-ONE

Sheriff Musard decided to go back to see Solomon. Something was troubling him greatly. Over lunch he had much to mull over. He had started at the beginning.

Who had attacked Gabbai? Was it Solomon? If not him, who? If it was Solomon, had Gabbai attacked him in revenge? But how did he get to him locked up in the gaol? How did Solomon get out of his cell and on top of the castle tower? What happened to Solomon? Did he commit suicide rather than be pushed over the battlements by the so-called 'uncircumcised men'? Who were these men?

And what of his wife, Comitissa? Was Solomon's ramblings merely that – the ramblings of a gravely ill man – or did she have something to do with his fall? Had he been hasty in locking her up? He needed to speak to Solomon. Hopefully he had recovered enough to start making sense. When he arrived at the infirmary, he found Solomon propped on a pillow.

'How are you today, Solomon?'

'I am not long for this world, sheriff. I would like to draw up my will while I can. I need five witnesses.'

'Who do you want? I'll send my guard to fetch them.'

Solomon immediately asked for Bonanfaunt. Then he thought for a moment and listed four more. The Warwick brothers, Abraham, Leo and Elias, and Moses, son of Aaron, who were newcomers to Gloucester. All prominent Jewish men within the Gloucester community. While they waited for the men to arrive the sheriff questioned Solomon further.

'Yesterday you said your wife tried to murder you...'

'Did I?' Solomon said, looking somewhat surprised.

'If I remember correctly, you said it was by her plot that you had been slain. Why did you say that?'

Solomon appeared confused. He rubbed at his temples, deep in thought. Then closed his eyes and seemed to drift off to sleep. Musard waited for him to wake up, eager to hear what else Solomon may say that might enlighten him. The witnesses arrived and when they were all assembled Solomon rallied and gave an account of the circumstances of his fall. He claimed that Abraham Gabbai had sought his destruction and that he wanted this to be officially recorded.

The sheriff listened carefully while Bonanfaunt wrote down Solomon's wishes. Solomon spoke clearly and appeared to be of sound mind yet here he was accusing Gabbai this time and not his wife. And there was no mention of King Saul.

Afterwards the sheriff spoke to Bonanfaunt.

'This is a peculiar business. I'd appreciate your thoughts, Bonanfaunt. Yesterday he accused his wife of trying to murder him and now he says it was Gabbai. I don't know what to think.'

'It's all very puzzling.'

'Months ago Gabbai came to see me to accuse Solomon of assaulting him. Now Solomon is accusing him of trying to murder him.'

Bonanfaunt shrugged his shoulders.

'It's hard to know who's telling the truth,' the sheriff said in an attempt to draw out Bonanfaunt's opinions.

Bonanfaunt remained silent.

The sheriff left Bonanfaunt and the others at the castle barbican and returned to the great hall. His mind was still whirring with questions as to who did what to whom and what was at the bottom of it all. He had some paperwork to do for the next halimot court and he needed to clear his mind. It was sometime later when a guard came to tell him that Solomon had died. The sheriff's mind began to whir into action again.

Was this a case of murder or suicide and how was he going to get at the truth now that Solomon was dead? He would need to seek out Gabbai and interrogate him and he needed to talk to Solomon's guards.

The sheriff made his way to the castle's kitchen where the prisoners' food was prepared – usually from the scraps – and where the gaolors came to fill up tankards of ale for their captives. The warm May weather coupled with the roaring fire which was almost constantly kept alight made the kitchen unbearably hot. How the kitchen workers could stand it he would never know.

On the other hand, the smell of roasting chickens and sides of beef, pork and lamb mixed with fried onions and leeks and fresh herbs was delightful. The sheriff's stomach rumbled in response. A carved chicken lay on the huge oak table looking inviting, so the sheriff helped himself to a chunk of breast meat. It was succulent and tasty, so he took another chunk.

The kitchen was a hive of activity. Loaves of bread were stacked on a wooden bench close to the bread oven. Maids were stirring large iron pots; others were preparing fresh vegetables. As the sheriff took in the scene, Andrew and Gilbert, the ale servers, walked in, carrying several empty pewter tankards.

'You two,' he shouted across the room.

The ale servers stopped their banter and stood still. The servants stopped what they were doing and looked over at the sheriff then back to the ale servers.

'Sheriff,' said Andrew with an acknowledging nod.

'On the day of Solomon's fall, were you present?'

The two men shuffled on their feet and looked down at the tamped earth.

'Answer me,' said the sheriff, walking towards the two men.

'We was, sheriff,' Gilbert began.

'Did you see anyone?' shouted the sheriff, becoming impatient.

The two men looked at each other, their gaze shifty.

'There was a Jew.'

'Which Jew?'

'Isaac of Lincoln,' answered Andrew.

'Mirabelle's son-in-law?'

'Yes, that's the one.'

'Was he there when Solomon fell?'

'Can't say for sure. Solomon asked if he could go up on the ramparts for some air.'

'And you let him?'

'We thought naught of it.'

The sheriff knew it was common to allow prisoners to take the air in exchange for a small pourboire, a fee. In fact, pretty much anything could be bought in the gaol. It had its own working economy.

'Did you follow them?'

Andrew wiped the sweat from his face. 'We had other prisoners to see to.'

'Did you see Isaac leave?'

The pair looked at each other, a gormless look on their bloated faces. Then they both shrugged. The sheriff's hackles rose. He didn't suffer fools well.

'I'll deal with you two later,' he said, storming out of the kitchen but not before he wrenched another chunk of chicken from the ravaged carcass on the table.

He returned to the great hall and ordered that Comitissa be released. Sometime later, as he crossed the bailey, he bumped into her. She was being led out of the gaol by two women, looking frailer and a good deal slimmer than when he last saw her. Wailing and sobbing she spotted the sheriff and made her way over to him.

'What are you going to do about my husband's murder?'

'We don't know that it is murder.'

'I know it is and what's more I know who's responsible. It's that treacherous rat Gabbai and if you're not going to do anything then I am going to London to petition Josceus.'

With that she sniffed a few times, leaned on her friend's arm, and walked away.

The Jew, Josceus, was the Arch-Presbyter of the Justices of the Jews based in London and highly influential. It was clear from Comitissa's remark that she was determined to cause him trouble over her husband's death. The sheriff could not have a woman, let alone a Jewess, making trouble for him. He would have to use all his skills to survive this meddlesome and pernicious woman.

For now he must seek out Isaac to get his version of events. He should have known that where there was treachery, it was only a matter of time before Mirabelle's name would be mentioned. Had she stooped so low that she was involving her feckless son-in-law? This news further complicated what was already a complex and tawdry affair. She was a formidable opponent in any financial dispute but murder... He could not make any sense of it. The more he found out the more confused he became.

Before he reached the safety of his private lodgings Baruch ran up to him in an agitated state.

'Sheriff, my daughter Ozanne is missing.'

The sheriff could not bear to be inconvenienced furthermore, let alone by a Jew, even if it was Baruch. They were responsible for their own affairs so why were they bothering him today of all days?

'What is it about the damn Jews in this city today?' he muttered under his breath. 'Since when?'

'Since last night.'

Baruch's daughter Ozanne was a comely lass but as to her character he knew nothing.

'I'm sure she'll turn up soon. She's probably gone to visit a friend or a member of the family, Baruch. I wouldn't worry.'

He flicked his hand towards Baruch in a dismissive gesture.

'You don't understand. She wasn't in her room this morning and her kinnor is gone. She would never leave that behind. Someone's taken her.'

'Baruch,' he said, coming to a standstill. 'I am a very busy man today. If she doesn't turn up by tomorrow come and see me.'

With that he continued towards the castle, leaving Baruch alone in the castle bailey.

THIRTY-TWO

That afternoon, the sheriff knocked on Mirabelle's door. He had wanted to catch Isaac alone without the interfering presence of his mother-in-law, but it seemed impossible so he had no option but to turn up at Mirabelle's where no doubt her formidable brood would be present.

Bonanfaunt answered the door. 'Good afternoon, sheriff. What can I do for you?' Bonanfaunt asked, a friendly smile upon his face.

'I've come to see Isaac. Is he in?'

'He is but may I ask why you would want to see Isaac. Are you sure it's not my mother you're after?'

Bonanfaunt was speaking very politely yet it irked the sheriff. Mirabelle had them all under her spell. He was sure that not one of them dare fart without asking Mirabelle's permission.

'No, it's Isaac I'm here to speak with. Can you bring him to me?'

'Please, come in,' said Bonanfaunt, opening the door wide and letting him into the fore hall. 'I'll go and fetch him.'

Bonanfaunt disappeared and came back some minutes later with Isaac, Mirabelle and Isaac's wife, Belia. The sheriff couldn't help noting how like her mother Belia was. As irascible to boot.

Mirabelle spoke. 'My son tells me you wish to speak with Isaac? What's it about?'

The sides of her thin nose flapped in and out as she pursed her lips and inhaled. The sheriff could sense she was in a confrontational mood.

'It's in relation to Solomon's accident.'

Mirabelle folded her arms. 'What has my son-in-law got to do with that?'

'If I could just speak to him for a moment.'

'Don't say a word, Isaac. I'll deal with this.'

She took a few steps forward leaving Isaac in her shadow. Isaac took on a sheepish look. He picked at his fingernails and kept his gaze to the floor. Belia placed a comforting hand on his arm.

'My guards have informed me that Isaac came to visit Solomon in gaol the morning of his fall. I'd like to ask Isaac if there is any truth in this.'

'I can confirm that Isaac was there. I sent him on an errand.'

'And what errand would that be, may I enquire?'

'You may. I merely asked Isaac to pay his respects to Solomon and enquire as to his health.'

The sheriff looked beyond Mirabelle and addressed Isaac. 'Is this true?'

Isaac's gaze was still fixed on the flagstones.

'Isaac,' the sheriff shouted. 'Answer me.'

Isaac jerked, looked up and nodded.

'When you left him, was he alive?'

Isaac glanced at his mother. Mirabelle nodded to him and answered for him. 'He was most definitely alive.'

'I'd rather he answered the question.'

Isaac finally found his voice. 'Yes, he was alive.'

Isaac's answers appeared to the sheriff to be rehearsed. He could just see Mirabelle drumming it into his head that if anyone asked him why he was in the castle he should give that very reply.

'I didn't think you were that close,' the sheriff said, suspicion rising.

'Solomon is an old friend,' Mirabelle said.

Another rehearsed response, thought the sheriff. He addressed Isaac directly. 'Did you go on the ramparts?'

'We did. Solomon wanted some fresh air. The guards let us go up there.'

'Did you have any other reason to visit him other than to ask after his well-being?'

Mirabelle answered. 'I've already told you.'

'May I remind you that this is a murder inquiry.'

At the mention of murder the colour drained from Isaac's face.

'Murder? Is he dead?' asked Bonanfaunt.

'A few hours ago,' replied the sheriff.

'I thought Solomon fell. In which case it was an accident. Surely?'

'Not according to his wife,' the sheriff answered.

'She has always disliked my family,' Mirabelle said, bitterly. 'It's a malicious accusation with no basis in fact.'

'Facts appear to be very thin on the ground,' the sheriff said.

Mirabelle smiled at him. 'I truly believe this to be malicious. Didn't Solomon himself accuse his own wife of murdering him?'

The sheriff scratched his ear. 'He did but then he quickly withdrew his accusation.'

'Well then, sheriff. I think we can help you no further.'

The sheriff sighed. He was becoming sorely frustrated by the whole affair. 'Nevertheless, the fact remains that Isaac was seen visiting Solomon on the day he fell, and Isaac has admitted that he did. As no one saw him leave I must arrest him and question him further.'

Mirabelle's eyes narrowed and she pursed her lips into a sardonic smile. Taking the sheriff by the arm she led him away from her front door. 'Come now, sheriff. Surely you don't believe Isaac had anything to do with this. I'm sure we can come to some arrangement.'

Mirabelle fixed her stare on him. She was offering him a bribe. The sheriff wanted nothing more than this whole business to disappear so he could go back to lunches with his friends. Safe, uncontroversial pastimes. He breathed in deeply.

'I'm sure that will be in order,' he said.

Mirabelle walked back towards her door where her family was still gathered.

'Then it won't be necessary to arrest Isaac as you're satisfied there's been no wrongdoing?'

'I am satisfied,' the sheriff said.

The sheriff left. Once again, he had been weak and succumbed to the allure of hard cash. After all, he wasn't getting any younger and he deserved some of the finer things in life in his advancing years.

As he marched back to the castle, he couldn't quite wipe away the filth of corruption sticking to what conscience he had left.

THIRTY-THREE

Baruch sat outside the Lich Inn cradling a tankard of ale in the crook of his arm. Sheriff Musard had been less than helpful, being far too busy with the Solomon Turbe murder case to bother searching for Ozanne.

Through his own enquiries earlier in the day he had managed to establish she had been seen at The Cross holding a musical instrument, then been seen walking towards the South Gate with a man. Baruch knew then she had run off with the troubadour Yvain. He would have to return home with the bad news. But he needed the courage to go home and face Brunetta. His mind was in turmoil. On the one hand, he was furious with Ozanne but then he felt like a hypocrite as he had done the same thing to his own mother by leaving to go on crusade. It was early evening, and he could stay out no longer. He had to face Brunetta and tell her the bad news. He drank the last of the dregs and walked home.

As soon as he opened the door Brunetta ran to him. 'You've been gone all day. Where is she?' Brunetta looked behind Baruch as if she expected to see Ozanne hiding there.

'She's left with that boy.'

'The French troubadour?'

Baruch nodded. Brunetta fell into his arms sobbing.

Douce appeared, her face stern as ever. She raised her chin and her eyes flicked open and closed in judgement. 'So the daughter takes after the father, not the son. This family is cursed.'

Brunetta turned to glare at Douce. 'Baruch is not–'

Douce huffed. 'I've heard enough lies in this family,' she said and walked away.

Baruch was shocked to hear Douce intimate that he was Ozanne's real father. The crafty old crone had known all along but he couldn't dwell on that. His only daughter had run off with a man and broken his and her mother's heart. Hearing Brunetta's sobs, he was convinced that this was retribution for his own misdemeanours. He took her into the kitchen and poured her an apple brandy then poured one for himself.

'What are you going to do?' she asked.

'What can I do?'

'You can find her and bring her back.'

Baruch shrugged and took a glug of brandy. 'I have no idea where they've gone. They could be anywhere in the country by now. I wouldn't know where to look.'

'What about that tavern in London where you first met him?'

'He was only working there. They travel all over the country and abroad following the work. You know that.'

'We can't sit around and do nothing.'

Baruch sighed. 'Whether you like it or not Ozanne has made her decision.'

'Douce is right, she's turned out just like you.'

'You say that as if it's a bad thing.'

Brunetta didn't answer him, nor did she look at him. She

took another sip of brandy and after a long silence she said: 'Maybe Tzuri isn't yours?'

Baruch sensed an argument was brewing. Brunetta had never questioned Tzuri's parentage. 'It's obvious Tzuri is mine. He looks like me.'

'He doesn't act like you.'

'He's mine. You know it and I know it. Why do you attack me when things aren't going your way?'

'I don't,' she shouted back at him.

Baruch heard a noise behind him. He turned to see Tzuri standing in the doorway with Vernisse.

'How long have you been standing there?' Baruch asked him.

'Long enough.'

CHAPTER

THIRTY-FOUR

Ozanne reached Southampton by horse and cart where, along with Yvain and Guillaume, she waited to board a ship to Bordeaux. The *Seintespirit* was a clinker-built cog, trading in Gascony wine. It was fitted with a single mast and a single square sail. Sailors were scurrying up and down the gangplank carrying barrels of wine and food provisions. The sight of so many men sent a fearful shiver down her spine.

What had she done?

On her way to the port it dawned on her that there were many questions she hadn't thought to ask. The swiftness of her decision to join Yvain left no time for questions.

'Will I be the only woman on board?' she asked her companions.

Yvain and Guillaume exchanged looks. Yvain looked away. Guillaume cleared his throat.

'Probably,' answered Guillaume eventually.

She hadn't given this much thought at all. How did she feel about being the only woman in the company of what appeared to be a bunch of uncouth-looking ruffians?

'Oh,' was all Ozanne could manage at this revelation.

She resolved to keep close to Yvain and never let him out of her sight.

When they finally boarded the ship at Southampton Ozanne was relieved. The journey had been demanding, and she was not used to travelling such distances and with so few possessions. When the captain showed them to their cabin deep in the bowels of the ship she wondered if the worst of the journey was about to begin. Having never set foot on a ship before she had no idea whether she would suffer from the *mal de mer*. The sickness of the sea.

There were lots of questions Ozanne had not thought to ask. On the first day on board, as they sat eating their evening meal, she fired one after the other at her companions.

'Why are you going to the Holy Land? Surely that's for Crusaders?'

'We earn our living as troubadours. We go where the work is,' replied Guillaume.

'So why did you leave the king's tour before it ended?'

'The king has no taste for another crusade. After the last one the zeal to take the cross has diminished.'

'Why do they go on crusade?'

'Because they believe what the Pope tells them,' Guillaume said.

'And that is?' Ozanne pressed.

'That by going on crusade they will be performing a sacred act, in God's eyes, by purging the Holy Land of Muslim rulers,' said Yvain.

They were like a double act, taking it in turn to answer her questions.

'The Crusades are not a religious war. The greedy Pope wants to grab land and power and he bribes loyal knights with promises of land if they help him,' said Guillaume.

'What happened at the last one?'

'It failed,' Yvain said.

'Were you there?'

'No,' they both answered.

'Is it dangerous to travel to the Holy Land if there's a war raging?'

'Yes,' said Guillaume.

'Not for us,' Yvain said, trying to reassure her. 'We're not warring pilgrims. We stay well away from the fighting armies. We perform for them before they go to war.'

Ozanne aimed her next question at Guillaume. 'Do you recite your heretical poems?'

Guillaume laughed and so did Yvain. Yvain said: 'They would feed him to the lions.'

'Are there lions out there?'

They laughed again. Yvain put his arm around her. 'Lions are everywhere!' he quipped.

After their meal, they retired to the cabin and she slumped onto the narrow built-in bed. Yvain joined her. She smelt the intoxicating aroma of his flesh. She was as eager as he was to make love again, but something was troubling her.

'Yvain, this doesn't feel right.'

He stopped what he was doing and raised himself up on one elbow. 'What's the matter?'

'I'm the only woman on the ship and I'm unmarried.'

'What are you saying, *cherie*?'

'I'd feel safer if we were married.'

'They've probably assumed we're married. Do we need to be?'

'I think so. For my own safety and for the sake of our...' She hesitated, trying to find the words. 'I would enjoy this more if we were married,' she said, pushing his hand away from her breast.

'What does it matter? What's the difference?' Yvain said.

'In my religion sexual relations are seen as a divine gift to be enjoyed.'

'In mine they're regarded as sinful. A necessary evil,' he said, exhaling.

'It's not sinful to show your love to someone in a physical way. I want to feel I am an equal participant. I need to feel secure to be able to be that person. I know it's silly and I should be less concerned with tradition–'

Yvain put his finger to her lips. He swung his legs over the side of the bed and stood up. 'You're right. I'll speak to the captain.'

He adjusted his clothing and left the cabin. Ozanne wondered why he needed to speak to the captain, but she was so exhausted she drifted off to sleep. When she woke, Yvain was back. The bed seemed to be moving beneath her.

'We've set sail,' Yvain said.

'Is that why everything seems to be moving?'

'That's the pitch and roll of the ship. You better get used to it. Do you have another robe with you?'

It seemed such an odd question to ask when they had been talking about the movement of the ship.

'I do. Why do you ask?'

'Because, *ma chérie*, we are going to be married.'

Ozanne sat up. 'How is that possible?'

Yvain came to sit next to her. He brushed the tresses of hair from her cheek. 'You don't know that a captain of a ship has the power to perform church services?'

Ozanne's cheeks were flushed from her slumbers. 'A Christian wedding?'

'What else?'

'I don't know. I hadn't thought it through.'

'What does it matter? We love each other. The ceremony

will be symbolic of our love. We don't need convention. We are above that.'

Ozanne put her arms around Yvain's neck. 'You're right. Our love transcends convention.'

Somewhere in the middle of the ocean the ship's captain performed a simple service. Ozanne wore a plain shift of cream organza, a lightweight sheer silk fabric. The ceremony was short. Guillaume acted as a witness. The captain said a few words and it was over. No *chuppah*. No breaking of pots. No celebration with a lavish banquet. No *ketubah*. It was liberating. Uncomplicated. At the end of it the captain shook her hand, Guillaume embraced her, and Yvain kissed her on the lips. A bottle of Gascony wine was opened and they made a toast.

'*L'chaim*,' Ozanne said.

Those gathered looked puzzled.

'It's Jewish. It means *to life*.'

'In France we say *santé*.'

'To health.'

'To life and health,' Yvain said.

They clinked cups and repeated the words together.

'I wish my family were here,' Ozanne said.

'That would not be a good idea. They'd throw me overboard,' Yvain said, squeezing her around the waist.

After several cups of wine they returned to their cabin accompanied by a few ribald comments. Ozanne giggled as Yvain took her hand and led her away. The wine had made her feel light-headed and incautious. She couldn't wait to lie with Yvain again.

THIRTY-FIVE

Tzuri could not be more content. He had married the woman he loved, she had shown her love for him by converting to the faith and now she was having his child. A Jewish child. The only dark shadow upon his life was Ozanne. Nobody had heard from her. It was generally acknowledged in the family that she had run away with the Occitan troubadour but all efforts to find her had been unsuccessful. His father had travelled to London but found no trace of her there. It was as though she had vanished. Baruch had taken her absence very badly and had started drinking in the local Christian taverns with the sheriff's men.

Before Ozanne's disappearance Tzuri had always viewed his family as straightforward, ordinary Jews living amongst other straightforward, ordinary Jews. It was only recently he had thought that maybe he had become the black sheep of the family by wanting to marry a Christian. That all changed the day Ozanne left.

Since Ozanne's departure there had been tensions in the household. His mother spent her time arguing with Baruch. In turn, Baruch spent his time out of the house with his

Christian friends either teaching swordsmanship or drinking at the local tavern. Then when he came home, they would row again.

Tzuri had battled with the overheard revelation that his stepfather may actually be his birth father.

'I don't know what I would do without you, Vernisse,' he said, kissing the back of her neck.

'What's brought that on?' she said, ruffling his hair in response. 'Are you still thinking about what your parents said?'

They were having a moment on their own in the back of Quinton's busy shop.

'I sometimes wonder if I dreamt what I heard.'

'You know it wasn't a dream. I was there when they were talking. I heard it too.'

Vernisse was sorting through bolts of cloth that had been delivered that morning from a trow docked at the port. Exotic silks of sarcenet, organza, baudekin, samite, taffeta and velvet. Tzuri had no idea there was so many different types of cloth until he started visiting the shop regularly. He was learning more every day. There was cotton mousseline and fine muslin. Bolts of woollen tiretaine, a fine woollen cloth called scarlet that was dyed with kermes – one of the most expensive dyes, made from crushed insects that lived on oak trees. It was all so fascinating. A bundle of treated furs Quinton used to trim garments had also been delivered that morning. Ermine from the winter coat of weasels, miniver from the grey fur of squirrels and strandling from the red squirrel, giving the shop an earthy smell.

'Do you think I look like Baruch?' Tzuri asked.

'There are similarities although you're much better-looking than him.'

'That's because I'm a lot younger and you're biased.' He swung her round to plant a kiss on her lips.

'What does it matter if he is your real father? You said yourself he's the only father you've ever known.'

'It was just a shock. How would you feel if you suddenly found out Quinton wasn't your father?'

Vernisse considered this for a while. 'I think I would be shocked like you but equally if he had been the only father I'd ever known, and he had been a good father – as Baruch has been to you – then I don't think I'd let it ruin my life.'

'I'm hardly letting it do that.'

'You never stop talking about it.'

'Sorry, but it's preying on my mind.' Tzuri walked over to a pile of miniver and ran his hand through the soft fur. 'You do realise if Baruch is my father, then my mother was unfaithful to her husband for most of her marriage.'

Vernisse was folding a length of heavy brocade.

'That had crossed my mind. But you weren't there and so I don't think you can judge her. It's obvious they're still in love after all these years, despite their arguments.'

Tzuri thought for a moment before answering. He was unsure how he felt about it all. He had never known Abraham so had no actual loyalty towards him and if he thought about it, did it matter if he was his real father or not because in truth Baruch had been the only father he had ever known. But his mother? How did he feel about her and her infidelity? Did it change his love for her? Not really. She was the same mother she had always been. Loving, kind, protective.

'You're right. She's still the same mother. Nothing has changed that.'

'And Baruch is still the same.'

Tzuri nodded.

'I hope we will still be that much in love at their age.'

Tzuri came out of his reverie and studied Vernisse. Everything about her was perfect, he thought. Her hair, a fiery shade of russet, glistened in the light. Her smile, her lithe body. He was discovering new wonders about her every day. Now he could add her wise council that he was beginning to rely on. He walked over to her and placed his hand upon her swollen stomach.

'I'm sure we will be,' he said.

THIRTY-SIX

'Where are you going?' Tzuri asked Baruch one day, even though he knew where he was going. 'Can I come with you?'

Baruch muttered something under his breath. Tzuri guessed he was nursing a hangover from the night before. His beard was untrimmed, and he had dark puffy bags beneath his eyes.

'You can't come where I'm going,' Baruch said, his voice deep and gravelly.

'Why not?'

Baruch grunted. He grabbed for his cloak. 'It's not a place for a Jew.'

'You're Jewish,' Tzuri said.

Tzuri was deliberately persistent in his questioning. He wanted to cause a reaction in his stepfather. It was time he said something. Although he had kept quiet, he had never forgotten what he'd overheard his mother say the day Ozanne went missing.

Maybe Tzuri isn't yours?

Baruch ran his fingers through his hair. Tzuri could tell he was getting more and more agitated.

'Your grandmother would never forgive me if I took you where I'm going,' Baruch said, wrapping his cloak around him.

'I know where you're going. I'm not stupid. Take me with you.'

'Why? Why this sudden interest in going with me?'

'I want to talk to you.'

'Lecture me, you mean?'

'That's Douce's job.'

Baruch managed a grizzled grin.

'She can be an ogre at times,' he said, scratching his cheek.

Baruch cast a glance behind Tzuri as if he was checking for someone. '*D'accord*. You can come on one condition...'

'Yes...'

'You never speak a word of this to your mother or Douce.'

Tzuri put his hand out to Baruch. Baruch took it, grinned, and shook his hand.

Tzuri had never set foot in a tavern before so was surprised to find the Lich Inn heaving with bodies and already merry before midday. Baruch must have seen his expression.

'It's market day. That's why it's busy.'

Tzuri nodded, keeping close to his stepfather.

'What are you drinking?' Baruch asked him.

'I'll have a cup of wine, please.'

Baruch grunted. 'Go and sit over there in the corner.'

Tzuri looked behind him and spotted an empty bench and table. He hurried over to it before anyone else could take it. When Baruch returned, he was carrying two large tankards. He put one of them down on the table in front of Tzuri. Tzuri looked at it as if it were a cup of poison.

'What's that?' he asked.

'You're already being stared at. Do you want to look more out of place drinking a cup of wine?'

Tzuri looked into the tankard at the foaming brown swill. As if Baruch could read his thoughts he said: 'Go on, it won't poison you.'

Baruch pitched half the contents of his tankard into his mouth, wiped his lips and slammed it onto the table. If Tzuri was going to get Baruch to open up, he would have to do the same. He picked up the heavy tankard with both hands and took several gulps then slammed it on the table following Baruch's example. The ale tasted bitter and made him quiver. He wished he was drinking wine.

'Why were you so eager to join me today? This kind of place isn't somewhere you'd feel relaxed in.'

A roar of drunken laughter came from a group of men and the shrill laughter of a questionable-looking woman made Tzuri look up.

'You're right, I don't feel relaxed,' Tzuri said. 'I just thought we should spend more time together.'

Tzuri had long been jealous of Baruch's closeness to Ozanne although he had not fully articulated this feeling to anyone. He took another gulp of the ale. It tasted marginally better. With Ozanne gone he wanted to see if he could get closer to Baruch.

'And seeing as how this is the place you spend most of your time, I thought I would join you.'

'Ouch,' said Baruch. 'I thought you said your name wasn't Douce.'

They laughed together and clinked their tankards in a toast. Baruch finished his and stood up to go to the bar.

'Where are you going?' Tzuri asked, feeling a little panicked his stepfather was about to leave him.

'To get another in,' Baruch replied. 'Come on, drink up.'

This was a side to Baruch that he hadn't seen. He began to understand how Baruch could work at the castle training men in swordsmanship. The Christians were certainly a different breed, he thought, as he scanned the tavern in his stepfather's absence. It wasn't long before Baruch arrived back with two more tankards.

'You need to drink up. They can't keep giving me a new tankard every time I go for a drink.'

Tzuri steeled himself to finish the ale, tipping it into his mouth and doing his best to finish it. There was so much he wanted to say to Baruch, but the words just wouldn't come out.

'How are you and Vernisse getting along? All well in that way?' Baruch said, winking.

'I'm very happy. Vernisse means everything to me.'

'You'll be a father soon. How do you feel about that?'

'Excited. I can't wait.'

'Marriage and family are the most important things in life,' Baruch said, looking into his tankard as if the answer to all life's mysteries lay there.

'Are you happy?'

Baruch flinched and fixed his gaze in the distance. 'I'm not sure how to answer that question,' he said.

'I know you miss Ozanne and you're grieving for Arlette and Zev. I worry about you.'

'No need to worry about me, Tzuri. I'm big enough and ugly enough to look after myself.'

'But *Ima* is not.'

'Has she said something?'

'No, but I can tell she's not happy. She's missing Ozanne as well.'

Baruch pressed his hands against his temples and dragged his straggly hair from his face. He had aged so much in the last few months. The drink was not helping.

'I've always been selfish, Tzuri. You'd do well in life if you didn't do what I have done. Vernisse is a lovely young woman. You should cherish her and never leave her.'

'Did you leave *Ima*?'

Baruch placed the palms of his hands over his eyes. 'I left them all,' he said, 'and now those I love are leaving me.'

Tzuri took Baruch's word as a slight on him. 'I'm still here and so is *Ima*.'

Baruch finished his ale and instead of going to fetch another he beckoned the serving wench over to order two more.

'I'm not worth loving, Tzuri. I've always thought of myself and now *Hashem* is punishing me.'

Tzuri thought his father was going to cry, so distraught had he become, but this was the very time when he could take advantage of his vulnerability and ask him the questions he'd wanted answers to all these years.

'Are you my real father?'

The words just tumbled out of his mouth. It must have been the ale; he was not used to it. Baruch's eyes widened. He opened his mouth to answer, faltered, then spoke as if he had changed his mind about what he originally intended to say.

'I am your real father.'

'Not Abraham?'

'No.'

'And Ozanne?'

'Mine too,' Baruch said, hanging his head.

'I thought so. Ever since I overheard the conversation between you and *Ima*.'

'I was afraid you'd heard too much.'

'It was the way *Ima* said, "Maybe Tzuri isn't yours?". I've never forgotten that.' And then you said, "It's obvious Tzuri is mine. He looks like me", and that's when I knew for sure I was yours.'

'You never said anything.'

'I didn't really want to acknowledge it. I thought it best the secret remained a secret. Did *Safta* know?' asked Tzuri.

'I think she did, though we never discussed it openly.'

'What about Douce?'

'She knows everything. There's not much she doesn't know, that old vixen.'

Tzuri could tell his father wanted to unburden himself. It was time to find out more.

'How did my father... Abraham die?'

Baruch took on a haunted look. It made Tzuri suspicious. 'Did you kill him so you could be with my mother?'

Baruch shook his head. 'It was nothing like that. Your mother and I committed a sin in the eyes of *Hashem*. She would never have left Abraham.'

'So what happened?'

'Remember what I said earlier about never telling your mother about me taking you here?'

Tzuri nodded, not wanting to upset the easy flow of conversation and secret-spilling that was happening before him. It was like a Christian confessional.

'Your father found out about us. He was in a dark place at that time. The business was suffering, and he lost his mind. He killed himself.'

Tzuri felt a cold shiver ripple through him. His father had committed suicide because of Baruch and his mother's infidelity.

'How did he kill himself?'

Tzuri had to know everything even if in knowing it would harm him.

'He hanged himself.'

'In the big house?'

'Yes. I found him but it was too late to save his life. He was already gone. I'm sorry.'

'At least you tried to save him.'

Tzuri finished his tankard and put it to one side. The wench arrived with another for Baruch.

'I'd understand if you hated me,' said Baruch.

'I don't know what to think. I have no memories of Abraham. I was only a boy when he... when he died. You're the only father I've ever known and now it turns out you're my real father.'

'I haven't been a great father or husband. I left when your mother was pregnant. By the time I returned you had been born and as soon as I saw you, I knew straight away you were mine.'

'I might look like you but I'm nothing like you in character.'

'We can thank *Hashem* for that,' Baruch said, gulping down his ale.

Tzuri was still struggling with his.

'I want you to know your mother has been completely blameless in all this. I took advantage of her feelings for me. I shouldn't have done that.'

'Is that why she gets angry with you?'

'Probably,' Baruch said with a wry smile.

'Are there any more secrets I should know?'

'I think that's enough for one day, don't you, my son?'

It was the first time Baruch had called him son. It sounded strange coming from him but maybe, thought Tzuri, it was his way of acknowledging he was his true son.

Tzuri, choked with emotion, replied, 'I think you're probably right, *Aba*.'

THIRTY-SEVEN

Baruch woke the next morning feeling out of sorts, but for the first time since Ozanne had gone missing, he was hopeful. Brunetta lay asleep beside him. He could hear her gentle and rhythmic breaths, her warm body stretched out next to him. He nuzzled into her neck. She moaned softly.

'Brunetta,' he whispered.

'Mm,' she said, still half asleep.

'I had a heart-to-heart with Tzuri yesterday.'

Brunetta turned on her side. 'Mm,' she repeated, pulling the bed cover over her shoulder.

'I told him I was his real father.'

Finally, Brunetta opened her eyes wide. 'You did what?'

'I told him I was his real father,' Baruch said, emphasising every word.

'Why did you do that?'

'He asked me outright.'

'Why would he do that?'

'I think he overheard us that day.'

'What day?' Brunetta was still not fully awake.

'Don't you remember the day when Ozanne went missing and Douce said the family was cursed and we argued?'

'I've been trying to forget that day.'

'I called him son. I've never felt like I could do that before.'

'About time,' Brunetta said.

'He said I was the only father he'd ever known. It made me so proud. That finally I could be openly acknowledged as his father.'

'Don't forget Ozanne. You're her father too.'

Baruch's heart ached at the sound of Ozanne's name. 'I know. I miss her so much.'

They were silent for a moment, caught up in their own grief.

'I think of Ozanne every day and wonder where she is, what she's doing, if she's happy, if she's alive even,' said Brunetta, snuggling into his bare chest.

'I worry about her too,' said Baruch, stroking her hair.

'What did Tzuri say when you told him?'

'Not a lot.'

Baruch kissed her on the top of her head. Brunetta responded by squeezing him tight.

'He also asked me how Abraham died.'

Brunetta pushed herself off Baruch and glared at him. 'You didn't tell him, did you?'

'I did.'

'*Oy lanu*,' Brunetta said, sitting up. 'Why?'

'He's a man now, he needed to hear the truth.'

'But not that. I thought we said we would never tell the children.'

'I never thought he'd ask.'

'Just because he asked, doesn't mean you have to tell him.' Brunetta's voice was rising with every word.

'Calm down, Brunetta, and speak quieter. You'll wake the whole household.'

'How can I be calm when you've just told my son his father killed himself?'

'He took it surprisingly well. He said he had no memories of Abraham and that he had always thought of me as his father.'

'What else have you told him?'

'Nothing more.'

'You didn't tell him about what else Abraham tried to do, please tell me you didn't tell him that?' she said, getting upset.

'I would never tell him or anyone about that.'

Brunetta sighed and sunk back into Baruch's hairy chest. 'It would destroy him if he ever knew.'

CHAPTER

THIRTY-EIGHT

When Sheriff Musard next saw Comitissa, following her return from London, he had already received his instructions from the justiciar, Hubert de Burgh, the king's representative, a very powerful man. The sheriff had no option but to carry out his orders. He had already seized Abraham Gabbai's chattels and all of his chirographs. These were to be kept until the outcome of an inquiry had been held into the circumstances of Solomon's death and it was up to the sheriff to arrange. More work, he thought.

Comitissa approached him in the bailey of the castle. He thought about avoiding her by turning back but she was almost upon him before he could do so.

'Why haven't you arrested Gabbai?' she demanded.

The sheriff was not in the mood for such a quarrelsome woman. He sighed openly.

'I haven't arrested him because he has only been accused of procuring your husband's death and not with his actual murder, as is the law.'

He thought this answer would shut her up, but no.

'That's as maybe yet those murderers, Gilbert and Andrew,

are still wandering around freely, as is Gabbai. Who knows what they might do next. Gabbai might murder me.'

The sheriff stifled a snicker. A wicked thought had popped into his head that his life would be a lot easier if in fact Comitissa were dead. She obviously had some sway in certain circles for the justiciar to get involved.

'I am arranging an inquiry into your husband's death, and you will be called to give evidence as will those you've accused. Until then, I'm a busy man and would be obliged if you would let me get on with my job.'

The sheriff did not wait for her response. He walked briskly towards the great hall where, if she were to follow him, he would tell the guards to deal with her.

Back in the great hall the sheriff drew up a list of people to serve on the inquiry. John Gooseditch and John Rufus, the two Christian chirographers, were the obvious choice. They were both in charge of the *archa*, the secure chest where all the financial transactions of the Jewish moneylenders were safely stored. It had been introduced after the York massacre when many Jewish bonds had been burned. They were both trustworthy and knew the Jews involved. He would need a few Christian men he could trust to be on his side, men he could bribe if need be. The Matresdon family would satisfy that requirement. The inquest needed to be arranged quickly before this whole situation got out of hand. If Mirabelle was involved, then who else was and what was really afoot?

THIRTY-NINE

Abraham Gabbai was the last person Mirabelle wanted to see at her door yet here he was. At liberty and not locked up as she had hoped he would be.

'What do you want?' she snarled at him.

'Charming. I have been almost beaten to death since I last saw you.'

Mirabelle huffed. Gabbai was most certainly exaggerating his injuries, which had long healed.

'Come in then.'

She shut the door but not before checking to see if anyone had followed him. Inside the great hall Mirabelle sat on her throne-like chair and offered Gabbai a seat.

'Why have you come here?'

'To ask for your help–'

'How do you think I can possibly help you? Why hasn't the sheriff arrested you? I heard Comitissa has formerly accused you and that our honourable Josceus has given her leave for an inquiry.'

'The sheriff can't arrest me.'

'How so?'

'Because I've only been accused of procuring Solomon's death. Not of murdering him.'

'Same thing, isn't it?'

'Not in the eyes of the law.'

'What possible help can I be to you?'

'The sheriff has impounded all my worldly possessions until the trial is over. My bonds have been taken from me and secured in the *archa*. I cannot carry out my business–'

'What do you want me to do about it?'

Mirabelle was being deliberately curt with Gabbai, cutting in before he'd even finished his sentences and being obnoxiously callous about his plight. This had not gone unnoticed by Gabbai himself.

'Why are you being so unfriendly?'

'We are not friends. We are merely business associates.'

Gabbai sighed. 'In that case may I appeal to your pecuniary nature?'

Mirabelle sat up in her chair. She sensed a business deal coming her way. 'I'm listening.'

'I need to borrow some money.'

'How much?'

'Ten marks.'

'That's rather a lot since your trial is next week.'

'It's not a trial.'

'Well an inquiry then,' she snapped. 'What happens to my ten marks if you are found guilty and sent to jail or worse, to your execution in the tower?'

She sneered at the mention of his execution. Gabbai sneered back.

'If you lend me the money then the likelihood of that will be greatly reduced.'

Gabbai was scheming something. Mirabelle was convinced he was behind the death of Solomon. Perhaps not at his own hand. What had worried her more was the implication of her son-in-law in Solomon's death. Needing to resolve that quickly she had secured his safety by the giving of a douceur, a sweetener, to the sheriff, of three bezants. He was to say, under oath, that he had asked Solomon if he had fallen as a result of a fright from Isaac and to confirm that he had said he had not. Mirabelle loved the way money gave her power.

'I will lend you the money on surety of the goods seized. Draw up a bond to that effect and we have a deal.'

'You're forgetting, I have no means of drawing or storing such a bond.'

Mirabelle huffed again. 'Then I will draw up the bond at one mark a day interest.'

'One mark a day–'

'You want the money, don't you?'

Gabbai scowled. Mirabelle knew he was trapped with nowhere to go. Hopefully Gabbai would do a deal with the sheriff or whoever and be released within the week and Mirabelle would be several marks richer.

CHAPTER

FORTY

Ozanne gazed out from the prow of an Angevin tarida at the many ships docked in Bordeaux's harbour, the Port de la Lune, named after the moon-shaped river that crossed the city, according to Yvain. The journey onboard the clinker-built cog had been lengthy and arduous. Ozanne was not used to life at sea, and it had taken some time to get accustomed to the constant movement of the ship. The *Seintespirit* traded in Gascony wine, some of which was now being transferred to the *tarida*, a horse transportation ship that would take them along the coast to a city called Lisboa in Portugal.

So far on the journey Ozanne had experienced a miasma of emotions. Elated at being with the man she loved one moment followed by nauseating guilt at leaving her family in such a way. She had agonised over whether she should tell them and then had thought better of it. They would probably have locked her in her room and then she would have missed her rendezvous with Yvain. The thought of him leaving England without her had been unbearable. Her family would know by now that she had left. Would they realise it was with Yvain? Her mother would guess. Douce would be appalled and never speak to her again. Her father? He would have mixed emotions. Sad to not have his daughter at home but maybe secretly proud of her for having flaunted convention. After all, he had done something similar.

Ozanne watched as the horses were led onto the ship. They would be kept in specially made slings on the decks below. She wondered how they would cope with the pitch and roll once out on the ocean. Ozanne had not yet been seasick even when they faced rough seas. Docking in Bordeaux harbour, she had been relieved to set foot on firm land but after a few days they were ready to sail again. The horses would be the last to board the ship. Then they would be at sea for another week before reaching Lisboa. From there they would arrive at the port of Marseille, and then across a vast ocean to an island called Sicily. That's when she would leave France, a country whose language and culture was familiar to her, and embark on a journey of discovery to an unfamiliar land. That's when the real adventure would begin.

Her life on board with Yvain could not be happier. In the day they sat in the sunshine and at night they played their musical instruments underneath the stars.

One evening Guillaume asked Ozanne to play one of her compositions.

'Yvain tells me you have composed some songs. Why don't you play one of them? He also says you have the voice of an angel. Will you sing for us?'

Ozanne had never performed outside of her household. At first, she refused then Yvain coaxed her into it. She decided to play the song she wrote after she met him. The one full of the pain of lost love. She picked up her kinnor and began to tune it. Then she started to play. The men on the ship sat quietly as her voice rose above the lashing of the waves. When she had finished, there was a roar and an enthusiastic clapping of hands.

Yvain came over to her. 'You are officially a *trobairitz*. Now you can earn your own money.'

Guillaume followed him. He held out his hand to Ozanne. 'Welcome to the troupe.'

Yvain said, 'She's practically your sister-in-law. Give her a hug.'

Guillaume hugged Ozanne and kissed her on the cheek.

'I'm so glad we're friends,' she said to him. 'I never want to break the bond you have with Yvain.'

'Yvain is the only brother I've known. And now I have a sister,' he said, grinning at her.

When Ozanne agreed to leave with Yvain, she hadn't much thought of how Guillaume would take it, but he seemed to accept her from the first day. She supposed that was what brotherly love was like. A willingness to want a brother's happiness.

'Did you really like the song? It isn't anywhere near as good as your compositions. You are so passionate about so much more than love.'

'But I am not in love, and you are. Write about love. It is more sustaining than writing about politics. When you get to the Holy Land, you'll experience all life has to offer. The good and the bad.'

'My father was at the battle of Acre in 1199. He fought with the king.'

'He will have seen many atrocities. *Un homme avec courage*,' Guillaume said, placing his hand on his heart.

'I've never thought of him like that, but I suppose you're right. He must be courageous to go into battle.'

'You have his courage, *mon amie*. Yvain is a lucky man.'

He walked away to join the sailors who were drinking wine and singing sea shanties.

Yvain took her hand. 'Come on, let's go aft.'

He led her to the rear of the ship where it was quieter. They lay down on their backs, held hands and looked up at the pitch-black sky peppered with a myriad of twinkling stars.

'Do you ever wonder what's out there?' Ozanne asked Yvain.

Yvain replied, 'God's splendour is a tale that is told, written in the stars.'

'That's beautiful, Yvain. Did you write that?'

Yvain laughed. 'No, it's a Christian psalm.'

'I thought you didn't believe in any of that.'

'I'm against any form of organised religion but don't forget I was raised a Catholic. These teachings are branded into your blood.'

'It's the same with Judaism.'

They lay for some time watching the mesmerising stars to the background noise of the waves as the ship cut through the ocean, the gentle flapping of the canvas sail and the creaking and groaning of the wooden ship.

'Come on, let's go to bed.'

Ozanne stood up. She was weary but not too tired for another night of lovemaking.

FORTY-ONE

The Booth Hall, a cavernous timber-framed building on West Gate Street, was packed to hear the inquiry of Abraham Gabbai. Gabbai sat with his brother, Judas, who had travelled from Bristol to be with him. They looked like twins. Comitissa sat with her sister and a friend opposite them. On a raised dais sat the sheriff with his men at arms. Armed guards had also been placed by the entrance doors. Sheriff Musard began the proceedings by explaining that this was an inquiry to determine the facts of Solomon Turbe's death. Mirabelle settled into her seat, Bonanfaunt on one side and Isaac on the other. The rest of her family were spread out along the bench seats.

'Murderer,' Comitissa said under her breath, fixing a cold stare at Gabbai.

Sheriff Musard banged his gavel so hard it echoed at the back of the hall. 'May I remind those present that these proceedings are not unlike a court, and I will have order throughout.' He fixed his stare on Comitissa, who shuffled in her seat. 'I call Comitissa Turbe to give evidence.'

Comitissa shot out of her seat, eager to have her say. She crossed to the bench seat to give her testimony and sat down.

'As you know I have petitioned the Arch-Presbyter of the Justices of the Jews in London regarding the circumstances of my husband's *death*.'

She pronounced the word 'death' with emphasis and made sure she caught the eye of the sheriff.

'Before the Arch-Presbyter and three good men, namely Isaac of Norwich, Master Alexander de Dorset and Elias Martin, I gave the following evidence which I now enter into this inquiry. That on the 31 May, 1220, whilst my husband Solomon was falsely imprisoned for the assault of Abraham Gabbai, he met his death by falling from the tower of the castle gaol. I further submit that said Abraham Gabbai bribed two persons with a payment of ten marks to throw my husband from the tower. These two men were...'

Comitissa pointed at the ale server and the guard, Andrew and Gilbert, and named them.

There was uproar in The Booth Hall. People stamped their feet, threw their hats in the air.

'Order,' bawled the sheriff.

Once the furore settled down the sheriff asked Comitissa how she knew this.

'I believe that Abraham Gabbai talked the sheriff into arresting me to keep me out of the way–'

The crowd began to howl and bay at Comitissa. After all, thought Mirabelle, she had just accused the sheriff publicly and in an official inquiry of being corrupt. This was off to a good start as far as Mirabelle was concerned. Unwittingly, Comitissa was playing into hers, the sheriff's and Gabbai's hands.

The sheriff calmed the crowd.

'That is a very serious accusation, Comitissa. Do you have any proof to back up these slanderous claims?'

'I heard it with my very own ears.'

The rest of Comitissa's words were drowned out by the roar. The sheriff slammed the gavel down repeatedly until the crowd came to some kind of order.

'Anyone found making a noise will be removed by my men and imprisoned. Understood?'

The hall fell silent.

'As I said, whilst I was imprisoned in the castle, near starved to death and fearing for my life, I heard those two men,' she pointed again, 'relaying how Gabbai had paid them ten marks to throw my husband off the parapet of the tower. I heard it with my own ears and believe that to be the truth. And furthermore, when my husband was asked who was responsible, he replied it was Abraham Gabbai.'

'Is that your testimony in full?'

'It is.'

'Please sit down.'

Comitissa walked back to her seat, her chin tilted upwards in triumph.

'I call Abraham Gabbai.'

Gabbai stood up and sat on the same bench Comitissa had just left.

'Abraham Gabbai, where were you on the day of Solomon's death?'

'I was in Hereford all day on business, sheriff, so I couldn't have thrown Solomon off the tower as he accused me. The man was off his head.'

There was a rumble of tittering. The sheriff stifled it with a stare.

'Comitissa has accused you of paying Andrew and Gilbert to throw her husband from the tower. What do you say to that?'

'Not guilty as accused. Ask them.'

'Do you have any more to say?'

'No, sheriff.'

The sheriff said, 'I call Andrew and Gilbert jointly.'

Gabbai sat and the two men approached the bench seat. They both tried to sit on it but being corpulent, had difficulty, causing Gilbert to fall off. The crowd, who had been silenced, fell about laughing. Comitissa scowled. Gilbert regained his composure and remained standing.

'You have both been accused of the murder of Solomon Turbe by his widow. Do you have anything to say?'

'It weren't us, sheriff. We have wives and babbers to support. Why would we do that?'

'Murder is committed for all sorts of reasons. You'd be surprised,' said the sheriff. 'Did anyone visit Solomon on the day of his fall?'

'Yes, sheriff. Isaac, son-in-law of Mirabelle the Jew was there.'

A communal gasp rippled through the hall. Mirabelle held her breath. Sheriff Musard interrupted.

'I would like to add to Andrew and Gilbert's statement. I became aware of Isaac's visit to Solomon on the day he fell. Whilst Solomon was lying injured, I asked him if he may have fallen as a result of a fright caused by Isaac. Solomon was very firm in his answer. He denied that Isaac had any involvement with his fall.'

Mirabelle let out the breath she had been holding. Her scheme had worked. Suspicion was no longer aimed at Isaac. In truth, Mirabelle had sent Isaac not to enquire about his health but to ascertain whether he had any proof as to the activities regarding her tallage returns. She had not ordered Isaac to kill him. He was such an incompetent fool he would have bungled that instruction.

The sheriff then called the two Matresdon brothers, Geoffrey and Henry, to give evidence. They both said the same.

That they had seen a bundle falling from the tower and on approach saw that it was Solomon. The sheriff then asked their father, Simon, the coroner to give evidence and Simon confirmed that Solomon had been so badly injured that he was not making much sense and that he had at one time confessed to suicide then accused his wife of plotting to kill him.

At that Comitissa burst into tears.

'May I remind members of this inquiry that neither the widow Comitissa nor Isaac are in any way being accused of Solomon Turbe's death. Having heard the evidence I am ready to rule that Solomon Turbe died as a result of suicide and that no one person was responsible for his death. Do the members of this inquiry agree with me?'

'We do, sheriff,' they said.

The sheriff slammed his gavel one final time, and the inquiry was over.

Mirabelle left The Booth Hall with her family and with Isaac's reputation restored, much to the relief of Belia.

FORTY-TWO

Tzuri and Vernisse were sitting in the back of Quinton's drapery sorting through the latest delivery of bolts of cloth. Vernisse's father was an old man and increasingly frail and Vernisse was practically running the shop with Tzuri's help. Quinton was becoming forgetful and had become a hindrance in the business. Although she knew she shouldn't, she encouraged her father to visit the local tavern for 'a rest' as she put it to him. He rarely argued with her as he was partial to a drink or two. Tzuri was standing on a stool with a bolt of cloth on his shoulder about to slot it into place on the top shelf when the door to the shop opened and Quinton came shuffling in. His face was as pale as a shroud.

'Have you heard the news from Oxford?' he said, looking from one to the other.

'No, what's happened?' asked Tzuri, hefting the bolt into place and stepping down from the stool.

'A burning at the stake outside Osney Abbey.'

'How terrible,' exclaimed Vernisse.

'Who was it?' asked Tzuri.

'I don't know his name, but they say he had converted to Judaism. They burned him alive.'

Vernisse cried out and put her fist to her mouth and bit down on her knuckles, something she did when she was nervous. She immediately connected her own situation with that of this poor man.

'He was originally Christian then he converted to Judaism and married a Jewish woman. But the religious bigots didn't approve and gave him an ultimatum: abandon the Jewish faith or be burnt at the stake.'

'They burned him for giving up his Christian faith?' asked Tzuri.

'It seems so,' replied Quinton.

'You're concerned for Vernisse,' said Tzuri, walking over to Quinton's daughter, who had turned pale on hearing the news.

'Well, obviously. My daughter is very precious to me.'

'And to me,' Tzuri said, taking hold of Vernisse's hand. 'I'll speak to my father. He's well connected in Christian circles. Maybe there's more to this. I can't imagine the powers that be in Gloucester would want to burn Vernisse at the stake.'

At the mention of her being burned Vernisse let out an anguished cry, relinquished Tzuri's hand and ran up the stairs that led to Quinton's private quarters.

'I need to speak to my father,' Tzuri said, rushing out of the drapers.

Tzuri could not settle until he had spoken to him. He felt sure Baruch would know if there was something bigger going on in the country that he should know about. He found Baruch sitting in the small garden at the back of the house enjoying the sunshine.

'Here you are. I need some advice.'

Baruch opened one eye, then the other, squinted and then raised his hand to shade his vision from the bright sun.

'What can I do for you, Tzuri? Women problems?'

'You could say that,' Tzuri said, sitting beside him on the wooden bench.

'What's troubling you?' Baruch asked him.

'I just heard from Quinton that they burned a converted Jew at the stake for not converting back to Catholicism.'

'Go on,' said Baruch.

Tzuri recounted the sad tale of the young man and his demise. When he had finished, Baruch rubbed his cheeks vigorously as if to wake himself up.

'Hmm. I can see why you would be worried. You're thinking of Vernisse?'

'Exactly. What if they come for her? I can't give her up. I thought you might be able to find out more about the circumstances. Why it happened.'

'It's certainly a very rare occurrence. I can't remember the last time I heard of someone being burned at the stake. There must be more to it than that. Perhaps he's upset someone. It doesn't take much. I'll make some inquiries. Find out what's going on. It might be an isolated incident.'

'And if it isn't? That's what I'm worried about. These things start as isolated incidents then spread across the country like an infection. Remember what happened to Zev.'

'That was a drunken mob looking for a fight. I think this may be something different. I don't think you need to worry.'

Tzuri's shoulders relaxed a little and he felt the warm sun melting away the tension. 'You're sure?'

Baruch placed his hand on Tzuri's shoulder. 'Leave it with me, son,' he said as he stood up. 'I'll go and see the sheriff now and see what he knows. Until then, don't worry.'

CHAPTER
FORTY-THREE

Baruch had told Tzuri not to worry but in truth he had his own concerns. Losing Zev in the way that he had, followed swiftly by his mother, had affected him deeply and he still felt their loss. The only thing that kept his spirits up these days was watching Samuel grow up. Vernisse had given birth to his first grandchild, and he could not be happier. Having new life in the family had eased his sorrow.

Why did these things keep happening? *Just because you are a Jew.* It was at times like this that he questioned his identity. Half Christian, half Jew. What was he? He straddled both worlds. When he was teaching swordsmanship and drinking in the taverns he felt like a Christian. At home and on his infrequent visits to the synagogue he felt like a Jew. When he was with Christians he felt like an outsider and when he was with Jews, he felt the same.

Baruch found the sheriff in his private lodgings in the castle.

'Come in, Baruch. Sit down. Would you like a cup of wine?'

'Thank you for seeing me, sheriff. I know you're busy.'

'Not so busy now that dreadful business with Gabbai is over.'

'He was acquitted, wasn't he?'

Sheriff Musard chuckled. 'Yes, the lying hound.'

'You seem a lot more relaxed than when I last saw you.'

'Yes, it was a troubling time. Murder doesn't happen in this city too often, thank God.'

'Except if you're a Jew...'

'You're referring to your father? That was a very unfortunate incident. I'm sorry we never found those responsible.'

'So am I but that's not why I'm here. It's my son's wife.'

'Ah, Quinton's lovely daughter, Vernisse. I trust she is well?'

'For the moment she is, but I am concerned for her safety.'

'Why?'

'Quinton has told Tzuri about a Jew being burned at the stake in Oxford. Do you know anything about it?'

The sheriff poured them both another cup of wine. 'Nasty affair.'

'Can you tell me what happened? Tzuri is understandably worried for Vernisse.'

'Oh, he shouldn't worry. Nothing like that will happen to her.'

'How can you be so sure?'

Sheriff Musard continued, ignoring Baruch's question. 'The Synod of Oxford was held there a few weeks ago–'

Baruch interrupted. 'What's that?'

'It's a gathering of Catholic officials.' The sheriff scratched his beard. 'If I'm honest, it's a gathering of religious zealots. Stephen Langton, the archbishop, was in attendance. They meet to discuss enforcing the decisions of the Lateran Council–'

'Like the one about Jews being forced to wear a badge, singling them out?'

'The very same. Apparently, during this Synod they heard

about a young deacon who had been studying Hebrew and whilst attending his lessons he fell in love with the Jewish tutor's daughter. So he got himself circumcised.' The sheriff winced at the thought. 'And married her.'

'But why punish him in such a way? Is this how it's going to be for anyone who wishes to convert to Judaism?'

'I doubt it. I think because it was one of their own it aroused violent passions in those present. It was more of an affront to them. More so than if it had been an ordinary citizen.'

'I see,' said Baruch.

'They wanted to try him for denouncing his religion but before it could go to trial the sheriff, Fawkes de Bréauté, a brute of a man–'

'I've heard of him. My old friend the marshal disliked him.'

'Most people do,' said the sheriff, helping himself to another cup of wine without offering Baruch one. The sheriff settled into his chair seemingly enjoying his role as storyteller. 'So Fawkes apparently swore by the throat of God the convert would go to hell and ordered he be burnt at the stake there and then.'

'So they made an example of him.'

'That's the crux of it.'

'But couldn't that happen here? They might want to make an example of Vernisse.'

'Gloucester isn't Oxford. We don't have religious zealots. The nearest equivalent is Abbot Blunt.'

Abbot Blunt was a kindly old soul who practised his religion in the true spirit of Christianity.

'I see what you mean,' Baruch said, letting out a sigh of relief.

'I can see you're still worried for Vernisse. I obviously can't promise but if I get a whiff of anything that might endanger her, I'll let you know.'

Baruch drained his cup of wine and stood up. 'I suppose that's all I can ask of you. I thank you for your time. Good day to you.'

As Baruch walked out of the castle, he couldn't shake the feeling of dread that had engulfed him after hearing of the young deacon's fate.

CHAPTER

FORTY-FOUR

'The port of Messina is in sight at last,' said Yvain. 'Come on deck.'

Ozanne put the knife down she had been using to gut the salted fish they had loaded at the port of Napoli two days ago. She wiped her hands and went up on deck. The ship had followed the coast since leaving Marseille. She was only aware that they had crossed into Italy when the language she heard spoken changed. Now she could see a narrow strip of sea separating the mainland and the island of Sicily.

'That's the Strait of Messina. From there we travel to the Greek island of Crete.'

'Greece. How fascinating,' Ozanne declared.

They had been sailing close to the Italian coast for the last few days, calling in at various ports to get fresh water for the horses and fresh provisions. The heat was more intense as each day passed and Ozanne needed fresh water not only to drink but to cool herself down. Her skin had darkened under the sun's rays and so had Yvain's.

As she surveyed the land mass ahead of her and as she

listened to the strange languages at each port they had stopped at, she felt like she was in another world.

She loved being with Yvain, but she missed her family more than she thought she would. As the only woman aboard, a lot of attention had come her way and so she kept very close to Yvain or Guillaume whenever she could. She had struck up a friendship with the ship's cook and he let her prepare meals sometimes when they had fresh provisions on board. Still, she couldn't wait to set foot in the Holy Land. A land she had dreamt of for so long. She was finally travelling in Baruch's footsteps.

When they docked at Messina, Ozanne couldn't wait to disembark. The port had been called Zancle when the Romans were there because it resembled the shape of a scythe. A natural spit of land curled around to form an enclosed harbour. Ozanne spotted a stretch of golden sands not far from where the ship was moored. Yvain had promised to teach her to swim, and she was longing to wade into the cool, aquamarine sea.

'The closest to being immersed in water was when I used to visit the *mikveh* in Gloucester once a month,' she said as she waded into the sea wearing only her undershift.

'Why do you have to do that?'

'To be clean. We're considered *niddah*, unclean, whilst we have our monthly bleeds and we're not allowed to have sex.'

'There's nothing unclean about you. You're gorgeous any time of the month,' he said, pulling her towards him.

She felt him stiffen against her and it excited her. They had been having sex every day since they set sail from England. Sometimes more than once. Ozanne couldn't believe what she had been missing all her life. Her vow to not marry had been ill-considered. Yvain had changed all that. He was handsome, virile, kind and loving. She wondered if her mother felt this way about Baruch.

Yvain pulled up her sodden shift and pressed himself against her thigh. Ozanne quickly checked to see if anyone was looking. The water and the beach were empty. She wrapped her thighs around his waist, which she found incredibly easy because of the buoyancy of the sea, and Yvain thrust himself inside her.

'You're supposed to be teaching me how to swim,' she said.

'Later,' he said, breathing heavily.

It was over in minutes. Yvain wiped the sweat and salt crystals from his forehead.

'Now we can swim,' he said, grinning.

Ozanne was not nervous in the sea. She soon discovered she was a natural at swimming. The freedom of kicking her legs in the water while wearing very little made her soul soar.

'Now you need to learn to float.'

Yvain turned on his back and put his arms out by his side with his legs wide apart. He wasn't moving any limbs, yet he was not sinking.

'If we get shipwrecked this might just save your life.'

'Don't say things like that. My father was shipwrecked somewhere in these waters.'

'And he survived,' Yvain said, planting his feet on the seabed. 'Come on, try it.'

Ozanne lay on her back, but she was not floating. More like flailing.

'You need to relax. That's the only way this will work.' He placed his hand beneath her head. 'Now relax.'

Ozanne closed her eyes. She could hear the gentle lapping of the sea and the warmth of the sun.

'There you are. You're doing it.'

Ozanne opened her eyes. She was indeed floating, and it was the most wonderful feeling.

Later, as they were drying off on the beach, Ozanne thanked Yvain.

'Thanks for what?' he said.

'For opening my eyes to a wonderful world I never knew existed.'

'It's a world of freedom.'

'You're so right, Yvain. If I hadn't met you, I would never have experienced half of what this life has to offer.'

'It's freedom from convention, from religion, from other people's narrow judgements.'

Yvain picked her up by the waist and twirled her around. They fell into the soft sand and kissed.

'This is what heaven must be like,' Ozanne said as she lay on her back, her eyes closed.

'Do Jews believe in heaven?'

'They do but I am no longer a Jew. I am a member of the human race.'

CHAPTER
FORTY-FIVE

'When will it ever end?' Bonanfaunt cried.

'What now, Uncle Bon?' Pucelle replied, using the affectionate diminutive she had for him.

Pucelle preferred to spend time with her uncle than her own father. Bonanfaunt was wise and knowledgeable, and she knew if she worked hard and studied the world of finance she could do well. Maybe as well as her grandmother although she didn't have the steely nature of Mirabelle. In that respect Mirabelle was unique.

'The king has levied another tallage.'

'What for this time?'

'His damn sister.'

'Who is his sister and why does he want money for her?'

'She's marrying the king of Scotland and we've been asked to contribute by way of an *auxilium*.'

'Uncle Bon, you know I don't know Latin. Speak in plain terms so I can understand you and who is "she"?'

'Sorry, Pucelle, I forget – but it's a language you need to learn if you're going to follow in *Safta*'s footsteps.'

'I'm trying, Uncle.'

'Good. An *auxilium* is an aid or a tribute and *she* is the king's sister Joan, and they want us to pay tribute to the marriage by bleeding us for more money. We'll have nothing left.'

'Ah,' said Pucelle. 'They're getting crafty by calling it an aid rather than a tallage.'

'People are struggling already. I thought we might fare better under the boy king, but it seems the barons have the real power, and you know they don't like the way we are bolstering the king's coffers but that's not our fault. That's just the way the law is.'

'And we don't make the laws,' Pucelle said.

'No, we most certainly do not.'

'If we were allowed to own land would that help?'

'I doubt it.'

'So if you lend money to a baron or a lord or suchlike and they die before they've paid back the loan, what happens?'

'Because we're not allowed to own land – because we're debarred from performing the ceremonial oaths of homage and fealty, even though we've lived here for years – then the debtor's land reverts to their master and that is–'

'The king,' interrupted Pucelle.

'So you do listen sometimes,' Bonanfaunt said.

Pucelle grinned at her uncle. 'So the king is amassing huge tracts of land, and we are inadvertently helping him and that's why the barons don't like us.'

'Yes.'

'Well, nobody likes us, really,' said Pucelle. 'When are we expected to pay and how much do they want?'

'It's set to be collected on the vigil of St John and they want one thousand marks from us.'

'Not just the Gloucester Jews?'

'No, from all of us.'

'When is that due?'

'The twenty-third day of June this year. Four days after the actual wedding.'

'So we don't have long.'

'You're right and there's no way of avoiding it. We'll just have to pay it. They are saying we will have to make prompt payment and any Jew who fails to clear his debt by that date will be mulcted in twice the sum. *Debet duplum*.'

'*Debet duplum?*' Pucelle repeated, not understanding the words.

'It means double the amount. We would have to pay double what they say.'

'That's harsh.'

Bonanfaunt shrugged his shoulders. 'What else did you expect?' he said.

Bonanfaunt sat down at the counting desk. A pile of parchment bonds lay on its surface. He busied himself by sifting through them. Then he picked up his quill and began making calculations.

'How is Mirabelle today?' he asked, almost as an afterthought.

'She's upstairs in her bedroom, resting.'

'I don't know what we'll do when she goes,' he said.

'Don't say that,' Pucelle said.

Mirabelle could be difficult at times but when it came to her family, she was a rock. The family wouldn't be the same without her.

'We have to face it, Pucelle. She's old and getting frailer by the day. She isn't going to last forever.'

'Her mind is still sharp.'

'I know it is, as is her tongue.'

They laughed.

'So, I've calculated our family's contribution to this outrageous *auxilium* is going to be in the region of five marks.'

'And ten marks if we don't pay on time.'

'Exactly. You're learning.'

'I have a good teacher. Five marks and we don't even get to go to the wedding,' Pucelle said in jest.

'Why would you want to? It's in Scotland.'

FORTY-SIX

After landing in Messina and briefly stopping at Heraklion in Crete, the tarida they were sailing on headed towards the island of Cyprus.

'So Crete is governed by the Venetians who are Italian not Greek, and Sicily was governed by the king of Sicily who is German and at the same time the Holy Roman Emperor and that's Italian...' mused Ozanne.

'Correct,' said Guillaume.

'It's all very confusing,' Ozanne said, peering over the side of the prow at the port of Amathus near Lemesos in Cyprus.

Eager to know the history of this new island, Ozanne questioned Guillaume who had proved to be a font of knowledge.

'So who governs Cyprus?'

'Cyprus is a fascinating kingdom. It's been in the hands of the Arab Muslims, the sultans of Egypt, the Knights Templar–'

'I went to the marshal's funeral at the Templar Church in London.'

'That's where we met,' said Yvain, putting his arm around Ozanne's waist.

'That fateful day,' said Guillaume, raising his eyes to the azure sky.

Ozanne giggled and hugged Yvain. Yvain released his grip on Ozanne and picked up his gittern. He began to strum a melody. Guillaume scratched at his beard and then recited a poem:

> *'That fateful day,*
> *'Who could say...'*

Guillaume halted, searching for words.

> *'To love the fairest one on earth,*
> *'The lady of most worth,*
> *'And this he'll do his whole life long,*
> *'For he's in love with one so young.'*

Ozanne squealed with delight. Yvain plucked at his gittern in a frenzied tone. Ozanne wanted to join this impromptu performance. Could she come up with a few lines of poetry to match the impresarios before her?

> *'And she hath love for no other...'*

Ozanne stopped.

'Why have you stopped?' Yvain asked her.

'I feel foolish. You're so much better at this than me.'

'Nonsense,' said Guillaume. 'Come, Yvain, play a melody so that our fair Ozanne can recite something.'

Ozanne listened to the rhythm of the melody and hummed along to it then the words popped into her head:

'Ah, sweet love, all my desire,
'In your soul flares subtle fire,
'I'll long for you forever,
'No other gives me pleasure,
'No other love do I profess,
'To soothe my soul I doth confess.'

Yvain stopped playing. He put down his gittern and put his hands together and clapped enthusiastically. Guillaume joined in and gave out a whoop of congratulations.

'That was inspirational, Ozanne. From the heart,' Guillaume said, patting his hand on his chest.

Yvain walked towards Ozanne. He wrapped his arms around her shoulders and held on tight. *'Je t'aime,'* he whispered.

Guillaume coughed pointedly.

'Excuse us, my friend, but I cannot keep my hands off this woman. She is all that I desire in this life. I would die for her,' said Yvain, still hugging Ozanne.

'Let's hope that won't be necessary,' Guillaume quipped.

FORTY-SEVEN

Their stay at the near deserted port of Amathus was only a matter of days. Ozanne watched as sacks of carob pods were loaded onto the ship. A strange-looking pod, a rich deep brown in colour that the locals called black gold. She couldn't wait to taste the sugary syrup that they made from soaking them. Henri the cook had promised to show her how to prepare them. Fresh vegetables of all shapes and sizes and citrus fruits followed along with amphoras filled with oil made from olives grown on the island. Sacks of wheat and barley for bread-making. Ozanne thought of the feast she and Henri would cook that night.

'When will we reach Acre?' Ozanne asked Henri as she was kneading fresh dough later in the galley.

'We are not going to Acre.'

'We're not? Where then?'

'We are sailing to the port of Damietta.'

'Where's that?'

'In Egypt at the mouth of the river Nile.'

'Egypt? That's not the Holy Land,' she said, wiping the flour from her hands. 'I need to speak to Yvain. I'll be right back.'

Ozanne found Yvain lounging with Guillaume on deck. She could not see a speck of land in any direction she turned. They were in the middle of the ocean.

'Did you know we weren't going to Acre?' she asked Yvain.

Yvain straightened up. 'I only found out once we'd set sail.'

'Why didn't you tell me?' Ozanne could feel the tears stinging. Was this going to be their first argument? Shattering her blissful paradise. Shattering her trust in him.

Yvain stood up and put his arm around her shoulder. 'I didn't know if I should say anything. I knew you'd be upset.'

'Why are we going to Damietta? What's there?'

Guillaume spoke: 'Our livelihood.'

Ozanne pulled away from Yvain. 'Henri said Damietta was in Egypt. How far is that from Jerusalem?'

Guillaume rubbed his chin. 'Not sure.'

Ozanne stood with her hands on her hips. Yvain and Guillaume could not lock eyes with her.

'Once we land in Damietta are we going to travel on to Jerusalem?'

'We need to stay in Damietta. That's where the Crusaders are.'

'But I don't understand–'

'The Holy Roman Empire in its wisdom has decided the best way to capture the Holy Land is by conquering Egypt and the sultan ruler Al-Kamil, and then the Holy Land.'

Yvain took hold of Ozanne's hands. 'We have to earn a living and that means going where the Crusaders go.'

'Did you know all along we weren't sailing to the Holy Land?'

Yvain didn't answer her straight away. She pulled her hands away from his and stormed off. 'Ozanne, please listen to me,' Yvain cried, running after her.

Ozanne reached their cabin, opened the door and almost

slammed it in Yvain's face. She flung herself on top of the bed and sobbed. A well of sadness and regret took hold of her and she could not stop. She missed her family, she missed England, she even missed the weather, she missed dry land, she missed kosher food. The only thing keeping her happy was Yvain and without him she had nobody. She would be alone.

Utterly alone.

At each thought she howled like a fox in the night.

If she couldn't trust Yvain, who could she trust? If he could not be honest with her about the trip what else could he not be honest about? Her father and mother had warned her about troubadours and their reputation. It was the first time she had questioned her love for him.

Was this the end?

After a few minutes the cabin door opened, and Yvain crept towards her. He wrapped her in his arms and rocked her, telling her all the while that everything would be all right.

'I don't know what's up with me. I don't know why I'm so upset.'

Yvain said nothing but carried on rocking her.

'I need to trust you, Yvain, you're all I've got in this world. I gave up my family, my home for you.'

'You're taking this the wrong way. I haven't been dishonest. I promise I only knew this morning that we weren't sailing to the Holy Land. We can still go. It's just not going to be straight away. We must make some money, or we won't survive out here.'

Ozanne's sobs gradually turned to sniffs. 'You promise?'

Yvain crossed his chest like a Christian. 'I promise.'

She threw her arms around him. 'I don't ever want to fall out with you again.'

'We didn't fall out. It was a misunderstanding, that's all.'

They kissed with renewed passion and spent the rest of the afternoon in bed.

FORTY-EIGHT

I t took only a few days to sail to Damietta. As they approached the harbour Ozanne could see a fleet of ships docked side by side displaying the distinctive red cross of the Crusaders. Attached to the forecastle were several swallow-tailed gonfanon baucents in black and white. They were like a heraldic flag with streamers attached, suspended from a crossbar.

'Why are they black and white and not red and white?' Ozanne asked Guillaume.

'It's meant to demonstrate on the one hand their ferocity towards their enemies and on the other their kindness towards their friends.'

'They don't look like kind people to me,' she said. 'They look ferocious.'

'Wait till you see them up close,' Guillaume said, grinning.

Venetian trading cogs and taridas were docked separately. Ozanne could see lots of activity onboard although from that distance they looked like insects crawling over the deck. The city had three rings of formidable fortifications. A tall stone tower by the mouth of the river dominated the skyline along with many smaller towers. When she got closer, she could see that the smaller towers had been built between the first and the second walls and within that a moat had been dug.

Ozanne could not wait to reach dry land. She had been at sea almost continuously since she left England, stopping only to swap ships or load supplies. She longed to eat a freshly cooked meal and sit at a table that didn't move.

'Where will we stay when we get there?'

'Guillaume has friends here already. They will have found somewhere. We can stay with them.'

Ozanne packed her few belongings, said goodbye to Henri, and walked down the gangplank holding Yvain's hand. Guillaume walked ahead of them, eager to meet his comrades. Ozanne's immediate concern was where she would sleep that night. She was sure she would settle once she knew they were not sleeping on the street.

The port was bustling with activity. Horses from the ship were being led to their stables. Once or twice Ozanne had to step over steaming dollops of horse dung. A group of Knights Templar came marching towards her. They wore white loose-flowing mantles over their chainmail armour displaying the red Crusader cross along with a neck coif made of mail. A cord was tied around their waists.

Whispering to Yvain, Ozanne asked about the uniform.

'They are a strict order of warring Christians, bound by a strict code of conduct. That cord around their waist signifies their vow of chastity. They're a strange bunch of men.'

'So pleased you're not caught up in all that,' Ozanne said, giggling.

Each Templar carried a large almond-shaped shield made of wood and covered in painted leather with the red cross. Ozanne moved out of the way to let them pass. The knight leading the group held a standard of two colours called a balzaus. The sight of them in full regalia and marching with dogged determination filled her with apprehension. There was no denying the fact that she was in the middle of a conflict. Christian pilgrims displaying the Crusader cross stitched on to their tunics in silk and gold thread followed the marching army.

Men wearing cloths twined around their heads with swarthy, lined faces and lecherous looks thrust trinkets and blankets and all manner of things in front of her to buy. Yvain pushed them away, but they persisted. Ozanne held on to Yvain tighter, squirming as she was assaulted by every street trader they passed. Once away from the port the traders didn't follow them but returned to their patch to harass some more unsuspecting travellers.

Guillaume walked fast despite the heat, making it hard for Ozanne to keep up. A building in the distance caught her eye. It looked like a church of some sort yet had a dome-shaped roof.

'What's that?' she asked Yvain.

Guillaume turned around. 'It's a mosque. Well, it was a mosque. The Christians have made it their own since the occupation.'

'We'd be better off without religion,' she said to Yvain.

Eventually, after walking through narrow streets of stone houses, Guillaume stopped. 'I think this is it,' he said, looking at a dusty wooden door.

That evening Ozanne ate a fresh meal at a solid table on the rooftop of the house they had been invited to stay in. The company, their friendliness, their willingness to share their food with them had lifted her spirits. Guillaume's friends were poets and jongleurs, all living outside of conformism. It was refreshing and liberating. One of the friends was a woman travelling with her husband and when Ozanne discovered she was also a *trobairitz* she was delighted.

'Introduce me,' she said to Yvain.

Yvain took her hand and led her to where the couple stood.

'*Bonsoir, monsieur, madame.* I am Guillaume's friend, Yvain, and this is my wife, Ozanne. She's also a *trobairitz*.'

The woman who was introduced to Ozanne as Beatriz let out a squeal of delight. She grabbed hold of Ozanne's hands. 'It is so good to meet a fellow *trobairitz*. We are few and far between. I think we will become great friends,' she said, smiling.

Ozanne felt her anxiety from earlier in the day float away. Once they had eaten and the food was cleared away the jongleurs began to sing cansos and tensos. Ozanne was not familiar with the format of the tenso, where one person takes a political stand, and another opposes it. She was fascinated by the debate Guillaume held with his friend. Guillaume began spouting heretical views about the Pope and the Crusades whilst his friend Bertran put forward a counter view.

Guillaume started with an impassioned condemnation of Rome: 'Treacherous Rome, avarice ensnares you. Because you are false and perfidious. Rome, you have your seat.' Guillaume paused and looked around at his audience, then delivered the last line. 'In hell,' he yelled.

Bertran cleared his throat: 'Rome, thou art miraculous. Your piety knows no bounds. Your fight is right. No man can condemn.'

Guillaume laughed and clapped at Bertran's response.

'These Crusader knights are not here for God's purpose but their own. The Pope promises them land and privileges if they fight for him and in return the Pope gets richer by the day. It's all about money. Nothing more,' Guillaume said.

Bertran replied, 'That's a very cynical view of the world, my friend.'

'But true nonetheless.'

'If anyone heard you talk like this,' said Yvain, 'they would drive a stake through your heart.'

'Or burn you publicly to show others not to speak the same heretical filth,' said another, laughing.

'We are among friends,' Guillaume said, holding up his cup of wine to toast those gathered.

'Isn't it a sin in your religion to take a life?' enquired Ozanne.

'Indeed it is,' answered Bertran.

'Then why does the head of your religion, the Pope, sanction such mass killing? Surely that's considered a sin.'

Guillaume sat up straight. 'That's where the hypocrisy comes in. Pope Urban believed the Crusades were God's work. He convinced these Crusaders that they were taking part in a sacred act so granted them remission of the temporal punishment in purgatory, that their sins would be remitted in that hour. An indulgence.'

'And for anyone who refused to go, he threatened them with excommunication,' Yvain said.

'Pope Honorius is cut from the same cloth,' said Guillaume.

'Also, don't forget the Pope believes that Jerusalem is sacred because that's where Jesus Christ walked, died and rose after his death,' added Bertran.

'The Jews would have something to say about that,' Ozanne said. 'They don't believe in Jesus as a divine being, an intermediary between us humans and God. They don't believe in him as a messiah, or holy in any way.'

'That's exactly why religion is so divisive. People are driven to fight for a cause that is not worth fighting for,' said Guillaume.

'It's sad that so many people have been killed in the name of religion,' Ozanne said.

Yvain whispered in her ear, 'I'm sleepy. I think I'll go to bed.' He kissed her.

'I think I'll stay a while longer. It's just getting interesting.'

'Are you sure?'

Ozanne nodded. Listening to the music and their political debates mesmerised Ozanne. It was like a drug to her, and she couldn't get enough.

FORTY-NINE

Cardinal Pelagius Galvani was chosen by Pope Honorius III to lead the crusade against Sultan Al-Kamil. When Ozanne first set eyes on the cardinal as he walked along the street surrounded by knights, she noted his large eyes in contrast to his small mouth and that his nose was as pointed as his three-peaked biretta cap. His black cape hung on his small shoulders, and he had a slight stoop. In his right hand was a golden crozier.

'He doesn't look very fearsome,' Ozanne said.

'That's why he never goes anywhere without his faithful Knights Templar.'

'Who are they?' she asked, pointing to some other knights dressed in black mantles emblazoned with a white cross. 'I haven't seen them before.'

'They are the Knights Hospitallers. They used to heal people in hospitals but then decided to take the cross,' Guillaume said.

'They look fierce dressed in black.'

'I wouldn't want to cross them,' Guillaume said, laughing at his own joke.

'Where is he going?'

'To the mosque, or should I say church now they've turned it into a Christian place of worship.'

'Who's that behind him?'

A man of impressive proportions, in his fifties with a long grey beard and thunderous expression stormed behind the cardinal. He was dressed in the traditional white mantle with the red cross. He had an air of superiority about him. He held a poleaxe in his left hand and a band of men followed behind him.

'That's John of Brienne,' said Guillaume. 'He isn't a happy man.'

'Why not?'

'Pelagius was offered a deal by Al-Kamil after the occupation of Damietta and John thought he should take it, but Pelagius declined it.'

'What was he offering?'

'The restoration of all the territory that was once in the kingdom of Israel, including Jerusalem and Bethlehem.'

'Isn't that what these crusades are all about? Taking back the Holy Land from Muslim control?'

'You're right, but Jerusalem, whilst it might be of spiritual importance, isn't of strategic or significant economic importance. Pelagius was of the opinion that the Muslims could easily take control of the Holy Land once Damietta was given up. He thought that if they were to be successful, they needed to capture Egypt. As he was the senior religious leader – the person appointed by the Pope – his word was unchallengeable.'

'It's all so pointless,' said Ozanne with a deep sigh. 'Such loss of lives and for what? A patch of land.'

'You're forgetting, Ozanne, the spoils of war equals great riches, wealth and power.'

'I know. It's like I said. So pointless.'

'That's because you're not a man,' Guillaume said. 'You don't think like a man.'

'If this is what it takes to be a man, I'm glad I'm not one. I'm proud to be a woman.'

She smiled at Yvain, and he smiled back, a proud look on his face.

'I'm also glad you're not a man,' Yvain said.

Ozanne slapped him lightly on the shoulder. 'Oh shush,' she said, blushing.

'I heard that they are planning to set up camp at Fariskur and then advance to the city of Mansurah.'

'Where's that?' asked Ozanne, still staring at the Pope's entourage as they marched past.

'It's south of here on the banks of the Nile.'

The phalanx of Crusaders walked past them, and Ozanne and her friends carried on to the port where they hoped to buy some fresh fish and get a drink at one of the many hostelries. Ozanne loved sitting outside with a cool glass of mint tea watching the world go by. It was one of her favourite times of the day.

Beatriz and Bertran were already sitting at a table. She gave Beatriz a kiss on both cheeks, adopting the French way of greeting people.

'We're going to Fariskur to follow the Crusaders.'

'When?' asked Guillaume.

'Tomorrow. They're marching to Mansurah to defeat Al-Kamil's men.'

'You better stay here, Ozanne. It's not safe for you to come with us,' said Yvain.

'Are you going, Beatriz?' she asked her friend.

'I'm staying here. I have no intention of being anywhere near the enemy.'

'I must confess I'm not feeling too well this morning,' said Ozanne.

'I'll look after you,' Beatriz said, giving Ozanne's hand a friendly squeeze.

~

Early the next morning Ozanne woke up and was immediately sick. Yvain fussed over her and made her go back to bed.

'I'll be fine. I think it must be something I ate. Beatriz is here. We're going swimming later.'

Yvain hugged her and held on tight. 'It's nice you've found a friend.'

'She's so sweet. Honestly, I'll be fine. Come back to me soon,' she said, kissing him languorously.

Once they were gone, she joined Beatriz at a nearby beach for a swim. The heat was searing and the only way she could cool down was to immerse herself in the blue waters of the sea. As she floated idly on the surface of the water, she realised her feelings of being sick had disappeared. She righted herself in the water and put her feet on the seabed below. She remembered her mother telling her how she had felt tired and was sick in the morning when she was carrying Tzuri. Then she realised her monthly bleed had not come around for some weeks. Could she be with child? They had done it often enough. It was entirely possible.

Beatriz, who was swimming out to sea, stopped and turned around. Treading water, she shouted across to Ozanne, 'Everything all right?'

'Perfect,' replied Ozanne.

'I thought for a moment you might have been stung.'

'Well, in a way I have,' Ozanne shouted back, giggling.

Beatriz swam towards her. 'You've been stung?' she said, concerned.

'You could say that. I'm with child.'

Beatriz laughed, then hugged Ozanne. 'Stung by your husband. There must be a poem I could write about that. I shall have to think on it.'

Ozanne beamed with happiness at the thought of having Yvain's child. *Wait till he finds out*, she thought. *He'll be thrilled.*

'Yvain will be so happy. He'll be able to teach him to play the gittern and to swim. I would teach him to read and to be a good person and to play the kinnor and of course, "he" could be a "she". No problem.' Ozanne laughed. 'We will bring the child up the same way whether it's a boy or a girl.'

CHAPTER
FIFTY

The first night without Ozanne was hard. Yvain could not sleep and so had taken to drinking before he lay down for the night. They had reached Sharamsah, a city in between Fariskur and Mansurah. After the capture of Damietta in 1219, Al-Kamil had moved his stronghold to the city of Mansurah. The cardinal hoped to capture the city and from there go onwards to Cairo to then capture the ultimate prize of Jerusalem.

Sharamsah was taken with little effort on the part of the Crusaders. The Knights Templar were first into battle chanting their war cry: a psalm. Yvain thought it incongruous to mix singing with bloodshed.

Non nobis, Domine. Not unto us, O Lord.

Sed nomine. But to your name.

Tuo da gloriam. May all the glory be.

They were chanting it like monks would in an abbey except they were going into battle. It did seem hypocritical. By the time they occupied Sharamsah food supplies were low. The Crusaders were becoming restless. Yvain felt uneasy.

'Some of the Crusaders have already left for Damietta. They can't do that, can they?' Yvain asked Guillaume.

'The Knights Hospitaller and the Templars can't but the others can. That's what they're saying at the camp.'

Guillaume had gone over to the tented camp earlier in the day to see one of the Knights Hospitaller to ask for some medicine for a pain he was feeling in his chest. He blamed it on the spicy food he had to eat.

'They're saying the sultan has blockaded the canal and the river so Cardinal Pelagius can't reach Damietta to restock supplies. And as you know, an army marches on its stomach.'

'This doesn't sound good, does it? Perhaps we should retreat with them? I miss Ozanne.'

'Let's see what happens.'

Yvain conceded to Guillaume's higher wisdom. He was usually right about these things. Besides, he needed to work so he could treat Ozanne when he got back.

Another month passed before Cardinal Pelagius finally ordered a retreat to Damietta. Yvain really wanted to get back to Ozanne. He was worried about her, but he couldn't leave on his own. It was too dangerous. When he woke one morning there was an air of desperation in the camp. Al-Kamil's ships were blocking the main route back to Damietta along the canal. Yvain realised they were trapped.

'What are we going to do, Guillaume?'

Guillaume had contacts amongst the knights and frequently went over to their camp to gain information about the campaign.

'Pelagius has ordered a retreat to Damietta. They're leaving under cover of darkness.'

As the day wore on Yvain became increasingly nervous. The Crusaders were drinking heavily, having nothing to do and reluctant to leave the amphoras of wine behind, they set about emptying them down their throats on an empty stomach. Yvain kept his gittern by his side, ready to run at a moment's notice. He kept watch on the Crusader camp as they drank and became more belligerent.

The campfire flames flickered in the darkness making it harder for Yvain to see what was happening. He thought he saw some movement in the bushes beyond the camp. Then moving shadows. He heard the flapping of a flag, the thundering of many feet and then a cry that sent fear deep into Yvain's bones.

'*Allāhu 'akbar.*'

The enemy were upon them.

CHAPTER

FIFTY-ONE

'Where is Yvain?' Ozanne asked as Guillaume came trudging towards her without her husband by his side.

Guillaume stopped before her and hung his head.

'Where's Yvain?' she screamed at him.

'He's dead, Ozanne.'

Ozanne staggered and put her hand to her stomach. 'Dead?'

Guillaume nodded solemnly.

Ozanne heard the word 'dead' but could not take it in at first.

Yvain was dead.

Her protector, lover, husband, her everything was dead. She let out a screech of piercing proportions and fell to the ground, wailing and clutching at her stomach.

Guillaume put his hand on her arm.

'Get off,' she screamed and carried on wailing and sobbing.

Beatriz came running towards Ozanne and knelt beside her. 'What is it, *ma amie*?'

'Yvain,' she breathed, barely able to speak through the sobs racking her body. 'He's dead.'

234

Beatriz turned her gaze to Guillaume. He nodded.

'*Mon Dieu*,' she said, putting her arm around Ozanne. 'Calm yourself.' Beatriz helped Ozanne to her feet. 'Come, Ozanne. Come with me.'

Beatriz led Ozanne upstairs into the room she shared with Yvain. Ozanne looked around at the few possessions he had left behind. She picked up his tunic, smelled it then threw herself on the bed screaming his name over and over again.

Ozanne was inconsolable. She sobbed for hours and just when she thought she could cry no more a memory of their life together popped into her mind, and she collapsed again. In her grief she had not asked how Yvain had died. She wasn't entirely sure she wanted to know. The thought distressed her. But she could not shake the question from her thoughts. She had to find out. She couldn't say why but it was important to her. When she had calmed down, she went in search of Guillaume.

'How did he die?'

'Do you really want to know?' Guillaume said.

'Yes.'

'He drowned in the river near Baramun just outside of Sharamsah.'

'How?' she asked. 'He was a good swimmer.'

'We were running away from Al-Kamil's marauders and to escape we had to cross the river. There was a surge of water. In the darkness Yvain lost his footing and was swept away. I never saw him again.'

'Take me there,' Ozanne pleaded.

'I can't. It's too dangerous. The place is surrounded by the Muslim hordes. Besides, I wouldn't know where to look.'

The pain in Ozanne's heart returned. Beatriz said, 'He's

right, Ozanne, it's better we leave here before the Muslim army arrives. They will spare no one, and you know what they do to women...'

Beatriz's words trailed off. The reputation of the Muslims to make slaves of captured women was well known. Ozanne knew her friend was talking sense but to leave without Yvain's body seemed such a betrayal. He was neither Jew nor Christian so he probably wouldn't want the usual religious observances to apply. Still, the thought of leaving Yvain, cold and alone in a land she would, in all likelihood, never return to, dragged her deeper into a dark place.

'The Crusaders are leaving Damietta now. The ships are already setting sail. We must hurry. The sultan has taken control, there are mass executions. We need to leave immediately. If we don't get on a ship today it will be the end of us.'

Ozanne put her hand to her stomach.

'Are you feeling unwell?' Guillaume asked.

'I'm with child,' Ozanne said, the tears welling once more.

Guillaume stared back at Ozanne, non-plussed. '*Un bébé?*'

'*Oui, un bébé,*' Beatriz said, defensively.

'You are having Yvain's child?'

'Yes.'

'Did he know?'

Ozanne burst into tears. 'I didn't get the chance to tell him. I wanted to be certain I was with child.'

'And you are?'

Ozanne nodded.

'*Sacré bleu*! As if I don't have enough to deal with,' Guillaume said.

Ozanne howled at the pain of losing Yvain, at her predicament. Alone in a strange country, the enemy advancing, and with child. The force of her screams shocked Guillaume.

'Guillaume, have some Christian charity,' Beatriz said.

'I'm sorry. I shouldn't have said that.' He put his arms around Ozanne's shoulders and drew her to him. '*Pauvre petite*,' he said in soothing tones, patting her shoulder. '*Pauvre petite*. I will look after you. Come on, gather a few things. We must find a ship that is sailing today.'

It still seemed unreal to Ozanne that Yvain was dead. That she would never see him again or feel his warm body next to hers. She held on to her stomach where the child was growing inside her.

'If it's a boy I'm going to call him Yvain.'

'And if it's a girl?'

'Maybe Douce after my grandmother.'

'*Bon. Allons-y.*'

Drifting like a ship in the doldrums, Ozanne allowed herself to be pulled along by Guillaume and Beatriz, each holding an arm, with Bertran trailing behind holding their meagre belongings, to join a hysterical throng of fleeing pilgrims and Crusaders towards the port of Damietta.

CHAPTER

FIFTY-TWO

E scaping Damietta was harder than Ozanne had expected. Ships were leaving the harbour in their droves, packed full of pilgrims and anyone else who feared the Muslim armies. Word had reached them that the sultan and his men were marching from Mansurah to Damietta to recapture the city.

The port had always been a place of bustling activity but today it was in utter chaos. Wounded Crusaders with bloodied bandages and terrified pilgrims rushed around begging to be allowed on board the ships docked in the harbour. Guillaume, Ozanne, Beatriz and Bertran pushed their way through the frantic crowds hoping to see the tarida they had arrived upon.

'It's gone,' said Guillaume.

'Are you sure?' Bertran said.

'Positive.'

'What are we going to do now?' asked Beatriz, her voice rising in panic.

Guillaume looked at Ozanne. She was staring out to sea, oblivious of her surroundings and their predicament.

'I don't know but we have to get Ozanne out of here.'

Guillaume set down his few belongings. 'Stay here. I'll see if I can get us passage on another ship.'

Everyone nodded. Beatriz led Ozanne to the edge of the wharf and told her to sit down. Ozanne obeyed her and swung her legs over the side and stared into the clear water below.

'What are we going to do if Guillaume has no luck? We can't stay here. We'd be sitting targets for the enemy. I heard they rape women and then cut their bellies in half,' said Beatriz.

'No more savage than what the Crusaders do to them,' said Bertran. 'Do you think you should be saying that sort of thing in front of Ozanne?'

'I don't think she can hear me.'

The midday sun blazed down on them like hot coals. There was no shade to be had on the wharf and all they could do was wait for the return of Guillaume. It was hours before they saw him hurrying towards them.

'I've found a ship's captain who's prepared to take us but it's going to cost. Does anyone have any money?'

Guillaume was met with blank faces. Ozanne continued to swing her legs against the wharf wall.

'Ozanne,' Guillaume shouted, 'have you any money?'

Ozanne lifted her head and spoke, her voice seemed far away. 'Cloak.'

'What's she talking about?' Bertran said.

'No idea.'

'Ozanne, do you have any money?'

Ozanne pushed herself backwards on the edge of the wharf and stood up. She walked over to her possessions that were lying on the ground wrapped up in a cloth. She rummaged inside the cloth and brought out a cloak.

'Here,' she said, holding it out.

'She's lost her mind, poor thing,' said Beatriz.

'I haven't lost my mind, I've lost Yvain,' Ozanne said,

seeming to come out of the fug she was in. She felt around the hem of the cloak and finding what she was looking for began to rip it open. 'My father told me to never go anywhere without a secret supply of money for emergencies.'

With that, several coins spilled from the hem onto the cobbles. Her friends gasped in wonder, then they cheered and clapped when they saw how much was there.

'Ozanne, you never fail to amaze me,' said Guillaume.

'That's what Yvain used to say.'

They picked up the coins and counted them.

'Is it enough?' asked Beatriz.

'I think it will do. Come on, we don't have much time.'

They gathered their belongings and trudged back the way they had come, stopping eventually in front of a trade ship.

'Is it going to England?' asked Bertran.

'Not exactly,' said Guillaume, 'but it will get us out of this hellhole.'

CHAPTER

FIFTY-THREE

'You can't think only of yourself, Ozanne. You have to think of the baby.'

Beatriz was right. She had someone else to consider. Yvain's child. By not eating she was damaging the baby. She took the piece of unleavened bread proffered by Beatriz and put it to her lips. The thought of eating it made her gag. She took a nibble despite feeling sick. She chewed it a long time until it felt soggy in her mouth then swallowed hard. Each swallow like eating dry twigs.

'There, that wasn't that bad. Another bite?'

Ozanne did as she was told. Each mouthful was an effort. It was as if her throat had closed up.

'Here, take some wine with it.'

Ozanne took the weak wine from Beatriz's outstretched hand and took a few sips.

'You have to be strong for the baby, Ozanne,' Beatriz said, urging her to eat the final piece of bread.

Ozanne pushed it away. She had had enough.

They were on a trading cog sailing to Crete, similar to the one they had travelled on from Southampton to Bordeaux. This time she was painfully aware of the absence of Yvain. A poignant reminder of the life she might have had with him, the plans they had made, the adventures she was looking forward to. All lost. The best she could hope for now was to reach home and her family and live the rest of her life as a widow and a shunned member of her community for her marriage to Yvain would probably not be recognised as legitimate. She worried how she would fit in once she was home as she was definitely not the same woman – girl – who had left.

She was now sharing a cabin with Beatriz. Guillaume and Bertran were in another. In the evenings her friends would sing and read poetry just as in the old days, but Ozanne had no interest in joining them. The aching void within her heart meant she could not bear to do anything that reminded her of him.

'You should come on deck this evening. The captain says there will be a full moon,' said Beatriz.

'I'll see,' she said listlessly. 'I'm tired. I'm going to lie down.'

It wasn't a lie. Ozanne had no energy or inclination to do anything. Not even eat or drink. The only reason she was surviving was because of Beatriz's good nature and gentle persuasions. All the vibrancy, energy and cheerfulness she was known for had deserted her. Is this how Arlette had felt inside? What trauma in her life would have caused her to be sad all the time? From the outside she had looked fine but inside there was a black shroud wrapped around her, covering her in dragging blackness.

Ozanne spent the day lying on her bed in the cabin listening to the sounds of men working, people chattering and the wind. When the sun set and there was a lull, she lifted herself up on her elbow and swung her legs over the side and sat up. She touched the empty space behind her with the flat of her palm. He was not there. Foolish woman. She stretched her foot out until her toes touched the wooden decking. That's when she felt it. A fluttering in her stomach. Instinctively she placed her hand on her belly. There it was again, like a swirling feeling. She panicked and rushed to find Beatriz.

'I think something's wrong with the baby,' she said.

Beatriz was sitting on the deck with Bertran and Guillaume. They were strumming and humming to some new songs they had composed. She shot up and took Ozanne's arm.

'Why do you say that?'

'I had a strange feeling in my belly, all swirly and fluttery.'

Beatriz had no children of her own, but she was the eldest of ten children and had lived through nine of her mother's pregnancies.

'I think that's what they call the quickening. It's nothing to worry about. It just means the baby's growing bigger and it's starting to move.'

Ozanne beamed at her friend. 'You're sure?'

'I'm positive. It's a good sign.'

Ozanne moved closer to Beatriz and spoke in a low voice. 'I think it was a sign from Yvain.'

Beatriz flashed a concerned look.

'I was thinking about him and then the baby moved.'

Beatriz smiled weakly at her but did not contradict her.

'It sounds crazy, I know, Beatriz, but...' she looked about her at the never-ending horizon, 'I feel so much better. May I join you?'

'*Bien sûr que non, ma amie.* Come sit with us.'

The dark shroud loosened its grip on Ozanne's spirit and for a moment it swept up into the clouds and soared there with the sea birds.

FIFTY-FOUR

O zanne held her baby daughter tight to her chest. She had given birth on the trader cog that had brought her back to England. The journey had taken months. Because they had little money left, they had been forced to disembark at ports along the way so that they could earn money from their performances. Ozanne had been further on in her pregnancy than she had realised and was surprised and terrified when her waters broke. Beatriz held her hand throughout and baby Doucette arrived safely in the middle of the night.

When they reached Bordeaux, Ozanne feared her friends would want to stay in France, but to her surprise they told her they had decided to come with her to England. Ozanne had burst into tears at their kindness. On arrival in Southampton they had thrust some pennies into her hand and bid her farewell and good luck. She had enough to pay a cartman to take her to Gloucester. Her friends went on to London in search of work. It had been an emotional separation, especially from Beatriz whom she'd come to rely on for emotional support.

The cart trundled down South Gate Street. At the gate they

were stopped by the porters, asked their business and allowed into the city. Everything about it was familiar to her. She had been across the world, seen many sights, eaten foreign foods, swam in warm Mediterranean oceans but none of that came close to the overwhelming feeling at the sight of The Cross and the throngs of people on market day. The pain in her heart eased and her insides relaxed at the thought of being home. She looked down at Doucette and wondered how her daughter would be greeted by the family. Or indeed herself. A nervous churning returned to her stomach. As if the child sensed her apprehension, she opened her eyes and howled. She put Doucette to her breast and the child suckled hungrily. The cart stopped at The Cross, and she stepped down into a sea of milling people. She reached for the shawl around her shoulders and pulled it over her head to conceal her face and the babe in her arms. Then she took a deep breath and made her way to the le Riche household and taking a deeper breath she knocked on the door.

As she heard the locks clank and the latch click open, she steeled herself for what was to come. She wished her grandmother Arlette could be the one to answer the door. She had always been the least judgemental of the family and the kindest of souls. The heavy wooden door opened slowly and Douce stood in front of her. She had aged a little and seemed frailer than she last remembered. Ozanne managed a greeting smile. Douce stared through her.

'*Safta*, it's me, Ozanne.'

'*Oy lanu*,' Douce exclaimed, putting her hands to her cheeks. '*Baruch Hashem*.'

She opened her arms wide to embrace Ozanne and at the same time shouted for Baruch. Baruch came running to the door expecting to find a thief.

'What is it, Douce?'

Ozanne smiled as she saw his mouth drop open.

'Is it you?' he said. 'Is it really you?'

'I've come home, *Aba*.'

'Don't stand at the door. Come in,' said Douce, ushering her into the kitchen where her mother, Brunetta, stood by the *foudron*.

She turned towards the commotion and as soon as she set eyes on Ozanne her expression changed. 'You have a child?'

Up to that point no one had noticed the babe in her arms, but Brunetta had spotted her immediately.

'A child!' Douce and Baruch said in unison.

Ozanne peeled back the shawl to reveal Doucette.

'*Oy lanu*,' said Douce, collapsing onto a chair.

'Whose is it?' Brunetta asked, her tone cold.

'Yvain's,' Ozanne replied, stroking her daughter's cheek.

'And where is he?' Brunetta asked, placing her hands firmly on her hips.

'He's dead.'

At that pronouncement Ozanne burst into tears. The baby woke up and bawled with her. Once she started to cry, she couldn't stop. Baruch gave Brunetta a helpless look. Brunetta huffed and strode towards Ozanne.

'Give me the child. You're upsetting the poor thing.'

Through her sobs she corrected her mother. 'Her name is Doucette.'

On hearing the first part of her name Douce stood up and went over to Brunetta who had hold of the baby. She peered into the bundle of cloths. Her face lit up. 'She's beautiful, Ozanne. And you named her after me. Give her to me.'

'Sit down and I'll place her on your lap,' Brunetta told her.

The two women fussed over Doucette, asking the baby if she was hungry or wet as if the child could tell them. Brunetta disappeared to fetch clean clothes. Baruch was ordered to fill a bowl with warm water so they could wash the child. Douce removed the grimy swaddling cloth to check on her grandchild. Doucette wriggled on her lap enjoying the attention. They were all ignoring Ozanne.

Ozanne sat on a chair at the table and tried to stop the sobbing. She had held her grief in for so long and seeing her family and feeling safe for the first time in months, it had all become too much for her. She had been dreading how she would be received having left in such a deceitful way, but apart from the shock of realising she had a child and Brunetta's brusqueness, they seemed pleased to see her.

Once the baby was washed and swaddled, Douce set about feeding her with watered-down frumenty. Ozanne was still breast-feeding as she had no money for food so when she saw Doucette being cared for with such gentleness and love she broke down again. It was only then the adults seemed to acknowledge her existence.

'Brunetta, take Ozanne upstairs and clean her up. She looks like she could do with a wash.'

Ozanne had been wearing the same clothes since she left Damietta. She must have looked a sight. No wonder Douce didn't recognise her at the door.

When she returned to the kitchen, pink with cleanliness and wearing one of her old shift dresses, she sat down at the table. Doucette lay in a bassinet fast asleep, Douce's hand gently rocking the basket. It was almost as if she had never left. Then the questions started. Ozanne answered them all until they asked what had happened to Yvain. The words caught in her throat when she remembered Guillaume returning without him.

Baruch stood up and put his arm around her shoulders. 'Don't upset yourself. What's done is done. The most important thing is you're home now and have brought with you the greatest gift ever.'

Baruch glanced over at the sleeping infant. Ozanne sniffed and gathered herself. A plate of roast chicken and fresh bread was placed before her. The smell of it made her realise how hungry she was and how much she had missed her mother's baking. Baruch set before her a glass of red wine. When she had finished eating and drinking exhaustion overtook her.

Doucette was safe. She was back home. Her struggles were over. The relief she felt was overwhelming.

'I need to lie down. I feel so exhausted I can barely talk.'

'*D'accord, ma petite*,' Baruch said. 'Your bedroom is where you left it.'

She stood up and put her arms around Baruch's neck. '*Merci, Papa.*'

As she left the kitchen Baruch said, 'Welcome home.'

CHAPTER

FIFTY-FIVE

'Can you believe it, that slippery eel Gabbai has been charged with another murder,' Bonanfaunt said. 'It's not long since he was acquitted of poor Solomon's.'

He was sitting on a stool next to his mother's bedside. Mirabelle was now bedridden following a fever. The joints in her hands and feet were terribly swollen, so much so they looked deformed and twisted. She complained constantly of painful aches all over her body and sometimes they were so bad she would scream out in the night saying she was on fire. Bonanfaunt visited her every day for even through her illness she controlled the family business with an iron fist.

'Who has he murdered now?' she asked, sitting up in bed.

'Allegedly, Abraham Folet's sister, Chera.'

Mirabelle sucked her teeth. 'Tsk,' she said. 'If I know Gabbai it won't be a *crime passionnel*. There will be money at the heart of this. That's his only motivation.'

'His nephew, Leo, has been charged with him. They've been arrested and are being held in Bristol Castle.'

'Bristol Castle.' Mirabelle sighed. 'Where your poor father

died.'

'I didn't mean to drag up painful memories, *Ima*.'

'They're old memories now. It won't be long before I join your father.'

'Don't say that. I don't like it when you talk like that.'

Mirabelle's face twisted. Her body stiffened and she stifled a groan.

'Are you in pain, *Ima*?'

'Not too much,' she replied. 'Go on with what you were saying.'

She winced as she spoke and Bonanfaunt could tell his mother was being stoical. A tincture bottle of distilled crocus root sat on the table by the bed. He stood up and took the glass dropper from the phial.

'Take some of this,' he said.

'It tastes vile,' she said, pursing her lips.

Bonanfaunt thrust the dropper in front of her. Like a child she opened her mouth, and he poured several drops onto her tongue.

'I'm not sure any of that works,' she said, after swallowing the tincture with a shake of her head.

'The physician has prescribed it so you must take it. Don't be stubborn.'

'All right, son. I'll be a good girl.' She smiled even though her body was wracked with pain. 'Now carry on with your news.'

'There isn't much more to tell apart from the constable of Bristol has appointed a jury of twelve men. Six Christians and six Jews who will decide his fate.'

'That will cost him dearly if he has to bribe them all. Maybe someone will get to him in the castle before the trial, you never know,' she replied, a cheeky glint of old appearing in her eyes.

'I never liked Gabbai. I always thought he was guilty of

Solomon's death.'

'I think he was responsible but not by his own hand.'

Bonanfaunt's expression changed. 'Isaac wasn't involved was he, *Ima*?'

'Not at all. I think Gabbai bribed the guards to kill him.'

Bonanfaunt let out a sigh of relief. He had always feared his brother-in-law Isaac was involved in some way. His mother was being uncharacteristically open and forthcoming. 'I'm relieved to hear that, *Ima*.'

'You must keep me informed about Gabbai's case. He may not be so lucky this time around.'

Mirabelle laced her gnarled hands together. 'I want you to promise me something, Bonanfaunt.'

'Yes, what is it?' he replied.

'You must be strong. I've made this family great with the help of your father in small part. You must promise me you'll keep the family's fortunes. Remember all I've taught you.'

Bonanfaunt opened his mouth to speak. Mirabelle silenced him with a sweep of her hand.

'We are a strong family. Three generations working together forming an association, a financial institution which in time will grow, become powerful and wealthy. It's been my life's mission. It's all I've ever strove to achieve. Everything I've ever done, every deceit, every douceur, I have done to protect this family.'

'I know, *Ima*. I know how much you've sacrificed for us.'

'I know you don't like some of my methods, but they have worked and kept us wealthy and powerful. Being completely honest in business doesn't always work. Sometimes you have to be crafty, use artifice–'

'Be dishonest, you mean, *Ima*.'

She waved her hand again dismissively. 'Call it what you will. It amounts to the same thing.'

CHAPTER
FIFTY-SIX

Ozanne held Doucette's hand as they walked towards the market. She had been back in Gloucester for almost two years, and it was as if she had never left. Her family doted on Doucette and the shame she thought they would punish her for never materialised. She thought about Yvain every day and sometimes spoke to him as if he were alive and standing next to her. She would tell him about Doucette's progress. Her first steps. Her first words. How foolish she had been, convincing herself that she never wanted children. Motherhood suited her and with her music Ozanne was as content as she had ever been in her life.

Spring had arrived after a long and cold winter. The early spring sunshine warmed her back as she made her way slowly to The Cross. The market was busier than she had ever seen it and there seemed to be a buzz in the air. As she turned the corner into North Gate Street, she saw what all the hubbub was for. Street musicians and jongleurs were performing. Her heart ached at the memories the sight evoked. Just as she thought she was getting over the death of Yvain.

She stood for a while listening to the music and explaining

to Doucette the scene before them. She thought for a moment she saw Guillaume, but it was only someone who looked like him. She started to walk away when a stooped young man with a limp caught her eye. There was something familiar about him that made her think she knew him. He turned to face her as if he could feel her stare upon him. His face was terribly scarred, and he had an eye missing, but there was no doubting it.

It was Yvain.

'Yvain,' she screamed, picking up Doucette and running towards him.

The man pulled his cap to one side to cover the disfigured part of his face and turned his back on her, picking up speed, his limp even more pronounced.

'Yvain,' she shouted louder, her voice frantic.

The man did not turn. Was she mistaken? Was it her mind playing tricks on her again, wanting her to see Yvain in every stranger she saw? The man continued to pick up speed. Doucette began to whinge, sensing something wasn't right with her mother. Ozanne shushed her as she bounced her on her hip whilst struggling through the crowds.

At last Ozanne saw him turn a corner. She rushed after him, holding Doucette tightly. When she finally reached him, she was out of breath. She called his name again, but he did not turn around or stop. She grabbed for his arm and pulled hard.

'No!' he shouted, shielding his face.

'Yvain, it *is* you. I thought you were dead.'

The man looked at her, his expression full of pain. 'I should be to you,' he said, a tear emerging from the closed socket where his eye should be.

'Yvain, I can't believe it. You're alive.'

She popped Doucette on the ground and told her to go and play in the wildflower meadow in front of them, then without thinking threw her arms around him and held on tight. She felt his body stiffen and then he peeled her arms from around his neck.

'What's the matter, Yvain? It's Ozanne.'

Yvain covered his face with his hands and turned his blind side away from her. Ozanne pulled his hand away.

'Look at me,' she said. 'I haven't changed. I'm the same old Ozanne.'

'But I am not the same,' he said, avoiding her gaze.

'I have thought of you every day. I have talked to you every day as if you were still alive, and you are. Why didn't you come looking for me?'

He put his outstretched palms to his face. 'I didn't think you'd want anything to do with me looking like this.'

'Why wouldn't I? You're my husband. Please, Yvain, don't push me away. Let's go somewhere to talk.'

She took his hand and led him to a quiet area of the meadow where she knew Doucette would be safe to run around and give them some space to talk. As she walked, her head was a cauldron of emotions. Her heart was bursting with happiness at knowing Yvain was alive but there was something wrong with him.

'Guillaume said you drowned in the river.'

'I nearly did. The current was stronger than I thought, and I lost my footing. It swept me several miles downstream until I was able to swim to the shore. That's when I was captured. They could see I wasn't a soldier because I wasn't wearing battle dress but still, they took me prisoner.'

'Where did they take you?'

'Some prison south of Mansurah. I had no idea where I was, and I couldn't speak the language. It was hard.'

'What did they do to you, Yvain?' she asked.

Ozanne was not as naïve as she used to be. Looking at him

and his disfigurements it was obvious he had endured hardships which had affected him deeply.

'They tortured me.'

His voice cracked and he put his head in his hands and began to cry.

Ozanne was overwhelmed with love for him. Like a bird with a broken wing, she would nurse him to health. She would never let him go. Keeping an eye on Doucette, who was happily plucking tufts of grass from the ground, she put her arms around Yvain and held him tightly until his sobs started to subside.

'Did they do anything else?'

Yvain's body stiffened again, his sobs grew louder and his whole body shook.

'I'm not going to let you go, Yvain. You must come home with me. Now.'

'I can't.'

'You can. You think because you're changed, I won't love you?'

Yvain regained some composure and still hugging her tight he said, 'All I could think of was you and escaping that hellhole of a gaol to be with you. But as the months turned into years, and the torture they exacted upon me for attempting to escape or refusing to do what they wanted of me grew more savage I thought less of myself, and then when they burned my eye out, I lost all hope of ever seeing you again. I didn't think you'd want anything to do with me.'

'You foolish man,' she said, stroking his scarred cheek.

'Once I'd escaped and landed in England, I wanted to see you just one more time without you knowing. Just to gaze upon your heavenly face. That was all. I didn't think you'd recognise me.'

Ozanne released him from her grip. He had been through

such a terrible ordeal she couldn't begin to contemplate. She had to make him whole again.

'Yvain, you haven't met your daughter yet.'

'I have a daughter?'

He looked over at Doucette, her dark ringlets swaying from side to side as she ran in the long grass chasing butterflies.

'Whose else would it be?'

'I thought maybe you had married...'

'I called her Doucette after my great-grandmother. I hope you don't mind.'

Yvain stared at her in disbelief.

'I know you think I'm crazy, but I believe I drew you back to me.'

'I did travel here against all my better judgement.'

'I used to say things to Beatriz about you being near or when certain things happened, I'd say "it's a sign from Yvain". She thought me quite mad.'

'You must be mad to want me back looking like this,' he said, hanging his head in shame.

Ozanne tipped his chin upwards with her fingertips and made a point of studying his features. He had been brutalised. His face was more scarred than her father's, but he was still her Yvain.

'Come home and meet my family.'

CHAPTER

FIFTY-SEVEN

'The world is changing, *Ima*. The king is getting wise to the practice of coin and forgery,' said Bonanfaunt.

His mother lay in bed, twisted and deformed from her painful illness. She rarely left her room, finding it hard to walk. Her feet and toes were deformed as were her hands. Whatever ailed her was cruel and ceaseless, yet it had not diminished her appetite for local gossip and intrigue.

'Talking of criminals, how is my adversary doing? Is he still in gaol?'

Mirabelle was referring to Abraham of Warwick. He had been arrested for forgery and was being held in the castle. For the first time, Mirabelle saw Abraham of Warwick's family and not the le Riches as the threat to her family's position as leaders of the community. For the last few years the Warwick family had been consolidating their position in the city, seeking out lucrative money loans and increasing their wealth.

'He's going before a jury this afternoon.'

'Who's on the jury?'

Bonanfaunt listed the members. Few were from Gloucester.

'The sheriff doesn't trust anyone local by the looks of it.'

'They're saying he's heading for the Tower this time to make an example of him. The king is angry at the Jews.'

'It's because of him that we Jews have to resort to this sort of deceit. He's bleeding us dry. They all are. It won't change after I'm gone. They'll still hate us.' Mirabelle winced with the pain.

'It doesn't do you any good to get excited, *Ima*. You should relax.'

'Are you going to the trial?'

'The whole community is going.'

'I wish I could be there.'

'Don't worry, I'll take notes and report back to you.'

'You should be taking notes to learn how he did it.'

'Do you want me to be imprisoned in the Tower or worse still, hanged?'

'That wouldn't happen if you were careful.'

'We've had this conversation before, you won't change my mind. I do things differently. I told you the world is changing. We must change with it.'

Mirabelle huffed and crossed her wizened arms. Bonanfaunt stood up and bent to plant a tender kiss on his mother's forehead.

'I'll see you later. I must go or I'll be late for the trial.'

'I shall miss all this skulduggery when I'm gone,' she said, listlessly.

That afternoon Bonanfaunt attended Abraham's trial. As he listened to the evidence presented, his mother's words echoed in his head. Was she right? That for business to be successful you had to adopt corrupt means? He had always been at odds with his mother over some of her more dubious business dealings. He listened and took notes as Sheriff Musard presided.

Abraham sat in the dock looking shamefaced. He had lost weight since his confinement, and he had an air of defeat about him. Mirabelle would find solace in his downfall, but Bonanfaunt could only feel sorrow for the man. Each and every Jew had suffered at the hands of the king who consistently put pressure on them to contribute more and more to the numerous tallages. There had been one in 1221, another in 1223 and the most recent in 1226. They were becoming more oppressive in terms of the amounts and at the same time the king was making it difficult for Jews to carry on in any other occupations to support their families. From her sickbed his mother had formed a consortium with Aaron le Blund and other leaders of the London community, along with David of Oxford, to stave off what seemed like the increasingly inevitable demise of moneylending. If the king banned them from moneylending it would be the end of the Jewish communities across England.

The sheriff was questioning Abbot Bredon. Sheriff Musard sat upon a raised dais flanked on both sides by his advisors. He had gained a considerable amount of weight, and his cheeks were flushed. He did not look a well man.

The elderly Abbot Blunt had died some years previous, and Thomas Bredon had taken over the reins at the abbey. He was not much younger than Blunt and at times seemed confused and yet when asked about the debt he supposedly owed to Abraham he was most exacting.

The sheriff summoned one of the Christian chirographers to come forward. John Gooseditch, a man with a moon face and bleary eyes, approached holding a parchment bond. These had replaced the old system of tally sticks.

'Can you hold up the bond in your hand, so everyone might see?' the sheriff asked him.

John dutifully held up the piece of parchment by the bottom and top corners. To Bonanfaunt it looked quite grubby.

'Abbot Bredon, do you recognise this bond?'

Abbot Bredon squinted his eyes.

'I do not, sheriff. As you know, before I became the abbot, I was responsible for all of the abbey's financial affairs. This is not my handwriting and furthermore the parchment has been washed.' Abbot Bredon pointed to the said document still upheld in the chirographer's hands. 'That is evident by the white chalk visible in the folds.'

John swivelled on his heels to show everyone the questionable parchment.

'And that's not all. The writing has been blackened with what looks like grease to give it the appearance of being much older than it is.'

Sheriff Musard glared at Abraham then turned back to the abbot.

'So in your most esteemed opinion, Abbot Bredon, this is a forgery.'

'I am certain this is a forgery.'

'Thank you, abbot.'

Abbot Bredon stepped down from the dais and the sheriff addressed Abraham and told him to take the stand.

'Abraham of Warwick, you have heard the testimony of Abbot Bredon. What do you have to say in response?'

Abraham gripped the side of the raised wooden bench to steady himself. The dark grey beneath his eyes and his hollowed-out cheeks gave him a ghoulish appearance. The evidence against him was damning and Bonanfaunt wondered what he would say in his defence to keep him from the gallows.

'I fear this is all a great misunderstanding. Unfortunately, Abbot Blunt is not here to testify or I'm sure he would defend me.'

A trickle of sweat ran down his temple and he began to shake.

'How did this charter come into your possession?'

'I bought the charter from a servant in good faith at the time when all charters were to be enrolled in the *archa*. I know of no fraud then nor now.'

'Can you tell us the name of this servant so that the court can call him to give evidence?'

Abraham's body shook uncontrollably. Bonanfaunt wanted to believe him but this account of how he came by the charter was beyond incredulous. His very demeanour marked him out as guilty. Surely the sheriff had already come to the same opinion.

'I don't remember the servant's name.'

'Does he reside in the city? Do you have his address?'

Abraham shook his head.

Sheriff Musard barked at him, 'Speak your answer for the court.'

'I don't know.'

The sheriff sighed out of frustration. 'Do you have any more to add?' he asked him.

Abraham shook his head, and then lowered it.

'Speak,' the sheriff shouted.

Abraham jumped at the sound of the sheriff's booming voice. 'No, sheriff.'

Sheriff Musard waited until Abraham was seated. He scribbled a few notes with his quill, then put it back into its inkwell and looked directly at Abraham.

'You have produced a charter for a debt of sixteen marks. The charter is obviously forged. You can offer no believable account of how you came into possession of the charter. I find you guilty of forgery and order that you be taken to the Tower of London for sentencing. Take him away.'

Abraham slumped in his chair before the sheriff's men took hold of him by both arms and dragged him out of the hall. He was surely a dead man. Bonanfaunt thought of his mother and how pleased she would be that he was no longer a threat to the family's ascendency.

It was a cruel world.

FIFTY-EIGHT

As Bonanfaunt had predicted, Sheriff Musard died some weeks after the trial of Abraham of Warwick and a new sheriff had been appointed. A man called William de Putot. Not much was known about him other than he was from Bitton, a small town in Gloucestershire, and as yet, he had not made his mark upon the city. Would he be stringent in the application of the king's law, or would he be open to a douceur or two as was Sheriff Musard? It was too early to tell. All Bonanfaunt knew was that England's sheriffs had been ordered by the king to root out coin clipping.

Bonanfaunt picked up one of the pennies he'd collected that morning. The short cross penny had been in circulation since the current king's father, King Henry II, and it had been designed so that it could be easily divided into half pennies. This one looked misshapen. He held it to the light to examine the edges. He couldn't be certain, but it looked like the edge of it had been sheared ever so slightly. *Gezzazah*, the shearing of coins was on the rise. A Jew named Vives and his co-conspirators Isaac and Aaron from Shropshire, along with their wives, had been arrested by the sheriff of their town and sent to the Tower for the crime of coin clipping. They were held in the Tower for months until the justiciar, Stephen de Sedgrave, visited London to hear the case. As far as he knew they were still languishing there.

The only way to check if a coin had been sheared was to weigh it. Bonanfaunt had invested in a set of balance scales for that very purpose. As he was putting the scales together his niece Pucelle walked into the cellar.

'What are you doing?' she said.

'Weighing these pennies.'

'Why?'

'To see if they've been sheared.'

Pucelle walked over to the pile of coins on the table and picked one up. 'It looks all right to me.'

'You need a trained eye to spot it. Here, hold it up to the light.'

She did as he instructed, keen as always to learn as much as she could about the moneylending business.

'See how it's not perfectly rounded?'

'Oh yes. I can see it now. How clever you are, Uncle.' She placed the coin back on the pile, chose another and inspected it in the same way. 'This one looks untouched.'

'The only way to really tell is to weigh them.'

'This pile looks shiny and new. Surely, they're not sheared?'

'They are freshly minted from our young friend Lucas Cornubius.'

'The moneyer who works at the Mint?'

Baruch nodded.

'So they should be the correct weight.'

Bonanfaunt held up the scales. They were made of brass and comprised of a beam, two folding arms and a pointer. Bonanfaunt held the scales by the beam, unfolded the two arms until they locked in alignment. At either end three cords were suspended from each arm. The balance was held by a loop pivoted in the hole at the base of the triangular pointer.

'I'm glad you're here. You can help me.'

'What do you want me to do?' she said, beaming with the privilege of being trusted with her uncle's work.

'If I hold it, can you position those brass pans on the end of the arms?'

'Like this?' she said, picking up a brass pan and balancing it evenly within the cords.

'Now the other one.'

Once the scales were set up Bonanfaunt asked Pucelle to place the newly minted coins onto one pan. The scales immediately fell to one side with the weight.

'Oh, what have I done?' Pucelle exclaimed, worried she'd broken them.

'It's supposed to do that, now place an equal amount of the used coins on the other pan.'

Pucelle did so and the scales tipped the other way. When the pans balanced out Bonanfaunt closed one eye and squinted at the beam on the scales. The weights should have been equal when the pointer aligned with the axis of the suspension loop. It didn't.

'I was right. There is a discrepancy in the weights.'

'What does that mean?'

'It means the money is not lawful and legally I shouldn't pass it on. By law I'm required to disclose forgers of deeds and coin clippers that come to my notice as it's theft. From the king no less. Treasonous.'

'*Oy lanu*,' she said.

'But if I tell the authorities about these coins, they will be taken from me and I will lose the money.'

'Mirabelle wouldn't like that,' Pucelle said, giggling.

'I don't think I dare tell her,' Bonanfaunt said, chuckling with her.

Despite her ill health, Mirabelle still insisted on Bonanfaunt giving her a daily account of the business. He reflected on the conversation he had had with his mother about being honest in financial dealings. Perhaps she had a point.

'What will you do?' Pucelle asked.

'If I'm caught in possession of these, I'll be arrested and sent to the Tower, so I need to get rid of them as quickly as possible.'

'Does everyone do it?'

'Do what?'

'Shear the coin?'

'I don't.'

'I know *you* don't but does everyone else do it?'

'It's hard to tell but I suspect the practice is much wider than anyone knows.'

Bonanfaunt put the sheared coins in a money pouch and locked them in his chest. Pucelle left to go to the market with her husband and her daughter. Bonanfaunt kissed her on the cheek at the bottom of the stairs and said goodbye then climbed the stairs to his mother's bedchamber. It was time for her daily update. He clicked open the latch and went inside. The room was eerily calm. Silent and still. He knew in an instant his mother was dead.

He approached her bedside. With each measured step a stifled sob escaped. He put his hand to his mouth to stop them. By the time he reached her still body the tears were streaming down his face and when he touched her cold cheek, he could not control the sobs wracking his body. He broke down and howled out his pain. His mother had been a difficult woman to love. His father would testify to that if he were still alive. Nevertheless, Bonanfaunt had loved and admired her and now she was dead he felt like he had been set adrift.

Mirabelle had been a visionary, a tour de force. She could be difficult, truculent, but above all she was a fierce protector of her family, fighting tooth and nail and not always fairly.

He was going to miss her.

CHAPTER

FIFTY NINE

When Douce heard of the death of Mirabelle she took to her bed. Had she been waiting for that very event to finally accept her own demise? Her thin body looked even thinner under the covers, hardly making a lump in the bed. Baruch and Brunetta; Rubin; Tzuri and Vernisse and their three children; Ozanne and Yvain with Doucette, who was now ten years old, gathered around her. Douce was delirious, muttering unintelligible words. Baruch held Douce's hand and leaned in close to see if he could make out what she was saying.

'Misabel. The witch. Is she gone?'

Baruch could hardly believe that Douce was still concerned about Mirabelle. Even on her deathbed she was still obsessed with the loathsome woman. It was as if she had been determined to win the last and ultimate battle.

'Don't concern yourself about her. She's dead.'

'Dead?'

'Yes, *Safta*. She's dead.'

A smile appeared upon Douce's lined face. Her hand went to her amulet, still around her wrinkled neck. She touched it and as if she had been released from a spell her sullen features relaxed, her complexion glowed with the radiance of a newborn baby. The rapture was short-lived. Douce tossed her head from side to side, muttering. He leaned in closer.

'I'm sorry, Baruch.'

'Sorry for what, *Safta*?'

'Moses. Is that you, Moses? *Mon amour*.'

'This is Baruch, *Safta*.'

Douce shut her eyes tight and became agitated. 'Why did you do it?'

'Do what, *Safta*?' She was making no sense at all, and Baruch feared she was nearing the end.

'A sin above sins.'

'Who has sinned?'

'Abraham. You were wicked. Not the children.'

Baruch flashed a look of horror towards Brunetta. Then he looked at Tzuri and Ozanne. Had they understood what Douce was about to say? That Abraham had tried to take them with him. How would they ever find peace if they knew that? Fearful that in her hysteria she was going to divulge a family secret that should never be spoken of, he reminded her of who was in the room, hoping it would bring her back to whatever senses she had left.

'Tzuri and Ozanne are here, *Safta*.' Baruch beckoned them both nearer. 'Say something to her.'

'We're here, *Safta*,' said Ozanne, reaching out to take her hand.

Douce gripped it with vice-like strength for someone so close to the end. 'Ozanne, you've come back. Wicked girl.'

Ozanne tried to pull her hand away, but Douce grasped it so tightly she had to prise it off.

'I wasn't expecting that,' she whispered to Tzuri.

'Take no heed,' said Brunetta. 'She doesn't know what she's saying. She's delirious.'

Douce tossed her head this way and that, muttering to herself until a moment of clarity fell upon her. Her eyes opened wide.

'Brito? Is that you? Be gone,' she cried, holding her thin arms in front of her face as if protecting herself from an unseen malevolent force.

It was faint but Baruch felt sure Douce had uttered his father's name. A name he had never heard spoken in the le Riche household. Why was Douce remembering him of all people? Why not mention Moses's name? He shot a panicked look at Brunetta. Had she heard it too?

'What about Brito?' Baruch asked.

'She doesn't know what she's saying,' said Brunetta.

'I think she does,' said Baruch.

'Brito. Is he here?' breathed Douce, her voice barely audible.

'Who is Brito?' asked Ozanne.

'No one,' snapped Brunetta.

'What do you want with Brito, *Safta*?' asked Baruch.

'His head. I see his head. On the virgin snow.'

'What are you talking about, *Safta*?'

Baruch wiped the beads of sweat from Douce's forehead with a damp cloth. She was the closest person to him now that Arlette had died. His heart ached with the pain of loss, knowing his grandmother had not long on this earth. He loved Douce, who had been like a mother to him. He would miss the tenderness his mother and Douce had shown towards him. It was that tenderness that had brought out the best in him.

'I told Moses we would take it to our graves,' Douce said. She opened her eyes wide and with great clarity spoke again. 'I have lived my life with the guilt of it but with no regret. Oh no, no regret.' She momentarily lapsed into her native tongue once more. '*Pas de tout. Je ne regrette rien.*'

'I don't understand,' said Baruch.

Douce remained agitated.

'*Nous ne comprenons pas,*' Ozanne said to Douce. 'We don't understand.'

Whilst with Yvain, Ozanne had learnt fluent French and Occitan. Baruch was grateful for her help. Douce had regressed back in time and perhaps by talking to her in her native language she could be coaxed back to the present.

'We had to do it.'

Baruch stood up and placed the cloth on the side table. He cleared his throat. 'I'd like to spend some time with my grandmother. Please leave us.'

Brunetta opened her mouth to protest. Baruch put his finger to his lips to silence her. She nodded at him. 'Come, everyone. Say your goodbyes to Douce and give your father some time alone.'

One by one they came forward, kissed Douce on the forehead, bid her '*adieu*' and left. Brunetta kissed Baruch on the cheek. It did not surprise him that she did not say her goodbyes to Douce. It seemed the lifelong acrimony between the two remained. Would Douce have wanted Brunetta to say her final goodbye? Probably not, thought Baruch.

Once he was alone with Douce, he dipped a clean cloth in the bowl of cool weak wine and put it to her lips. She seemed to revive a little.

'Baruch, my boy,' she said, reaching out her hand to him.

He took hold of her bony fingers. Hearing her call him 'my boy' caused a lump to form in his throat and his eyes began to smart. There had been too much death in the family. Losing Douce, even though she was in her nineties and ready for the end, he would feel the loss as keenly as he had felt his mother's.

'I'm here, *Safta*. What did you want to tell me?'

'Tell you?'

Her eyelids fluttered.

'You were talking about Brito.'

Douce looked about her, terror in her eyes, as if by saying his name he had conjured the presence of Brito into the room.

'We killed him.'

He had always hoped Brito had been killed by one of his many enemies and the conversation he had heard all those years ago on Moses's deathbed had been nothing more than the delirious ramblings of an old man. Never in his wildest dreams had he suspected Douce was involved. He could remember the conversation he'd had afterwards with the marshal like it was yesterday, when he told him his father was dead. At the hand of brigands, he had said. Not at the hands of his own grandparents.

'What are you saying, *Safta*?' he said.

Douce stared back at Baruch. 'We did it for her,' she said.

'For whom?'

'Your mother. He wronged her.'

Douce knew about the rape. And so did Moses. They had kept secrets from everyone in the family for all these years. He had to know it all. Once and for all he had to know the truth. From now on, no more secrets.

'What did you do, *Safta*?' Baruch pressed.

'We killed him,' she said, her expression like a crazed person.

'You and Moses? Did Moses kill my father?'

'Zev was your father,' she said, squeezing his hand until he felt the sharpness of her long nails.

'*Safta*, I've known for a long time that Zev was not my real father and I know that Brito raped my mother and that I was the result of that attack. I've known for years.'

'My dearest boy, your mother loved you just the same.'

'I know. I know that now.'

'And Zev. He loved you in his own way.'

'I know that now too, *Safta*. I didn't for a long time. I know Zev struggled with his love for me. My behaviour towards him didn't help.'

Douce smiled. 'It's hard for any man to accept a child that is not his own, let alone one that has come into this world in such circumstances.'

'I know and I respected Zev for what he did. He loved my mother.'

'No one could have loved your mother more than he. He saved her from ruin.'

'So you also know that Brito was my real father? And you kept that secret for all these years.'

'We did it for Arlette. She went through a lot in her life. What woman could survive such an ordeal?'

Douce was more lucid now. The outpouring of long-held secrets seemed to rouse her from her delirium. He had to ask her again. He had to know everything and Douce was the last person who could reveal it.

'Did Moses kill Brito?'

He thought of how Brito had died. The marshal said whoever killed him cut off his head. Did Moses do that? The thought of his grandfather wielding a sword was almost unthinkable but was it true?

Douce shook her head and a weak smile appeared on her lined lips. 'Moses could not hurt a living creature. He was a kind soul.'

'Who then?'

'We paid the Irish king.'

'Dairmait?'

She nodded. 'We paid him good money.'

273

Brito had been a much-hated man but to hear that Douce and Moses were behind his death was still a shock. He looked at Douce, frail, gentle. It was barely believable. And Moses. A kinder man could not be found. It made sense it was not at their own hand.

'Forgive me, Baruch. He was your father.'

The pain of guilt was etched on Douce's face. She seemed to be reliving the event over again.

'*Safta*,' Baruch said, bringing Douce's hand to his lips. 'Brito was no father of mine. Zev was always my true father.'

Douce slumped back into the covers of the bed, absolved. She closed her eyes.

'*Safta*, do you want to say the *viddui*?'

Douce nodded, her eyes still closed. Baruch walked over to the cupboard and brought out Moses's tattered prayer book. He flicked through the well-thumbed pages until he came to the one he wanted. He recited the prayer.

'I acknowledge before You, Lord my God and the God of my fathers, that my recovery and my death are in Your hands. May it be Your will that You heal me with total recovery, but, if I die, may my death be an atonement for all the errors, iniquities, and wilful sins that I have erred, sinned and transgressed before You, and may You grant my share in the Garden of Eden, and grant me the merit to abide in the World to Come which is vouchsafed for the righteous.'

Douce recited the prayer in unison with Baruch in a soft, barely audible voice: 'Master of the Universe, may it be Your will that my passing be in peace.'

Baruch continued: 'We have transgressed, we have acted perfidiously, we have robbed, we have slandered. We have acted perversely and wickedly, we have wilfully sinned, we have done violence, we have imputed falsely. We have given evil counsel, we have lied, we have scoffed, we have rebelled, we have provoked, we have been disobedient, we have committed iniquity, we have wantonly transgressed, we have oppressed, we have been obstinate. We have committed evil...'

A tear spilled from the corner of Douce's eye. 'May it be Your will that my death be an atonement for all my sins,' she breathed.

Baruch halted for a moment.

'No need of tears, *Safta*. You have led a righteous life. *Hashem* forgives.'

He could tell Douce had not long. Her breathing was shallower.

'...we have acted perniciously, we have acted abominably, we have gone astray, we have led others astray. We have strayed from Your good precepts and ordinances, and it has not profited us. Indeed, You are just in all that has come upon us, for You have acted truthfully, and it is we who have acted wickedly.'

The door of Douce's bedroom opened a crack and Tzuri appeared. Baruch beckoned him to join them. He was followed by the others who quietly and reverently gathered by the bedside.

A sublime smile lit up Douce's face. She looked angelic lying in her sumptuous bed.

'She's happy she's joining Moses at last,' Ozanne said, tears streaming down her pink cheeks.

Moments passed in silence. Douce's breath came and went with longer and longer gaps until she took her last.

CHAPTER

SIXTY

Baruch had always wondered what Douce and Moses had promised to take to their graves and now he knew. He had long suspected it had something to do with Brito's death. Knowing that his grandparents had conspired together to have him killed shocked even him – the battle-weary knight who had seen many a man killed and killed many himself. They had done it for the sake of Arlette. He had never known his father and only knew what he had heard from the old soldier and the marshal, neither of whom had much good to say about him. He imagined Brito to be a difficult man. Perhaps he was pestering Arlette. Persecuting her. They had done it to protect her. Keep her safe.

That he was a brute who had raped Baruch's mother was never in doubt. Ever since he'd heard those words, he had struggled to come to terms with who his father was. Having acknowledged that he had certain traits of his father, he had worked hard in his later years to change, to make amends. To atone.

One good thing had come out of it – he had become a better person. He had become a better son to his mother, a better son to Zev, a loving husband to his wife and a doting father to his children. With Douce's death he finally understood the marshal's words when he said he felt as if he had ventured into a wild sea where sailors found no shore or anchorage. Douce had been the glue keeping the family together. That glue had melted away and cast him adrift. It was up to him, as head of the family, to step into her shoes. Baruch let out a deep sigh and an involuntary tear fell from his eye. In a few short years he had lost his mother, his father, his brother and his grandmother. How could *Hashem* be so cruel? But equally *Hashem* had restored Ozanne to him and blessed him with another grandchild. Her husband, Yvain, had been barely recognisable when he saw him but despite him taking Ozanne from them, the family had welcomed him into their home. Ozanne had never been happier.

He felt an arm across his shoulders. Brunetta had arrived to keep him company. He squeezed her hand.

Acting as *shomerim* until her burial beside Moses in the cemetery his grandfather had built, Baruch reflected on the le Riche dynasty. The family had been part of Gloucester's seminal Jewish community for almost one hundred years. They had suffered greatly. Massacres, rape, imprisonment, untimely deaths, hardship. Yet they had survived. With Douce's death the dynasty had died. There was no one who could step into the place Moses had created.

The great magnate Moses le Riche.

Douce, the matriarch.

The end of an era.

THE END

Also by Christine Jordan

The Hebraica Trilogy

Sacrifice

Massacre

~

Writing as CJ Claxton

MisPer

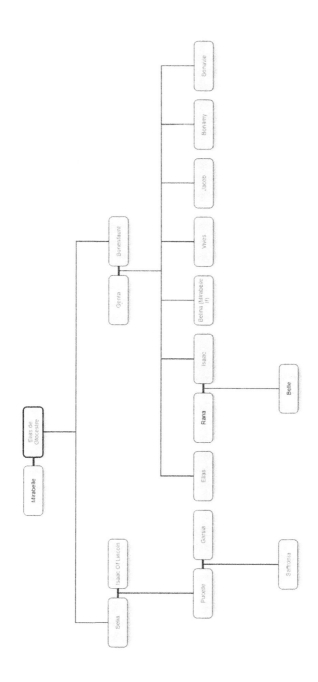

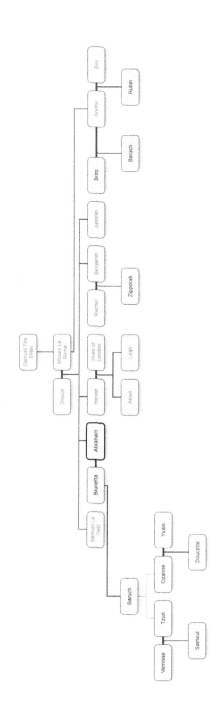

HISTORICAL NOTE

1. For the music at King Henry III's coronation in Gloucester I have relied upon the research of Dr G R Rastall FSA, Emeritus Professor, Leeds University.
2. The crowning of Henry III in Gloucester was one of the very few post-Conquest coronations to take place outside Westminster Abbey. However, as there may have been some irregularities with the 1216 ceremony, Henry III was crowned a second time on 17 May 1220 in Westminster.
3. For the account of the death of Solomon Turbe I have relied loosely upon Jo Hillaby's account in *Testimony from the Margin: The Gloucester Jewry and Its Neighbours* and Emma Cavell's blog.
4. For the burning of a Jewish convert in Oxford in 1222 I have relied upon Cecil Roth's account in *A History of the Jews in England*.
5. For the account of fraud I have relied loosely upon the case of Brun the Jew as outlined in the *Select Pleas of the Jewish Exchequer*, J M Rigg.

6. Medieval trobairitz were Occitan female troubadours of the 12th and 13th centuries, active from around 1170 to approximately 1260.

7. For descriptions of Jewish culture and religious services I have relied upon Rabinowitz's book, *The Social Life of the Jews of Northern France in the XII-XIV Centuries*, L Rabinowitz, M.A. 1938.

GLOSSARY

Aba: Father.

A bientôt: See you later.

Archa: An official chest, provided with three locks and seals, in which a counterpart of all deeds and contracts involving Jews was to be deposited in order to preserve the records.

Balzaus: A standard of two colours.

Baucent: The name of the war flag (*Vexillum Belli*) used by the Knights Templar.

Baruch Hashem: Thank God.

Bet Din: Means *house of judgement.* Jewish tribunal empowered to adjudicate cases involving criminal, civil, or religious law.

Challah: Egg baked bread served on the Sabbath.

Chuppah: Wedding canopy.

D'accord: Okay.

Garçon amoureux: A boy in love.

Gezzazah: Shearing (coins).

Giyoret: A convert to Judaism who came to her faith not by birth but by choice.

Gonfanon: A type of heraldic flag or banner, often pointed, swallow-tailed, or with several streamers, and suspended from a crossbar.

Hashem: Literal translation: "the name". Used in Judaism as the name for God.

Ima: Mother.

Jusqu'à demain: Until tomorrow.

L'chaim: A toast.

Ma chérie: My darling (to a female).

Melec Sha'ul: King Saul.

Mikveh: Sunken bath for ritual cleansing.

Oy lanu: Woe is us.

Pas de problème: No problem.

Safta: Grandmother.

Shabbat: Jewish Sabbath.

Sheol: Hell.

Shomerim: A person who sits with the dead body out of respect, literally a guard.

Shtar Giur: Certificate of conversion, certifying that the person is now a Jew.

Skirmiseur: A fencing master.

Tallage: Tax.

Talmud: A central text of Rabbinic Judaism.

Tevillah: A full body immersion in a mikveh.

Troubadour: An Occitan composer and performer of Old Occitan lyric poetry.

Trobairitz: Occitan female troubadours of the 12th and 13th centuries.

Viddui: Jewish deathbed confessional prayer.

A NOTE FROM THE PUBLISHER

Thank you for reading this book. If you enjoyed it please do consider leaving a review on Amazon to help others find it too.

We hate typos. All of our books have been rigorously edited and proofread, but sometimes mistakes do slip through. If you have spotted a typo, please do let us know and we can get it amended within hours.

info@bloodhoundbooks.com

Printed in Great Britain
by Amazon